MESSAGES FROM HITCHCOCK'S MISFORTUNE COOKIES

"Death is nature's way of telling you to slow down."

"A kill in time saves nine."

"The family that slays together, stays together."

"Suicide is for sissies—murder is a man's game."

"The female of the species is more deadly than the male."

"Do to your neighbor what he would like to do to you—and do it first."

"Use organic arsenic."

And for fuller explorations of the nature of evil, turn to the terror treats waiting for you on—

MURDER-GO-ROUND
14 excursions into freezing fear

MURDER-GO-ROUND

Alfred Hitchcock

A DELL BOOK

Published by
Dell Publishing Co., Inc.
1 Dag Hammarskjold Plaza
New York, New York 10017

Dell ® TM 681510, Dell Publishing Co., Inc.

ISBN: 0-440-15607-6

Printed in the United States of America
First printing—January 1978

ACKNOWLEDGMENTS

FAT JOW AND THE WATCHMAKER by Robert Alan Blair—Copyright © 1975 by H.S.D. Publications, Inc. Reprinted by permission of the author and the author's agents, Scott Meredith Literary Agency, Inc.

DOCTOR'S DILEMMA by Harold Q. Masur—Copyright © 1975 by H.S.D. Publications, Inc. Reprinted by permission of the author.

A NICE WHOLESOME GIRL by Robert Colby—Copyright © 1968 by H.S.D. Publications, Inc. Reprinted by permission of the author and the author's agents, Scott Meredith Literary Agency, Inc.

DINNER WILL BE COLD by Fletcher Flora—Copyright © 1963 by H.S.D. Publications, Inc. Reprinted by permission of the Estate of Fletcher Flora and the agents for the Estate, Scott Meredith Literary Agency, Inc.

POACHERS' ISLAND by Richard Hardwick—Copyright © 1967 by H.S.D. Publications, Inc. Reprinted by permission of the Estate of Richard Hardwick and the agents for the Estate, Scott Meredith Literary Agency, Inc.

NOBODY TO PLAY WITH by Irwin Porges—Copyright © 1968 by H.S.D. Publications, Inc. Reprinted by permission of the author and the author's agents, Scott Meredith Literary Agency, Inc.

GALLIVANTIN' WOMAN by Wenzell Brown—Copyright © 1965 by H.S.D. Publications, Inc. Reprinted by permission of the author.

HARDHEADED COP by D. S. Halacy, Jr.—Copyright © 1965 by H.S.D. Publications, Inc. Reprinted by permission of the author and the author's agents, Scott Meredith Literary Agency, Inc.

TIME TO KILL by Dick Ellis—Copyright © 1970 by H.S.D. Publications, Inc. Reprinted by permission of the author and the author's agents, Scott Meredith Literary Agency, Inc.

MURDER OUT OF A HAT by Henry Slesar—Copyright © 1961 by H.S.D. Publications, Inc. Reprinted by permission of the author and the author's agents, Raines and Raines.

THE ELECTRIC GIRL CAPER by Edward D. Hoch—Copyright © 1976 by Davis Publications, Inc. Reprinted by permission of the author.

A GOOD HEAD FOR MURDER by Charles W. Runyon—Copyright © 1974 by H.S.D. Publications, Inc. Reprinted by permission of the author and the author's agents, Scott Meredith Literary Agency, Inc.

ROUNDHOUSE by Frank Sisk—Copyright © 1971 by H.S.D. Publications, Inc. Reprinted by permission of the author and the author's agents, Scott Meredith Literary Agency, Inc.

THE DAY OF THE PICNIC by John Lutz—Copyright © 1971 by H.S.D. Publications, Inc. Reprinted by permission of the author and the author's agents, Scott Meredith Literary Agency, Inc.

CONTENTS

MURDER-GO-ROUND

INTRODUCTION

During a recent brief period of enforced idleness (I had been attacked by a savage beast that my physician, in his typically blasé fashion, chose to refer to as a "flu bug"), I became acutely aware of radio stations that broadcast the news round the clock.

I will never be the same. The flu bug, having had its way with me, has flown. But I am now the victim, and perhaps carrier, of an illness that I will call Triviaphobia—an abnormal fear of the inconsequential information that these stations pass off as news.

The merest hint that I am about to learn the name of the young lady who has been named Queen of the Sunflower Seed Festival sends me hiking off to my closet, where I remain in isolation for hours. A lead-in to an item that threatens to tell me the results of a study by a group of Harvard biologists of the mating habits of the inch worm— and how it explains the Gay Liberation movement—causes me to stuff my ears with cotton.

I understand, of course, how these fillers get on the air. When there are twenty-four hours to fill with news—or at least sound—and perhaps, at the most, a half hour of actual news to work with, some compromises must necessarily be made. Stories that back in the old days—when newscasts were five minutes long and served mainly as a means of giving the disk jockey time to deal with his kidneys— would have been relegated to the trash basket, are now delivered to us in the doomsday tones of the announcers as if they actually mattered.

My phobia, I suspect, stems from what this overly generous employment of trivia portends. Eventually, the listeners will become inured to it and switch off their sets (nothing lasts forever—where are the hula hoop, spats and Shipwreck Kelly today?). Ratings will plunge. In panic, station

managers, doing what they do best, will fire all the secre-
taries. That won't help. Someone will have to *think*.

In time, naturally, the someone who is doing the thinking will emerge from the tank with the conclusion that the
trivia must be made exciting. As we have learned from the
history of failing TV situation comedies, the solution to
plummeting ratings is an injection of guest appearances by
motion picture stars. And, monkey see, monkey do.

For a while we will have guest reporters. John Wayne
will advise us that the school board in Bigfoot, Wyoming,
has banned all Norman Mailer books from its library on
the grounds that they stimulate the growth of pre-pubescent
chest hair. Raquel Welch will report to us that the new
Miss America, in an effort to bridge the ideological gap
between the traditionalist homemakers and the radical fem-
inists, hopes to become the first housewife–surgeon to remove a brain tumor with a vacuum cleaner. And so on.

Unfortunately, that tactic will fail, as, previously, it has
always failed to keep afloat sinking TV situation comedies.
I say unfortunately because the failure will undoubtedly
drive the radio news people to use more drastic means to
revive the ratings. From the think tank this time will come
the idea of the stations creating their own news events. The
notion will be irresistible. For it will bring order to news-
casting. There will be no more long, dull waits for exciting
news stories to occur. They can be brought on as needed, a
half-dozen-or-so, say, to the hour.

At 6:07, for example, the station's demolition team will
blow up a delicatessen, providing the station's reporters not
only with a hot story but cold cuts to boot. At 10:17, the
station's yeggs will hold up the city's largest bank, at
one and the same time giving the station an exciting event
to cover and solving the station manager's problem of how
to finance his coming vacation in the Bahamas. At 7:50 the
next morning, the station's team of backseat drivers will
initiate a chain reaction collision on the main roadway
linking the city and the suburbs, thereby shutting down the
roadway for from three to five days and bringing on the
city's total economic collapse. But it will be worth it, because the motorists, trapped in their automobiles, will be
listening to the reports on the calamity on their car radios,
and ratings will soar.

But perhaps I'm just an old pessimist. Maybe none of

these sorry happenings will come to pass. Perhaps when the ratings begin to dip, the stations will revert to disk jockeys and five-minute newscasts, leaving the trivia to the newspapers to cover, as it was in the good old days.

Of one thing I am certain. The stories of mystery and the macabre that follow are as up-to-the-minute as tomorrow's news. And, equally as pleasing, you will find no commercials separating them.

—Alfred Hitchcock

FAT JOW AND THE WATCHMAKER

by Robert Alan Blair

And what will it be today?" Fat Jow asked the children ringed about his park bench.

The Saturday afternoon air shrilled with their cries: "The golden pagoda! The dragon! The nightingale! The demon!"

"I think it is time for the nightingale," said Fat Jow when quiet had returned.

The children offered no protest, but contentedly settled themselves to listen.

Three generations of Chinatown children had made a ritual of this Saturday visit to St. Mary's Square, to hear Uncle Jow relate one from among the many old stories his mother had brought from China.

As the old emperor regained health and strength through the singing of the genuine nightingale after the mechanical substitute had fallen to pieces, Fat Jow had his reward in the rapt faces and shining eyes of his audience.

He failed to notice the leathery little Occidental on the next bench until the children were scattering to return to their play. The stranger arose and came toward him.

"Good day, sir," he said in fluid Cantonese. "May I sit down?"

Fat Jow's astonishment delayed his reply only briefly. "Please do."

The other seated himself. "I could not help overhearing. A delightful story. My compliments."

"Thank you. It was their weekly lesson, although they do not recognize it as such. Truth is more palatable when candy-coated with parable."

"You are the one called Fat Jow?"

"You have the advantage over me, sir. Not only do you know my name, but you are fluent in Cantonese."

"For thirty years I had my watch-repair shop in the Street of the Lame Ox in Canton."

Fat Jow nodded in sympathy. "I have heard of the White Russians who fled China ahead of the forces of Chairman Mao."

"Now I am here, too old to do more than make a beginning. It is difficult to make one's way in a strange land—doubly so, if one is my age. Allow me to introduce myself. I am Fyodr Skarin."

Immediately to Fat Jow's mind came the image of the beautiful Eurasian woman whom he knew as an agent of the mainland Chinese. "I seem to have heard the name."

"Dunya's father."

That Dunya's father lived in San Francisco he knew; but always before, Fyodr Skarin had been a name, a figure out of Dunya's past, partaking of no reality. Yet here he was, sharing a bench in St. Mary's Square. "I am honored to know you, sir. Despite the identity of her employers, I hold only the highest regard for Miss Skarin. You brought her here and educated her in American schools—why then did she choose to go back to her Chinese mother, and espouse the cause of the People's Republic?"

"Who knows the minds of one's children these days? Her mother's arguments were more effective than mine. And her mother, as you may know, has risen steadily in the ranks of the Party. She had more prestige to offer Dunya than I, a struggling watchmaker." Fyodr clasped his hands in his lap. "I have not heard from Dunya for some time, and I am more worried with the passing of the months. Have you seen her?"

"Not for nearly a year. Surely you understand that she fears, not only for herself, but also for the trouble she would bring upon you as the father of a subversive operative?"

"Do you have a means of communication?"

"Nothing direct. I may leave a message with a certain local importer, but he must wait for her to call him."

"Will you leave a message for me?"

"It will please me, sir, but I cannot guarantee results."

"Only say that her father wishes to see her. And there is another reason that I come to you. Without going into meticulous detail, I invite you to visit my shop on Divisadero

Street, at your convenience. If you are able to come back with me now, so much the better."

"My herb shop is closed for the weekend; I am at your service, sir."

The two men rode the bus to Fyodr's shop on lower Divisadero near Haight, a semicommercial neighborhood boasting on shop fronts proud old names like Naremkin, Solovieff, Goronsky, Saharoff.

Originally the shop had been one square enclosure with an entrance at the middle. A partition had been installed dividing the one into two, the entryway recessed to permit two angled doors adjoining one another. The next shop window bore an arching legend in large block letters of gilt: "A. Gum, Jewelry, Loans," and in smaller letters on the lower right corner, "Fine engraving done here."

Fyodr went into the rear room and reappeared with a chair. "Please sit down and wait, and I shall fetch my friend." He stepped into the next shop.

Within a few minutes he returned with a tall Chinese of commanding appearance. A shock of thick black hair barely touched with gray capped a broad brow and keen black eyes. Fyodr said, "I shall not compromise you by speaking my friend's actual name. He avoids Chinatown because he would be subject to pressures by agents of both Peking and Taipei, both of whom would like to recruit his talents for their governments. But politics is not the reason I have brought you here, Master Fat."

A. Gum said after a slight bow, "Allow me to to explain, sir. While I do not choose to live in Chinatown, I am saddened that my children do not attend Chinese language classes after school. Mr. Skarin has heard of you through his daughter, and he has suggested that you may be willing to recommend someone of discretion to tutor them."

Fat Jow stroked his wisp of silky beard. "Anyone I recommend would himself be in Chinatown, and I presume that if you do not visit the area, neither do you wish your children to go. How many are there, and what are their ages?"

"A boy twelve, and girls nine and fourteen."

"I had not looked upon myself as a schoolmaster," said Fat Jow, smiling, "but I have found certain reward in giving my young grandnephew lessons in calligraphy at home. Since I live not in Chinatown but in an apartment west of

Van Ness, you could offer no objection to sending your children to me."

· A. Gum took his hand. "This is beyond all my hopes," he said sincerely. "Please state your conditions."

"I impose no conditions," Fat Jow said in some surprise. "I am happy to serve. My life is renewed by continuing communication with the young." He wrote on a piece of paper. "Here is my address and telephone number. Please call before you bring them. After a few visits, I am sure you will allow them to travel the bus by themselves."

As Fat Jow was leaving the shop with the thanks of both these new friends, Fyodr Skarin said, "You will not forget Dunya?"

"I plan to visit the importer before I return home this afternoon," said Fat Jow. "This is all that I may promise."

The shop of the importer was a few doors below the herb shop on the steep street two blocks above Grant Avenue, the red and gilt pagoda facade of Chinatown. The shopwindow had long since been replaced, and the priceless Sung Tusk, exquisite ivory carving, restored to its place of honor in a glass display case. The politically-motivated theft of the Sung Tusk and its subsequent recovery by Fat Jow had been the last occasion of his seeing Dunya Skarin.

The importer was waiting upon an Occidental couple whose camera straps and gay summer-weight clothing marked them as tourists. Fat Jow stood patiently before a counter of costume jewelry until the customers had made a purchase and departed. The importer remained behind the cash register. "I am fairly sure," he said dryly, "that you are not here to buy."

Fat Jow did not like the man, who acted occasionally for the mainland Chinese for no personal motive except money. He dispensed with the customary niceties of social exchange. "Has the *Celestial III* been returned to you as yet?" He referred to the importer's cabin cruiser which Dunya had used in the abortive attempt to accomplish the defection of the nuclear physicist On Leong-Sa.

"Not as yet," replied the importer. "She required it for further assignments."

"When did you last hear from her?"

"Perhaps six or seven months ago."

"Do you have means of direct communication?"

"The *Celestial III* has a radio, of course, but she forbids its use. She communicates when it is *her* wish—not mine."

"When she does," said Fat Jow, "please inform her that her father wishes to see her."

"Is he ill?"

"He is a father who is concerned for his daughter—I ask no more than that."

The importer nodded coldly. "I shall convey your message, when it becomes possible."

"Thank you." Fat Jow gave him a stiff bow and left the shop.

He heard no more from Fyodr, A. Gum, or the importer during the following week. On Saturday afternoon, after he had finished his storytelling session with the children and was relaxing on the bench with head tilted back to allow the welcome spring sun to warm his face, he saw a frail old man with a stack of round wicker baskets on his shoulder shuffling into the park. He passed in front of Fat Jow, stumbled, and the baskets clattered to the ground. One rolled beneath the bench, and Fat Jow bent to retrieve it.

When their heads came close in rebuilding the stack, the old man said without looking at him, "Once again my disguise is effective. Do you not know me?"

It was the voice of a woman, and a familiar voice. Dunya Skarin had returned to San Francisco.

Fat Jow covered his surprise by leaning back once more upon the bench. "Are you being watched?" he asked.

"I do not err by underestimating the skill of your authorities. Therefore I must assume that I am under surveillance at every moment. Where may we meet secretly? Make haste—I must be seen to leave here."

Fat Jow pondered briefly. "The fowl market of Ng Har. He may be trusted."

Dunya shouldered the baskets and hurried away, head down. She was soon lost to sight among the Saturday crowds. For some minutes longer Fat Jow sat under the benevolent steel gaze of Dr. Sun Yat-Sen, then took himself up the hill to Grant Avenue.

The fowl market was normally crowded. Fat Jow lingered near the window, ostensibly studying the rows of naked chickens and ducks hanging from stretched wires, until Ng Har came to him and said, "I believe I have what you wish, Master, if you will come with me." He led Fat Jow to the rear of the store and into the freezer, then to a small door opening into a storage room that gave upon a narrow alley beside the building. Ng Har did not enter with him, but returned to his customers.

Her stack of baskets set aside, Dunya Skarin was standing slim and straight beside them, looking out the dusty window, through which a fragment of Grant Avenue traffic might be seen, if only obliquely. She had removed the soiled felt hat, and her black lustrous hair fell richly to her shoulders.

She turned to meet him. "My friend," she said simply, taking both his hands.

"You received my message sooner than I had anticipated," said Fat Jow.

"I received no message; I am here on an assignment."

"I left a message with the importer. Have you talked to him?"

"The importer is stupid and dangerous—I do not tell him of my comings and goings. What message was it?"

"That your father wishes to see you. Will you go to him?"

She turned away to look out the window again. "It is unwise that I go to him. Will you bring him aboard the *Celestial III*? Be sure you are not followed or observed. If you suspect watchers, do not come to the boat, but take your ease on the green until you may leave again without your visit's appearing anything other than a casual stroll." With a few deft moves of her hands she put up her hair and concealed it beneath the old hat. "I cannot remain here longer."

Once more Fat Jow helped her with the wicker baskets. "I receive an impression that your assignment here pertains to your father. I was seen in his company, and I am being pressed into service."

"I am not permitted to discuss it," she said gravely, almost with reluctance.

"You are not alone on this mission?"

She looked at him without answering immediately. "Will you come?" she asked, making of the question a gentle plea.

"Was there ever any doubt?"

"Come as soon as you can. If I know my father, he will want to come at once. It will be better to wait for dark." She pulled open the outer door, looked up and down the alley, and shuffled toward Grant Avenue, where she turned right and vanished.

Fat Jow went back through the freezer to the market. To delay his departure, and to lend credence to his visit, he purchased a small dressed pullet to take home to Hsiang Yuen.

Shortly before sunset and the swift dusk of the coastal country, Fat Jow arrived alone at the marina green and strolled lazily along the water's edge, pausing once to activate coin-operated binoculars. After scanning the usual sights of the Golden Gate Bridge, Alcatraz and Angel Islands, and the Marin hills beyond, he swung the binoculars full circle to study the traffic along Marina Boulevard. Nothing that he saw, moving or parked, suggested a police car; but it would not be only the police for whom to watch.

He sat down on a bench and stretched his arms along the back. He had been lounging thus for the better part of an hour, and the dusk had given way to night brightened by the myriad lights around the Bay, when Fyodr Skarin came.

Fyodr said, "I did as you recommended: changed buses twice, and watched following traffic. I am reasonably sure that I have led no one here. I must express my gratitude that you take such precautions to prevent the arrest of my daughter."

"I like Miss Skarin," said Fat Jow, rising. "I can still hope that she will decide to become an American once more, and not under duress. You must try to exert more of an influence than her Chinese mother has ever done."

"I do not know how."

"Be a loving father, ask no questions, and do not demand more of her than she is ready to give. Accept her as the person she is, without seeking to change her."

Fyodr nodded. "I *have* been guilty of that." He looked around. "Where is it that we are to meet her?"

"Come," Fat Jow said, and he set off toward the St. Francis Yacht Harbor and the filled causeway leading to the breakwater.

The *Celestial III* rode quietly at her mooring between two narrow floating docks. Her portholes were brightly lighted, but no one was on deck when they came aboard.

As if the new rocking of the boat with their added weight had been a signal, light streamed up the companionway where the hatch slid back, and footsteps sounded on the ladder. A shadow blocked out the light from below. A strongly-coupled Chinese in blue dungarees and white T-shirt stepped upon the deck. He wore his hair cropped close, and something in his bearing suggested the military man, even before he spoke. "Good evening, gentlemen," he said with a smart salute. "Song Ja at your service."

"Rather," said Fat Jow, "at the service of the armed forces of the People's Republic, is that not so?"

Song Ja smiled thinly. "My congratulations. If I can judge you from what Miss Skarin has told me, you are not about to attempt anything heroic and foolish."

"First I would know why I should be expected to act so," Fat Jow replied.

Fyodr Skarin spoke up. "I am here to see my daughter. Where is she?"

Song Ja planted his hands upon his hips. "So you are the father. I have a small errand for you before you may see her."

"I do nothing," insisted Fyodr, "until I know she is safe. If you have harmed her, you will have to kill me."

"Nothing so dramatic." Song Ja turned and called down the open companionway. "Come on deck for a moment."

Dunya appeared, but had no time for more than a fleeting embrace before Song Ja ordered her below again. She went without protest. Song Ja slid the hatch cover closed with a bang, and secured it with a small combination padlock. "Now we may talk business, gentlemen." He sauntered astern to the padded benches lining the cockpit. "Sit down—we may as well be comfortable." When neither man moved, he laughed and sat down. "Father and friend. The one responsible for the person she is, the other for the person she thinks that she wishes to become. My superiors have been most curious about this Fat Jow, who has so seriously curtailed the efficiency of our valued agent Miss Skarin. You are here because you both can be of service to us. We are reasonably confident of your cooperation because of certain personal ties: Mr. Skarin with his daughter, and Fat Jow with his little grandnephew. First order of business is Mr. Skarin. Have you heard the name Chen Woei?" He looked sharply at Fyodr, watching his reaction.

"I was a merchant resident of Canton many years," said Fyodr. "It is obvious that I should know this person high in the ranks of the Kuomintang. At one time he was talked of as one of the five men closest to the generalissimo."

"Chen Woei did not flee to Taiwan with the forces of Chiang. Our agents in Taiwan have established that the Chiang government also would like to find him. His acumen in political science is a coveted asset for either side. Our people throughout the world have been supplied with his picture and dossier for years, with the hope that someone somewhere would recognize him. An exhaustive study of his history revealed that in Canton he had an acquaintance with whom he took tea almost weekly, a watchmaker in the Street of the Lame Ox. Because the watchmaker was the husband of a minor party official in Canton, we were able to identify him as Fyodr Skarin, who had settled in San Francisco. Last year we assigned an agent to watch Mr. Skarin, but the agent was inefficient, and it was not until our agent watching Fat Jow saw Mr. Skarin's colleague on Divisadero Street that the jeweler A. Gum was recognized as Chen Woei. We need his familiarity with the intimate details of the Chiang regime, and are prepared to offer him an enviable responsibility with our own. You are to bring him to me before midnight, on one pretext or other."

"While you hold my daughter hostage," said Fyodr.

"While I hold both your daughter and Fat Jow. You continue to be watched and any attempt on your part to communicate with the local authorities will be transmitted immediately to me. I shall then speed out of the harbor to international waters, to rendezvous with one of our nuclear submarines. Pending the outcome of this mission, we have deferred your daughter's trial for treason. If I am obliged to depart in haste, the trial will be deferred no longer."

"And Fat Jow?" Fyodr asked.

"He is scheduled for a conference with my superior. He has a potential of becoming our most valued operative, through his knowledge of Chinatown and the respect he commands among its people." Song Ja stood, his lazy air vanished. "As you see, I am not armed, although arms are readily available. But I trust that you will not make violence necessary." He unlocked the padlock and slid the hatch cover back. "Fat Jow, you are to go below and wait for Mr. Skarin to return."

Fat Jow exchanged glances with Fyodr, then with a

shrug descended the ladder. He heard the cover slide shut behind him, the lock click, voices conversing quietly as Song Ja gave Fyodr final instructions, and Fyodr's footsteps receding along the floating dock.

Dunya Skarin was seated on one of four tiered bunks built into the bow, elbows on knees, chin resting in her cupped hands. "I am sorry," she said. "This has come as a shock to me, too. I did not dream that I was to be as much of a pawn as you."

"You heard?" he asked gently.

"I heard enough."

"And you are disillusioned? When last we talked aboard this craft, you were undecided. Are we to wait meekly until your father returns, or are we to employ the time to mutual advantage?"

"I am willing to help you," she said dully. "If I am to be charged in any court, I prefer that it be in America. But what may we do against Song Ja? He is still my superior, and I am long conditioned to obey orders."

Fat Jow heard her only partially, as he was inspecting the quarters closely. The only exit was up the ladder, and the portholes were screened by heavy wire mesh locked in place. He rapped with his knuckles on the deck end of the wall. "Mahogany," he said. "Of what material is the hull constructed?"

"Fiberglass."

"And can it be worked with common hand tools?"

"Yes . . ." She raised her head, and her eyes brightened. "The tool locker!" She hurried to the galley area abaft the ladder, pulled open a drawer, and beckoned him.

Fat Jow looked among the contents of the drawer, came up with a brace and bit and a keyhole saw. "I must remember to reimburse the importer for whatever damage I do," he said. Experimentally he drilled a hole in the mahogany paneling close beneath the deck, in a shadowed spot well aft, where a casual glance from the ladder would not discover it. He followed this with a second hole no more than a quarter inch away, and a third, until he had a row two feet long. He continued his row downward another two feet. When he joined the rows, he had outlined a square two feet on each side. "My inspiration," he said, "is a postage stamp." With the saw, working very slowly and cautiously, he began joining the holes.

A rattling of the padlock on the hatch cover then paralyzed him, and they stood shoulder to shoulder, backs against the marks he had made, hands behind them holding the tools.

However, Song Ja did not come down. He called through the open hatch, "Fat Jow, come on deck. I want to talk to you."

With a meaningful glance at Dunya, Fat Jow slipped her the keyhole saw and hurried up the ladder. The moment that he stood on deck, Song Ja locked the hatch again. He waved Fat Jow to a stern bench, and this time the herbalist did not decline. He felt suddenly weak.

Song Ja stood with one foot on the bench, looking out over the stern toward the brilliance of the city. "Waiting can be a wearying time," he said.

"You allow yourself the debilitating luxury of loneliness?" Fat Jow taunted.

Song Ja looked long at him, but with no change of expression. "The strongest and most dedicated of us have moments when the Party seems far away. Secret agents in imperialist strongholds are subject to them. Here, for example, Miss Skarin goes ashore with far more equanimity than I. She knows the city and its customs, while I must be ever on my guard. I retain my sanity by continually reminding myself that in effect this craft is a vessel of the People's Navy, and I as its captain have a fragment of China beneath my feet."

"It is my understanding," said Fat Jow, "that the importer owns the *Celestial III*."

"A technicality. He is one of our agents, therefore the craft is ours." Song Ja smiled faintly. "I have been warned to choose well my words with you."

"Why am I so important to you? You must know I am not in sympathy with your cause."

"Yet you are proud of the achievements of China. This much you have told Miss Skarin."

Fat Jow nodded. "No matter what their political affiliation, Chinese everywhere in the world must look with pride at China's strides toward an independent position among the family of nations. Yet I had hoped that my last task for you had been performed, for the sake of keeping my grandnephew."

"I must inform you, sir, that in releasing the boy to you

before we had utilized your potential, Miss Skarin acted impulsively. Her mother has certain influence, and was able to ameliorate the charges. But when she failed in her mission to effect the defection of the nuclear scientist back to China, largely through your efforts, the charges against her were too grievous to ignore. We have elected to give her the opportunity of succeeding at this mission, through her father, and through you. Mr. Skarin is at this moment fulfilling his designed function. Now we turn to you. We know that you can be a valuable man in Chinatown."

"So the San Francisco police have been saying for years—but they have learned that I cooperate only within limits."

Song Ja laughed warmly. "You will do! Whatever Miss Skarin has said of you is true. To be brief: the importer has long been our principal permanent contact in Chinatown, but he is stupid, stupid! While the People's Republic was young, he was adequate for our purposes, but we are becoming more sophisticated, and so our representation must become the same."

"You must know that *I* cannot be your representative. What little I did, I did under coercion."

"Look upon it another way," Song Ja pursued patiently. "Your government has been seeking lines of communication with China. What better level than people like you, the merchant citizen?"

"Communication—and that is all?"

"You are suspicious—that is good. I shall be honest with you. Your choice is simple: either accept the terms I offer tonight, and become our man in Chinatown, or accompany me to my later rendezvous at sea, where more influential persons than I are waiting to speak with you." He waved his dismissal. "You may go below again—you have a few hours yet to make your decision, and I do not wish to distract you." He unlocked the hatch and slid it back only long enough for Fat Jow to descend the ladder. The padlock clicked once more.

Fat Jow told Dunya, "I too am scheduled for a sea voyage. I trust that we may cancel the reservation."

"I have been working while you were on deck," she told him, showing him a panel of mahogany two feet square that she had removed from the paneling at the deck line, exposing the rough inner surface of the fiberglass hull.

"Excellent," he said, running his hands along the serrated edges of the wood. "It promises to be a tight squeeze for someone like me. We have no wish to drill beneath the waterline. Do you know where it is?"

Dunya traced a line with a lipstick. "About there. Allow a few inches on either side."

"Even tighter." Fat Jow took up the drill again. "Hide the panel of wood, and try to devise something to seal this opening if Song Ja should come below."

"Be sure he will watch on deck until my father returns. He slept most of the day in preparation for this night."

Cutting of the fiberglass was even slower, not because of the material, but of the increased need for quiet on this outer surface, where sound might carry more readily to Song Ja on deck.

As he reached the last three drilled holes, Fat Jow stopped sawing. "We cannot permit this panel to fall outward," he said. "Perhaps some small hooks to insert in the holes and hold it in place?"

"I have hairpins." Dunya fashioned hooks of two hairpins, inserted them in holes at the top and bottom of the cut section, and held the ends.

Fat Jow turned out the lights, and then worked the saw through the last holding snags, stopped again. "It is free," he told her. "Pull—very gently."

The fiberglass panel stirred in its frame, and a tiny edge came under his fingers. Fat Jow pressed first with one hand, then the other. The edge came free, and he lowered the panel to the deck. Before them opened a square black aperture through which they saw the shadowy form of a yacht in the next slip. The slapping of water against the hull sounded quite clearly.

"Do you swim?" whispered Fat Jow.

"Yes."

"It will not be wise to use the floating dock to go ashore. Slip into the water, dive under the next boat if you can, and do not come up until you are away from here. If we are separated, go at once to my home, and ask Miss Baxter to let you wait there for me."

"And you?"

"I shall be not far behind you. Go now, and good luck. I am happy to have your help."

"You are helping me far more than I you."

"Miss Skarin, you help only by confirming your faith in me. Please go."

He helped her to crawl through the opening he had made. She hung by her hands on the edge of the hole for a moment, then slipped with hardly a ripple into the black water between the hull and the next floating dock. Fat Jow strained his eyes, but could not detect her.

He waited until he thought she had time to clear the next boat, and inched himself through, feet first. Being stouter than Dunya, he stuck at the middle, his legs protruding into the night, his head and shoulders inside the cabin. He struggled, but made no progress. He dared not make a sound lest he attract the attention of Song Ja.

Bracing his hands flat upon the mahogany on either side, he succeeded in pushing himself back into the cabin, where he crouched on the deck, regaining his breath and thinking. With the keyhole saw he worked some more on the lower edge of the hole, but it was not far enough above the waterline to offer much space for widening.

When he stopped sawing, he looked about the cabin. The proximity of the water to the hole suggested a means of keeping the *Celestial III*, and with it Song Ja, in the harbor. Fat Jow did not wish to subject himself to drowning while squeezing through an opening slightly smaller than his girth. He took up the drill again, squatted and drilled a hole in the paneling below the waterline. The bit broke through, and he pushed on to find the fiberglass hull. He drilled more, again broke through, and when he withdrew the bit it was wet to the touch.

The leak was small, and would be long in revealing itself. The space between hull and mahogany paneling would have to fill before water reached the hole in the mahogany.

Again he tried the opening, and beyond a small restraint at the middle, encountered no difficulty. As he hung suspended by both hands, his legs and feet were already in the water, cold at any time of the year, and he trusted himself to the Bay. He took a deep breath and allowed himself to sink. He called upon what little he knew about swimming, and after a fashion made his way beneath the hull of the adjoining yacht.

He found Dunya waiting on the steep rock slope of the

breakwater. "If we try to walk out," she said, "he will see."

"Then," said Fat Jow, unperturbed, "we must swim again, across the slip. It is not far."

They returned to the water, and swimming with a slow dog paddle to avoid splashing, moved across the strip of water between the ranks of boats.

From a public telephone Fat Jow called the police. He told them only, "There has been an attempted kidnapping aboard the *Celestial III* at the St. Francis Yacht Harbor," and he hung up. His next call requested a taxicab.

It was not long before he heard a siren, and saw a police car swing from Fillmore into Marina Boulevard. When the car slowed at the lane leading to the yacht harbor, he heard also a sudden rumble of marine engines behind him, and looking, saw the *Celestial III*, backing out of its berth. Even as the police car skidded to a stop at the telephone booth, the cruiser nosed around the end of the breakwater and into the open waters of the Bay. Once clear of the breakwater, it increased power, the bow went up and the stern down, upsetting the level of water which had been filling the bilges through the little hole he had drilled, and lowering the edge of the square aperture to the waterline.

The *Celestial III*, instead of gaining speed, simply up-ended itself at a steeper angle, until the engines died and the bow was pointing straight up to the night sky. A Coast Guard cutter summoned by the police was drawing near to rescue the unfortunate yachtsman. His identity would be a matter of interest to the authorities.

Fat Jow and Dunya Skarin gradually worked free of the crowd that had gathered and climbed, still dripping, into the waiting taxicab. Fat Jow gestured her in ahead of him, and gave the driver the address of the Baxter mansion. "Miss Baxter will have some dry clothes for you," he said, "although I fear they may be somewhat out of date. Then we shall attempt to telephone your father or A. Gum, and allay their fears. And in the morning, if you are still of a mind, you and I shall pay a visit to Lieutenant Cogswell of the San Francisco police."

Dunya did not answer, but sat silently during most of the ride. As they were turning the corner of Van Ness into the street of the Baxter mansion, she said only, "I am of a mind."

DOCTOR'S DILEMMA

by Harold Q. Masur

As soon as we reached the courthouse corridor Papa's face convulsed like a baby's in torment. "I'm dying," he moaned. "I'm bleeding to death."

"You're fine, Papa," I said. "You'll outlive us all."

"Ten grand." A sob caught in his throat. "I posted bail for that lunatic client on your say-so, Counselor. 'Don't worry,' you told me. 'There's no risk.' So where is he? Why didn't he show up in court?"

Papa was Nick Papadopolous, bald, swarthy, barrel-shaped, with capillaries tracing a ruby pattern across his ample nose. "You're a bail bondsman," I said. "There are risks in every business. You win some, you lose some."

It wrung a groan of anguish from his throat. "You have to find him, Counselor. You owe it to me. I trusted you. You heard what the judge said. Have him in court by ten o'clock tomorrow morning or forfeit bail. If he took off, so help me, Jordan, I'll finish you with every bondsman in town. You'll never be able to raise another nickel."

"He'll be here, Papa. I'll have him in court tomorrow morning if I have to carry him. Jaffee is not a bail jumper. He has too much at stake."

I believed it. Would a trained physician, a hospital intern, risk his career and his future by jumping bail and holing up somewhere because he's charged with felonious assault? Not likely. Dr. Allan Jaffee, a splendid physical specimen, young, handsome, studious, ambitious, seemed to have everything—except willpower. He was an obsessive gambler: poker, craps, roulette, sporting events, anything. He had already run through a sizable inheritance and now, with no liquid assets, he was in the hole to his bookie for four thousand dollars. So he stalled. So the bookie had dispatched some muscle to pressure the doctor, which turned out to be a mistake. Young Jaffee, a former collegiate wel-

terweight champ, had inflicted upon the collector a bent
nose, the need for extensive dental work, and various mul-
tiple abrasions, contusions, and traumas.

Because it was a noisy affair, someone had called the
law. The cops shipped the collector off in an ambulance
and promptly processed Jaffee into the slammer.

At the preliminary hearing, despite my plea of self-
defense, the judge agreed with the assistant D.A. that high
bail was appropriate under the circumstances. He sternly
labeled the fists of a trained boxer as dangerous weapons,
and set the trial date.

So at 10:00 this morning, the clerk had bawled: "The
People of the State of New York versus Allan Jaffee." The
judge was on the bench, the jury was in the box, the prose-
cutor was ready, defense counsel was ready, everybody on
tap—except the defendant. He hadn't shown.

"Your Honor," I said, "the accused is a medical doctor
training at Manhattan General. It is possible that he was
detained by an emergency. So it seems we have a problem—"

"No, Counselor. *We* have no problem. *You* have a problem. And you have twenty minutes to solve it." He called a
recess.

So I had sprinted out of the courtroom, down the corridor to a booth, and got on the horn to the hospital, but
they had no knowledge of Jaffee's whereabouts. I tried his
apartment. The line was busy. Apparently he hadn't even
left yet.

When the twenty minutes were gone, I approached the
bench and I said to the glaring judge, "If it please your
Honor, I would beg the Court's indulgence for—"

He cut me off. "The Court's indulgence is exhausted,
Mr. Jordan. This is intolerable, a blatant disregard of the
State's time and money. A warrant will be issued forthwith
for immediate execution by the marshal. If the accused has
left the jurisdiction of this Court, bail will be forfeit. Your
deadline is tomorrow morning, sir. Ten o'clock." He
rapped his gavel and called the next case.

Papa's agitation was understandable. With a worldwide
liquidity crisis, ten grand was important money. I disengaged his fingers from my sleeve and went back to the telephone. Still a busy signal; I tried twice more—no change.

So I said the hell with it and went out and flagged a cab and rode up to East 79th Street.

Jaffee lived on the second floor of an aging brownstone. He did not answer the bell. The door was open and I walked into utter chaos. The place had been ransacked and pillaged. I headed for the bedroom, expecting the worst.

He was on the floor, propped up against the bed. This time he had been hopelessly overmatched. Somebody, more likely several somebodies, had worked him over good. His face was hamburger. He tried to talk, but it was an incoherent guttural croak. The doctor needed a doctor, but soon.

I looked for the telephone and saw the handset hanging off the hook, which explained the busy signal. I hung up, jiggled, finally got a dial tone, and put a call through to Manhattan General. I told them that one of their interns had been injured, that he was in critical condition, and I gave them his name and address, adding, "This is an emergency. Better step on it if you don't want to lose him."

I turned back and found him out cold, unconscious— probably a blessing.

When the ambulance arrived, I was allowed to ride along, and sat beside the driver while first aid was being administered in the back. We careened through traffic with the siren wailing, running a few signals and frightening a lot of pedestrians.

"Who clobbered him?" the driver asked.

"I don't know. I found him like that."

"You a friend of Doc Jaffee's?"

"I'm his lawyer."

"Hey, now! He was supposed to be in court this morning, wasn't he?"

"You know about that?"

"Sure. He was on ambulance duty this week and he told me about it. Said he owed a bundle to his bookie but couldn't raise a dime. Said he banged up a guy who came to collect, strictly self-defense, but his lawyer told him you never know what a jury might do. So he was pretty jumpy yesterday morning. Man, Jaffee was one sorry character, and that's why I couldn't understand the change."

"What change?"

"The change in his mood. All morning he's got a long jaw, his face at half past six, and then suddenly he's walking on air, laughing and full of jokes."

"When did it happen?"

"Right after we got that stewardess."

"What stewardess?"

"The one from Global Airlines." He made a face. "Poor kid. She had taken one of those airport limousines from Kennedy and it dropped her off at Grand Central. She was crossing Lexington when the taxi clipped her. Boy, he must've been moving. She was a mess. Jaffee didn't think she'd make it. I don't know what he did back there, but he was working on her, oxygen, needles, everything, until we got her to Emergency. It was after he came out and hopped aboard for another call that I noticed the change. It was weird. Nothing chewing at him anymore. Smiling from ear to ear."

"Do you remember the girl's name?"

"Korth, Alison Korth. I remember because Doc Jaffee was so busy helping the Emergency team that I had to fill out the forms."

He swung the ambulance east one block, cut the siren, turned up a ramp, and ran back to help wheel the patient through a pair of swinging doors, where people were waiting to take over. A formidable-looking nurse blocked my path and ordered me to wait in the reception lounge.

I sat among gloomy-faced people, thinking about young Jaffee. The obvious assumption was that his bookie, a man named Big Sam Tarloff, could not sit back idly and do nothing after one of his collectors had been so injudiciously handled by a deadbeat. People would laugh. Under the circumstances, how could he keep potential welshers in line? So he would have to make an example of Jaffee.

I was restless and fidgety. Curiosity precluded inactivity. So I got up and wandered over to the reception desk and asked the girl for Miss Alison Korth. She consulted her chart.

"Room 625."

I took the elevator up and marched past the nurse's station, found the number and poked my head through a partially open door. The girl on the bed was swathed in bandages, eyes closed, heavily sedated, left arm and right leg in traction, her face pitifully dwindled and gray.

A voice startled me. "Are you one of the doctors?"

I blinked and then saw the speaker, seated primly on a chair against the wall. She looked drawn and woebegone.

"No, ma'am," I said.

"Well, if you're another insurance man from the taxi company, go away. We're going to retain a lawyer and you can talk to him."

"That's the way to handle it," I said. "Are you a friend of Alison's?"

"I'm her sister."

"Stick to your guns. Don't let any of those clowns try to pressure you into a hasty settlement."

She stood up and came close, her eyes dark and intense. "Did you know Alison?"

"No, ma'am."

"Who *are* you?" I gave her one of my cards and she looked at it, frowning. "Scott Jordan. The name sounds vaguely familiar. But we haven't asked anyone for a lawyer. Are you an ambulance chaser?"

"Hardly, Miss Korth. I don't handle automobile liability cases."

"Then who do you represent?"

"Dr. Allan Jaffee."

"The intern who treated Alison in the ambulance?"

"Yes."

"He's very nice. He looked in on Alison several times yesterday while I was here." Her frown deepened. "I don't understand. Why does Dr. Jaffee need a lawyer?"

"It's a long story, Miss Korth. I'd like to tell you about it over a cup of coffee. There's a rather decent cafeteria in the building." She looked dubious and I added, "There's nothing you can do for your sister at the moment, and the hall nurse can page you if anything develops."

She thought for a moment, then nodded and accompanied me along the corridor to the elevator, stopping briefly to confer at the nurse's station. The elevator door opened and a man stepped out. He stopped short.

"Hello, Vicky."

"Hello, Ben," she said, without warmth.

"How is Alison?"

"About the same," she replied.

"Has she regained consciousness?"

"Just for a moment, but they gave her some shots and she's sleeping now. She shouldn't be disturbed."

He lifted an eyebrow in my direction, a tall, blunt-featured man with dark curly hair, wearing sports clothes. Vicky introduced us.

"This is Captain Ben Cowan, the copilot on Alison's last flight. Scott Jordan."

He nodded fractionally. "Were you just leaving?"

"We're on our way to the cafeteria," I said.

"May I join you?"

"I think not," Vicky said. "Mr. Jordan and I have some business to discuss."

He registered no reaction to the rebuff. "I see. Well, would you tell Alison that I was here and that I'll look in again?"

"Of course."

Going down in the elevator there was no further dialogue between them. Captain Cowan left us on the lobby floor and we descended to the lower level. I brought coffee to a small corner table.

"You don't seem overly fond of the captain," I said.

"I detest him."

"Is he a close friend of Alison's?" I pursued the thought.

She made a face. "Alison's infatuated, crazy about him. And I don't like it one tiny bit. I think Ben Cowan is bad medicine."

"In what way?"

"Call it instinct, feminine intuition. Alison and I have always been very close. She shares my apartment whenever her flight lays over in New York. She started going with Cowan about a year ago and she's been moonstruck ever since, sort of in a daze. She used to confide in me. But now, since Ben, she's become withdrawn, even secretive. Alison's not very practical. She was always naive and trusting and I worry about her. And now this—this—" Her chin began to quiver, but she got it under control and blinked back tears.

I sipped coffee and gave her time to recover. After a while, in a small rusty voice, she asked me about Allan Jaffee. So I told her about the gambling debt, the fight and the assault charge, and his failure to appear in court. I told her about going to his apartment and finding him half dead from a merciless beating. Vicky was shocked, but it took her mind off Alison only briefly. She grew fidgety, so I took her back to the sixth floor and then went down to find someone who could brief me on Jaffee's condition.

I spoke to a resident who looked stumbling tired and furiously angry; tired because he'd been working a ten-hour tour and angry because they kept him repairing damages inflicted by people on people. "I'm sorry, sir," he told me. "Dr. Jaffee can talk to no one."

"Not even his lawyer?"

"Not even his Maker. For one thing, his jaw is wired. For another, we've got him under enough sedation to keep him fuzzy for twenty-four hours."

"Will he be able to write?"

"Yes. After a couple of fractured fingers knit properly. Try again in a couple of days."

A couple of days might be too late and I was in no mood to wait. So I went out and was waving for a cab when a hand fell on my shoulder. It was Captain Ben Cowan of Global Airlines.

"I'm sorry if I seem persistent, Mr. Jordan," he said. "But I'm terribly worried about Alison and I can't seem to get any information at the hospital. Everything is one big fat secret with those people. I thought, since you're a friend of Vicky's, you might know something."

"Why don't you ask her yourself?"

He looked rueful. "Vicky and I are not on the same wavelength. I don't think she likes me."

"Well, the fact is, Captain, I don't have any information myself."

"Haven't the doctors told Vicky anything?"

"We didn't discuss it. I don't know either of the girls very well, Captain. I met Vicky only today."

"Oh?" A deep frown scored his forehead. "Vicky gave me an entirely different impression. I thought you'd gone to the hospital to see her."

"Not her. A client of mine."

"A client?" he said, puzzled.

"I'm an attorney. I represent the intern who treated Alison at the accident."

"Jaffee?"

"Right. Dr. Allan Jaffee."

"Well, then, I guess you can't be much help."

"Afraid not," I agreed as a cab pulled up in answer to my signal.

* * *

Tarloff's was a secondhand bookstore on lower Fourth Avenue, a large and profitable establishment stocking a few splendid first editions and managed by the owner's brother-in-law. On the second floor Sam Tarloff operated a frenetically busy horse parlor with half a dozen constantly ringing telephones manned by larcenous-eyed employees. Big Sam, a heavy, bear-shaped man with an incongruously seraphic smile, sat on a platform watching everything and everybody.

He recognized me and said cordially, "Well, Counselor, good to see you. Let's use my private office." I followed him into a small room. He beamed at me. "And what is your pleasure, Mr. Jordan?"

"Nubile young cheerleaders," I told him. "Right now, however, I would like to see your hands."

"What for?"

"Come off it, Samuel. You know as well as I do that Dr. Jaffee is in the hospital."

"Where else should he be? He works there."

"Not as an employee at the moment. As a patient."

"What happened to him?"

"Somebody clubbed him half to death. I want to see if you have any bruised knuckles."

"Me? You think I did it?"

"You, or one of your men. It's a logical conclusion."

"Because he hurt one of my employees?"

"That, yes, and because he still owes you money."

"You're wrong, Counselor. He does not owe me money. He paid off last night, every cent, in cash, including interest."

"Samuel, I'm an old hand. Where would Jaffee get that kind of money on an intern's salary?"

"Not my business, Counselor. I gave him a receipt. Ask him."

"He can't talk. His jaw is wired."

"So look in his pockets. He's got it somewhere."

After countless hours of grilling people on the witness stand, you develop an instinct for the perjurer. Tarloff was not lying. I believed him. "You have lines out, Sam. Tell me, who do you think worked him over?"

He turned up a palm. "I don't know. But it was in the cards, Counselor, it had to happen sooner or later. Jaffee is a very reckless young man. He gambles without capital.

Who knows, maybe he was into the Shylocks for a bundle too. I'll ask around if you want."

"I'd appreciate that."

"How about a little tip, Counselor, a filly in the third at Belmont? Only please take your business to an off-track betting window."

"Not today, Samuel. May I use one of your phones?"

"Be my guest."

I rang Manhattan General and got through to Vicky Korth in her sister's room, still keeping the vigil. I asked her if Alison was close to anyone else at Global. She gave me a name, Ann Leslie, another stewardess, who generally stayed at the Barbizon, a hostelry for single females. Vicky offered to phone and tell her to expect me.

I found Ann Leslie waiting in the lobby, a slender girl, radiating concern, wanting to know when she could visit Alison.

"In a couple of days," I said.

"Darn!" She made a tragic face. "We're flying out again on Wednesday."

"Where to?"

"Same destination. Amsterdam. Same crew too, except for Alison. I'll miss her."

"I imagine Captain Ben Cowan will miss her too."

She squinted appraisingly. "You know about him?"

"Vicky told me. And she's not happy about it."

Ann Leslie tightened her mouth. "Neither am I. That Cowan—he's a chaser, a womanizer. He uses people. He made passes at me too, before Alison joined the crew, but I wouldn't have any part of him. I just don't trust him. Have you met Ben?"

"Yes. He seems genuinely fond of Alison."

"It's an act, believe me."

"Is he openly attentive to her?"

"They're not keeping it a secret, if that's what you mean."

"Would you know why he didn't accompany her into Manhattan yesterday when you put down at Kennedy?"

"Yes. Because he was held up at Customs. They wanted to talk to him in one of those private rooms. I was there and I heard him tell Alison to go ahead without him and that he'd meet her later."

"Are members of the crew usually held up at Customs?"

"Not as a rule. They never bothered me. But it couldn't have been much because I know he's flying out with us again on Wednesday, on our next flight."

We talked for a while longer and I thanked her and promised to tell Alison that Ann would be in to see her as soon as the doctors permitted it. I left and cabbed over to Jaffee's apartment. The super recognized me and let me in.

I stood and surveyed the chaos. Nothing had been left untouched. Even the upholstery had been razored open and kapok strewed over the floor. Desk drawers were pulled out and overturned. I hunkered down, sifting through papers. I did not find any receipt from Sam Tarloff, but after about an hour I did find something even more interesting: a duplicate deposit slip from the Gotham Trust, bearing yesterday's date, and showing a deposit of $34,000.

I straightened and took it to a chair and stared at it, wondering how Jaffee, presumably broke, without credit, could manage a deposit of that magnitude. I saw that it was not a cash deposit. The $34,000 was entered in the column allotted to checks.

But a check from whom? And for what? As I studied it, I felt a sudden surge of excitement, of anticipation, because the Gotham Trust was my own bank, an institution in which I had certain connections. Bank records are not quite as inviolate as most people believe.

Twenty minutes later, I marched through the bank's revolving doors and approached the desk of Mr. Henry Wharton, an assistant vice-president for whom I had performed a ticklish chore only four months before. He rose to shake my hand. Then he sat back and listened to my request. He frowned at Jaffee's deposit slip and rubbed his forehead and looked up at me with a pained expression.

"Well, now, Mr. Jordan, this is highly irregular."

"I know."

"It is not the policy of this bank to make disclosures about our depositors."

"I know."

"You're making it very difficult for me."

"I know."

He sighed and levered himself erect and disappeared into some hidden recess of the bank. I waited patiently. He was perspiring slightly when he returned. He cleared an obstruction from his throat. "You understand this is strictly confidential."

"Absolutely."

He lowered his voice. "Well, then, according to our microfilm records the deposit was made by a check drawn to the order of Dr. Allan Jaffee by the firm of Jacques Sutro, Ltd. I assume you recognize the name."

- "I do, indeed. And I'm deeply indebted, Harry."

"For what? I haven't told you a thing."

"That's right. Now, would it be possible for me to get a blowup of that microfilm?" He turned pale and a convulsive shudder almost lifted him out of the chair, and I added quickly, "All right, Harry, forget it. I'm leaving."

He was not sorry to see me go.

Mr. Jacques Sutro is a dealer in precious gems, operating out of the elegant second floor of a Fifth Avenue town house. Sutro, a portly specimen with silver hair and a manner as smooth as polished opal, folded his beautifully-manicured hands and listened to me with a beautiful smile that displayed some of the finest porcelain dentures in captivity.

"And so," I concluded, "as Dr. Jaffee's attorney, I would appreciate a few details about any transaction you had with him."

"Why not discuss it with your client?"

"I would if I could, Mr. Sutro. Unfortunately, Dr. Jaffee had an accident and he's a patient at Manhattan General under very heavy sedation. It may be days before he can talk. In the meantime I'm handling his legal affairs and it's imperative for me to fill out the picture."

Sutro pursed his lips thoughtfully. "Would you mind if I called the hospital?"

"Not at all. Please do."

He got the number, spoke into the mouthpiece, listened intently, then nodded and hung up. He spread his fingers. "You must understand that I knew young Jaffee's father before the old man died."

"So did I, Mr. Sutro. As a matter of fact, he took me into his office when I first got out of law school. That's why I'm interested in the son's welfare."

"I see. Well, the old gentleman was a valued customer of mine. He purchased some very fine pieces for his wife when she was alive. And later he even acquired some unset stones as a hedge against inflation. Young Allan liquidated them through my firm after his father died. Then yesterday afternoon, he came here and offered to sell some additional stones he had inherited."

"Merchandise you recognized?"

"No. But young Jaffee assured me that his father had bought gems from various other dealers too. I examined the pieces and offered him a very fair price."

"How much did you offer?"

"Forty thousand dollars. He said he needed some cash right away, an emergency in fact, and that he couldn't wait for my check to clear the bank. He said if I let him have four thousand in cash, he would knock two thousand off the total price. So I gave him the cash and a check for the balance, thirty-four thousand." Sutro looked mildly anxious. "Nothing wrong in that, is there, Counselor?"

I shrugged noncommittally. Within a very short time, Mr. Sutro, I suspected, was due for a severe shock, but I was going to let someone else give it to him. He was chewing the inside of his cheek when I left.

What I needed now was Vicky Korth's cooperation. I went looking for her at the hospital but she was not in Alison's room and neither was Alison. The room had been cleaned out, the bed freshly made; there was no sign of any occupancy. I felt a cold, sinking sensation and headed for the nurse's station.

Two girls in white were on duty. My inquiry seemed to upset them both. Their response was neither typical nor brisk. Alison Korth had suddenly developed serious respiratory problems and despite all efforts they had lost her.

I had no way of knowing whether Vicky wanted to be alone or would welcome company. My own experience led me to believe that most mourners crave the solace of visitors. I checked her address in the telephone directory and rode uptown.

Vicky answered my ring and opened the door. The shock of Alison's death had not yet fully registered. She looked dazed and numb and she needed a sympathetic ear.

"Oh, Scott," she said in a small trembly voice, "it didn't really have to happen. They were careless . . ."

"Who?" I asked.

"The nurses, the doctors, somebody . . ."

We sat down and I held her hand. "Tell me about it."

"She—she was having trouble breathing and they put her in oxygen. It's my fault. I left her alone. I went down for a sandwich and when I came back I saw that something was wrong. Her face was dark and I saw that the equipment had come loose, the tube from the oxygen tank, and Alison was—was . . ." Her eyes filled and she hid her face against my chest.

I said quietly, "You couldn't have anticipated anything like that, Vicky. You must not condemn yourself for lack of omniscience."

After a while, she sat back and wanted to reminisce, to talk about their childhood. She was touched by nostalgia and bittersweet memories. It was good therapy. She even smiled once or twice.

When she finally ran out of words, I began to talk. I put her completely into the picture. I told her about my interviews, about my deductions and my conclusions. I told her that Alison had been used, and that I needed her help, and told her what I wanted her to do.

She sat quietly and brooded at me for a long moment, then she got up and went to the telephone. She dialed a number and said in a wooden voice, "This is Vicky. I thought you ought to know, Alison died this afternoon. I'm calling you because she'd want me to. The funeral is Thursday. Services at Lambert's Mortuary. . . . Oh, I see. Well, if you wish, you can see her in the reposing room this evening. I made arrangements at the hospital when they gave me a package with Alison's things. I'll be there myself at six. Please let her friends know."

It was almost seven o'clock. I sat alone in Vicky's apartment and waited. My pupils had expanded to the growing darkness. A large brown parcel lay on the coffee table. Behind me, a closet door was open and waiting. Traffic sounds were muted. I kept my head cocked, concentrating, an ear bent in the direction of the hall door.

I was not quite sure how I would play it if he came. I was not even sure that he would come, but then, without warning, the doorbell rang. It seemed abnormally loud. I did not move. There was a pause and it rang again. Standard operating procedure: ring first to make sure no one is at home. I held my breath. Then it came, a metallic fum-

bling at the lock. I glided quickly into the closet, leaving
the door slightly ajar, giving me an adequate angle of vi-
sion.

Hinges creaked and a pencil beam probed the darkness.
A voice called softly, "Vicky, are you home?" Silence.
Overhead lights clicked on. He came into view and I saw
his eyes encompass the room in a quick circular sweep. He
walked to the coffee table, picked up the parcel, and tore
open the wrapping. He spread out the contents, staring at
Alison's clothes.

"It's no use, Cowan," I said, showing myself. "You won't
find them here."

His head pitched sideways and he stood impaled, jaws
rigid.

I said, "You are one miserable, gold-plated, card-
carrying, full-time rat. Conning a naive and trusting little
cupcake like Alison Korth into doing your dirty work."

"What the hell are you talking about?"

"That's a dry hole, Cowan. Step out of it. You know
what I'm talking about. Diamonds. Unset stones from Amsterdam. Your moonlighting sideline as a copilot on
Global. You suspected you were under surveillance and
you got Alison to smuggle a shipment off the plane and
into the country for you. Concealed on her person. That's
why you were clean when they fanned you at Kennedy yesterday."

His mouth was pinched. "You've got bats loose, Mr.
Lawyer."

"Save it, Cowan. The deal was blown when Alison had
an accident and was taken to the hospital. You thought the
stones were discovered when she was undressed and you
sweated that one out. But when nothing happened you began to wonder and reached a conclusion. The ambulance
intern would have to loosen her uniform to use his stetho-
scope, so he must have found the stuff taped to her body.
You checked him out and that's why you knew his name
when I told you that the intern who'd treated Alison at the
accident was a client of mine.

"You asked me what happened to him. Why did anything have to have happened to him? I'd go to the hospital
if I wanted to see him because he worked there, wouldn't I?
But you already knew what happened because you made it
happen. You broke into his apartment to search for the

loot and you heard him come back and you ambushed him. You hit him from behind, but Jaffee is not an easy man to cool, and even wounded he fought back. I don't know, maybe you even had help. Maybe you tried to make him talk."

Cowan stood like a statue carved out of stone.

"You got nothing from Jaffee," I said, "and nothing from his apartment. So maybe you were wrong about him. Maybe Alison had concealed the stones somewhere in her clothes and nobody had found them. That's why you came here tonight after Vicky told you she'd brought Alison's belongings back here to the apartment. You had to find out, and you knew Vicky would be at the mortuary."

He took a step toward me.

"Careful," I said. "You don't think I'd tackle a murderer by myself."

"Murderer?"

"Yes, Cowan. I'd make book on it. You're a shrewd specimen. You had to cover all contingencies. Suppose the hospital *had* found the diamonds and *had* notified the cops and they were keeping a lid on it until they could question Alison. A girl like her, she'd melt under heat. They could turn her inside out. She'd make a clean breast of it, and you'd be blown. So she had to go. She had to be eliminated. So you loitered and waited until you saw Vicky leave, and then you managed to slip into Alison's room and tamper with the equipment. You cut off her oxygen and watched her die. The cops know what to look for now and they're checking the hospital equipment thoroughly for your prints."

That tore it. He thought he could cut his losses by splitting, so he whirled and slammed through the door, but I hadn't been kidding. The cops were all set for him outside in the corridor.

It seldom comes up roses for all.

Vicky lost her sister, but gained a suitor—me. U.S. Customs descended on Jacques Sutro and seized the smuggled diamonds. Sutro's lawyers attached Jaffe's bank account and recovered the $34,000 check he had deposited. Mr. Sutro still wanted his four grand cash and I referred him to Big Sam Tarloff. Fat chance.

Allan Jaffee healed nicely. The episode may even have

cured his gambling addiction. He copped a plea on the gem charge and turned State's evidence against Ben Cowan. Cowan was going to be out of circulation until he was a rickety old man. For me, representing Jaffee was an act of charity. I never got paid.

Only Nick Papadopolous emerged unscathed. The judge canceled forfeiture of Jaffee's bail bond and Papa got his money back. He was delirious. He invited Vicky and me out to dinner. That was two weeks ago. We're still trying to digest the stuff.

A NICE WHOLESOME GIRL

by Robert Colby

Late in the afternoon, under a misty dome of San Francisco fog, Seaman Wallace Dunbar descended awkwardly from the Treasure Island bus. Trim in his dress uniform, having just been "separated" from the navy, he carried the sum total of his service possessions slung over his shoulder in a seabag weighing close to fifty pounds.

He eased the bag to the sidewalk with a grunt of relief, and for a moment stood glancing about uncertainly while gulping the cool, damp air of his newly won freedom. It was exhilarating to be divorced from the tight wedlock of the navy, but the feeling was mixed with confusion and loss. For two years they told you exactly what to do and how to do it by the book, while surrounded by some pretty close buddies in the same boat.

Suddenly they turned you loose in a strange city a couple of thousand miles from a place called home and a way of life you weren't quite ready to embrace—not until you got the kinks of confinement out of your system with one or two free-wheeling days of transition in this exotic city, the very name of which had always held a kind of magic.

Your wallet was fat with the cash of accumulated pay, and your winnings from a recent month of poker games—in all, eleven hundred bucks you would exchange on Monday for traveler's checks. To this add unlimited and undisciplined time and you had it made—except that now you were alone at the edge of Friday evening and did not know where to look for a girl of the sort you did not find in the Philippines.

Seaman Wally Dunbar, twenty-three, was a radioman who had, after six months of training, been deposited during his year and a half of overseas duty at Subic Naval Station in the Philippines. Though there had been some self-made highlights of excitement, it had been largely a dull and lonely tour of duty, as routine and familiar as his morning face in the shaving mirror.

There had been plenty of passes to the nearby town, which was almost within howling distance of the base. It was a small, shack-strewn, honky-tonk city which shamelessly boasted some four hundred bars, was in fact one great chain of squalid dens connected by crumbling, mud-mottled streets. Attached to the bars, as fixed as shabby mannequins in tired store windows, were close to two thousand mocha-skinned B-girls who wore paid smiles and said things like, "Hey, Joe, I love you—no bull! Buy me drink?"

In the beginning, Wally Dunbar had been amused and even a bit fascinated by the girls who provided instant companionship—while the pesos lasted. Yet he was not shallow. When he found that even those who had a fair understanding of English were only vacuous dolls who were about as deeply responsive and spontaneous as language-lesson recordings, he quickly lost interest.

After his pockets had been picked, his watch literally torn from his wrist by a street kid on the run, even his navy-issue raincoat lifted, he gave up in disgust. He rejected the passes, no longer went to town. Remaining in barracks, he dozed on his "rack," wrote letters, read, or played endless rounds of stud poker, at which he was a pretty consistent winner. Time thus crept toward his moment of release in this city of the Golden Gate to freedom.

On a night's leave from the separation center at Treasure Island, Wally had frequented a few bars along the Strip, but now he was in no mood for commercial entertainment or B-girls, nothing at all which had that Philippine flavor of pumped-up joy and counterfeit affection at a dollar a smile.

Rather, he hungered for a simple, uncomplicated American girl who wanted nothing more than to spend a simple, uncomplicated American evening with Wally Dunbar. The cost of the evening, with eleven hundred bucks on the hip, was of no importance. That is, within reasonable bounds it didn't matter how much was spent, just so long as the expense was never a bargaining point, a condition of friendship.

Having formed an attitude, but only the vaguest plan of action, Wally Dunbar, a middle-tall, middle-sized young man who was altogether undistinguished in the physical sense, hailed a cab, hoisted his seabag to the seat beside him, and ordered the driver to take him to one of the better hotels in a "nice, quiet section of town."

The hotel, sprouting, like most everything else in the city, from a rising hill, was tall and imposing. Its formidable, gray-stone exterior had a look of long-established dignity. The solemn-faced doorman neither snickered nor sneered when Wally alighted beneath the marquee, a Santa Claus of a gob with a bulging seabag in tow. On the contrary, the doorman graciously carried the bag to the rim of the lobby, where a bellhop continued it on its ponderous way to the desk.

Signing himself into a twenty-dollar-a-day room, Wally was carried aloft to the fourteenth floor. The bellhop, who was not much taller than the seabag and half as wide, wrestled it into the room and departed with a handsome tip.

Poised at a window, Wally sighed happily while inspecting an awesome view of the city, the darkening bay in the distance beyond, gracefully spanned by the Golden Gate Bridge. He was at last back in the States where most people treated you like a human being, where most girls did not look upon you as purely a money tree to be stripped clean and then deserted until you grew another batch of Uncle's green.

The thought gave him a secure feeling, a warmth for everything American. Still, as he lighted a cigarette and tried to conjure a delightful picture of the evening ahead, he could not project himself beyond dinner.

Rick Endicott, a fast buddy acquired at Subic, was visiting with a cousin in Oakland. They would meet at five next afternoon, on the Top of the Mark. Meanwhile, what—?

Probed by the cool finger of loneliness, Wally turned from the window in search of the phone. He called his mother long-distance, then, somewhat cheered, took a lazy, luxurious bath, shaved and went below to the dining room.

Shortly after dinner, an odd little incident took place in the lobby, and that was when he met the girl. He had thought that he might begin the evening by taking in a movie, and for that reason he was at the newsstand, buying a paper. There was a light tap on his shoulder, and when he turned his head, the girl was standing there.

She was a petite, dark-haired, dark-eyed girl in her twenties. Her small features were pert, if not pretty, she had long lashes and pale, flawless skin. She was dressed rather primly in a gray, tailored suit.

The moment she looked into his face, her mouth sprang open and she winced, recoiling with embarrassment.

"Oh, excuse me!" she exclaimed. "I thought you were—someone else. From the back you looked exactly like another sailor I know, a friend of my brother's."

As she began to turn away, he dug feverishly for something witty to keep her in conversation.

"Sorry about that," he quipped. "From the back we all look alike in uniform."

"Yes," she said, "that's so true." Her face had closed and she seemed a bird already on the wing.

"Even from the front," he continued hastily, "you can't tell one from the other without a program."

She smiled then. The smile gave her face a look of guileless charm. Still, she said nothing to encourage him.

"I hope you won't think I'm corny," he went on, closing the gap of silence as if it might swallow her, "but it's great to meet a nice, wholesome, American girl."

"How sweet. And thank you."

"I just got back from the Philippines and the sort of gal a sailor meets over there—well, you know what I mean . . ."

"My brother is stationed in Hawaii," she said. "He's in the navy too. He's a petty officer, third class."

Though this was only a rank above his own, he tried to look properly impressed, but he didn't want to talk about the navy. At heart, he was already a civilian.

"He'll be calling me from Hawaii in a couple of hours," she was saying. "He phones every Friday night at nine, seven o'clock their time. It must cost him a fortune. But he hasn't much else to spend his money on and we're very close, always have been."

"I suppose you're married," he said abruptly.

"No, do I look married?"

"It was a loaded question," he said honestly, and grinned.

"Well, I'm not married, I'm just a plain, ordinary working girl."

"A working girl, maybe. But not the rest of it. Are you a secretary?" People were milling about the stand and they had moved to one side.

"No, I—I work here—in the hotel beauty parlor. I was just on my way home."

He nodded. The little ball of certainty had rolled into the winning slot and he felt the timing was right. "How about a drink, then? Just one for the road."

She glanced at her watch. "I don't have an awful lot of time, but—"

"Plans for the evening?"

"Nothing special, no. But I'll have to be home at nine for that call from Hawaii. My brother, remember?"

"Sure, I remember."

"It takes a while on the bus."

"Yeah, but in a taxi, maybe only a few minutes. I'll see that you get there with time to spare."

She beamed at him and he began to guide her toward the hotel bar, exchanging names. Hers was Gloria Baxter.

"Now that you're out of the service, how long will you be in town?" she asked over a third drink. "This isn't your home, is it?"

"No, I live in St. Louis. I'll only be here a day or two at the most. Got a plane ticket. Special rate for the military, you know."

"I know." Her wide eyes fastened upon him, then the lids lowered shyly. "Guess you've got a girl back there in St. Louis."

"Nope. I wasn't six months in the Philippines when she got married. My father's dead, there's only my mother now."

"Too bad. About your girl, I mean."

"Well, that's the way it goes, Gloria. Except for Mom, there's no reason for me to hurry home. But it's lonely in a strange city and sooner or later the ol' bankroll will thin out and I'll need a job."

"A city doesn't have to be lonely or strange, Wally," she offered. "Not when you know someone, a friend to guide you about."

"Is that a promise?"

She chuckled. "That's a promise, Wally. And now I really must go, if you don't mind."

Crossing town in the taxi, he began to talk freely about himself. In the drink-widened expanse of his mind she was already his girl; he would not go home except for a visit, he would remain and make a new life for himself. Maybe something deep and lasting would develop between them. In any case, he would not be lonely.

It was a white stucco building of three stories on a narrow, climbing side street. She had suggested fixing him a drink while she waited for the call, after which, since she did not have to work on Saturday, she had agreed to help him celebrate his release from the navy with a tour of the city's most exciting night spots.

Her second-floor apartment was neatly, though sparingly, furnished in early American, frail, feminine pieces with bright splashes of color. It seemed a cozy, cheerful atmosphere and he sank onto the sofa with the feeling that he already belonged.

"The phone is in the bedroom," she explained, "so I'll just crack the door enough to hear it, then I'll make us a drink."

She went away but in a couple of minutes returned with tall highballs. "I don't have anything but bourbon and ginger," she apologized. "Will that do?"

"Why not? Another cocktail and I'd forget my name."

"Long as you don't forget mine, Wally."

He took the glass from her and sipped. "How could you forget a name like Gloria Baxter? Sounds like a movie star." He twirled the ice in the glass and drank deeply. "But I wouldn't like you if you were a movie star, Gloria. I'm just a plain guy and I like plain, uncomplicated girls. Know what I mean? *Real* people."

"A nice, wholesome American girl?" Her winged eyebrows ascended as she settled herself at the other end of the sofa.

"That's it," he answered. "Cornball or not, that's just what I'm trying to say. You spend a year or so on the other side of that ocean and you come home a square. I'm not ashamed of it—I'll drink to it."

He lifted his glass, they drank in unison.

He said a few other things after that, but later he could not remember them. He could remember only the faintly mocking twist of her smile as she toasted his approval of her.

It was morning. At least, a pale light seeped through the panes of an uncurtained window. He lay sprawled upon the uncarpeted floor of a small, perfectly barren room. It was the general size of a bedroom, and there were a couple of closets, but there were no other clues to its intended purpose. There was not a stick of furniture, not so much as a scrap of debris to give the room a name.

Wally was not alone. Draped about the floor, in a deep slumber and in a variety of unlikely postures for sleep, were two sailors and a marine sergeant. That the trio of their snores did not awaken them was a round of discordant applause in praise of Gloria Baxter's secret formula for hypnotic drinks.

Wally awoke with a sense of absolute disorientation, but, forgetting the foul taste in his mouth, he suffered no painful effect. His head felt weightless as a balloon but did not throb or ache. Also, his mind was lucid enough. He could, up to a point, remember word-for-word, action-for-action, the entire charade of the previous night.

Glancing about, he decided at once that he shouldn't even bother to hunt for his wallet, but there it was in his hip pocket. Not only that, it contained cash—four one dollar bills. She—they?—had, with big hearts, left him just enough for carfare and a deluxe breakfast.

If he had then been in possession of his eleven hundred, he would have been willing to bet all of it that his hapless companions, those staggered victims of a long, astonishing night of plunder, would not find their slenderized wallets in much better shape.

Looking out from that second floor window, Wally was quite certain that he was in the same building on the same street where the cab had deposited him with—Gloria Baxter? Well, that was at least a wiser choice than Liz Taylor.

Yet, when he stumbled into what had to be the living room, it was also naked, desolate. The bright, cozy furnishings were gone. In the kitchen there was only an ancient refrigerator.

He went out the front door and down the steps to the street. He came back thoughtfully, taking his bearings. Yes, the same building, same apartment. It was a clever scheme, skillfully executed. Although he could not guess the small details, he now felt that he understood how it must have been done.

A series of violent shakes and slaps failed to awaken the others. "Dream on, suckers," he muttered, "you got a surprise coming." He went out and down the stairs again.

Pausing before a door designated, "Manager," he beat upon it loudly.

A chesty, tousle-haired man, his eyes puffy with sleep, appeared in a faded robe and slippers. "Beat it!" he growled. "You got a nerve, this hour of the morning!"

When Wally explained that the police would be right behind him, the manager agreed to tell what he knew about apartment 2B. It had been rented by a man from Los Angeles who had paid up the entire year's lease. He had intended to use it as a place to hang his hat during frequent business trips to San Francisco. However, he had not been seen since and a letter mailed to him was returned. The man had moved without leaving a forwarding.

Furniture? No, all the apartments were rented unfurnished and not a single piece had been delivered for installation in 2B.

Wally smiled a secret smile and went away. It was a good story and doubtless the manager would be able to prove it with legal documents. At least Wally now had a better picture of the way the game was played and he was going to get his eleven hundred back, one way or the other.

His plan did not include the police, but it would be interesting, if not profitable, to check their reaction. He flagged a passing patrol car.

"You fell for one of the oldest gags on the books," the cop told him. "Hard-boiled dames with sweet-kid faces are cleaning the military all over town."

"Why don't you put a stop to it?"

"We try, fella, we try. We catch a few amateurs but the real pros are too slick. They only take the boys in transit to their home towns, the ones who can't or won't hang around long enough to appear in court, even if we could find these hustlers and bring them in.

"I won't kid you, sailor, you got about one chance in a thousand of getting your dough back—what's left of it."

The cop filled out a report and promised an investigation. He shook his head woefully when Wally said he was just another gob separated from service, pausing for a night or two on the town before flying home.

Shortly after five on the following afternoon, Wally was peering down from a window seat at the Top of the Mark.

". . . So when I got a peek at this manager and heard

his phony tale," he related to his navy pal, Rick Endicott, "I had the whole score figured. The manager is in on the deal and gets a nice fat cut. The minute the girl has her sucker doped off into dreamland, she lifts his cash, then goes down and raps on the manager's door. This character goes up with her and they move the poor stiff into an empty bedroom. It doesn't have to be furnished since the mark never gets to see it until he finally wakes up.

"And that's not until morning, because they give all these boobs like me a mixture that would wipe out an elephant. So now the road is clear for the next victim, and how long does it take a gal with any looks to con some half-boozed squid up to her pad?"

"About ten minutes," said Rick, a rangy, fun-loving sailor from Fort Worth. He grinned. "But when they've got all those crazy squids in the bag, what do they do with the furniture?"

"Well, what else *could* they do with it if they didn't just haul it right into an empty next door, saved for the gag? Pick up a few light pieces in the living room, roll up the rug, pull down the flimsy curtains—a fifteen minute job at most."

"Yeah, but why bother? Why not leave it?"

"Because it might help to confuse some guys. They might think they were in another building, another pad. But try this for size: you're a squid who's just been rolled for his full head of cabbage and you wake up in this joint, everything gone but the furniture. What do you do?"

"I find something heavy and I bust the furniture into kindling wood. Then I make a neat pile in the corner of the room and I burn the lot, every blasted piece."

Wally chuckled. "Any other questions?"

"Yeah, how come they never get caught? Suppose some guy goes back the next night and waits around to collect his dough or his pound of flesh?"

"He collects a little fresh air, and that's all, buddy, that's all. I'll bet twenty to one they don't use the gimmick more than two or three times a month. They wouldn't dare chance it, though they might have other pads in other buildings if it's a big, organized con game. Regardless, one play like last night's could net three or four grand."

He paused. "That phony Gloria with her phony call from her phony squid brother in Hawaii—she had me in the palm of her hand, eating my heart out. Some night, somewhere, I'm gonna catch up with her. And then I'll squeeze her till she coughs up eleven hundred bucks—with interest!

"Oh man, I can't wait for that scene. Meantime, I'm staying on here to take the takers. I'm gonna dangle myself all over town as human bait—a nice juicy, innocent squid on the hook with a big roll in his pocket, just ready to be gobbled up.

"And when they take the bait, I'm gonna catch a whole mess of Glorias with overstuffed purses full of navy-issue cash. All that cash is gonna wind up in my pocket, and then you'll hear me laughing all the way to St. Lou."

"Sounds like a real kick," Endicott said. "What do you plan to use for bait? I mean, you got to show at least a Philadelphia roll—stack of ones wrapped in a couple of hundreds, maybe."

"That's where you come in, Ricky-boy. You supply the green and you'll get it all back, with a neat profit. Anything over my eleven hundred, we split right down the middle. How does that grab you?"

"It grabs me right where I live—in my wallet. Do you do all the dirty work?"

"With pleasure, Rick. With pleasure!"

Rick was thoughtful. "You got a deal," he said, and reached for his money.

About ten o'clock that same Saturday night, in a crowded Strip bar, Wally set his bait and soon hooked a big one. She sat down beside him and coyly pretended indifference while he played it a little drunk and loudly demanded a drink, peeling a hundred from his dollar-padded roll, telling the complaining bartender he didn't have anything smaller, but hell, if it was any big problem, he would buy a round for the entire house.

After a while she couldn't seem to locate a match for her cigarette and when he produced his lighter, she found her personality and turned it on full-smile. She said her name was Sheila Marshall. He gave her the treatment, dropping the plan that he was flying home in the morning, had the ticket in his pocket.

The way she got him to her apartment was even more transparent. She ordered a tall rum drink mixed with sticky cola, then suddenly made a nervous gesture and spilled the entire mess into her lap.

"It won't take a minute," she said when she returned from the Powder Room. "We'll run over to my place—it's practically around the corner. I'll do a fast change and we'll be on our way again. Okay?"

He was a bit worried when he got a look at her furniture; that is, he was really bleeding for the guy who had to move it. The aging junk was built in the days of bulging, solid-wood construction, supporting massive chairs and giant sofas.

He sat down comfortably and waited for the play to begin. The curtain rose immediately when she came out of the kitchen with a couple of long ones, offering him the glass which seemed to contain a darker liquid.

Stalling with the lighting of a cigarette, he set the glass on a table beside him. "Listen, while I get on the good side of this drink, why don't you hop into a fresh rag?"

"Well sure." She crossed her long legs and adjusted her skirt. "You in a hurry?"

"Bet I am, baby! We got a lotta livin' to do yet. I came eighteen months and ten thousand miles for this night. I got ten yards of lettuce and I'm gonna spread at least a yard all over town. So hop to, sugar. Go-go-go!"

"Well, all right, then," she said obediently. Standing, she put down her drink and went off to another room. Was it empty, but for a dress in a closet?"

He got up quickly and switched the drinks. He was about to return to his chair when he noticed her pocketbook, left on the coffee table. *Why not?* he thought, and opened it.

He found a billfold jam-packed with currency. *Why not?* he thought again. Taking the bills, he began a hasty count.

Sensing a presence, he glanced up. She was standing there, framed in the doorway, eyeing him coolly.

"I forgot my purse," she was saying. "I see that you were about to bring it to me. How thoughtful—darling."

Rocked off balance for a moment, he groped for a sharp reply.

"I don't understand," she said, her face truly puzzled. "It's not as if you were broke and there was nothing left for you but to steal my money. If you were hard-up, I'd be the first one to let you have a few bucks. What kind of a guy are you, anyway? Really, I should call the police. That's just what I should do!"

"Be my guest," he said, the bitterness and boldness flooding back to him. "Call the police. And while we're waiting for them, we'll have a little drink. You're gonna drink from *my* glass, and I'm gonna drink from yours. By the time the cops get here, you'll be fast asleep. They'll carry you down like a rag doll and drive you to the station where they'll put you beddy-bye in a nice, cozy cell."

"Sorry," she said frigidly, "I don't get the joke. Is there supposed to be something wrong with the drink I made for you?"

"Nothing wrong with it, sister. Not if you like knockout drops in your whiskey."

"I see. And which was your glass?" she said evenly.

"This one." He extended it toward her.

She took it from him and with some effort and much swallowing, got all of the drink down her throat. Then she sat calmly and studied him.

"How long is it supposed to take?" she asked bitingly. "Ten minutes? Twenty?" She glanced at her watch. "If I should fall asleep, then I want you to keep the money as a gift. If I don't, then I'll call the police. Fair enough?"

He sat in moody silence for a time, then got up and returned the bills to her purse. "I'm sorry, Sheila," he said, "I'm terribly sorry. It was a mistake. Let me tell you what they did to me last night and I think you'll see this in another light."

She listened patiently as he unfolded the complete story, including his plan to bait the con-girls with his Philadelphia roll.

For a long moment she was grave and pensive, then she smiled a sad little smile. "Well, I *do* understand," she said. "And I can see how you might think of me as one of those—B-girls. Would you like to know how I happened to be in that bar, for the first time in my life really looking for a pickup?"

"Well, yeah, I am a bit curious."

"You see, I had a date with a guy I liked in a big way. He's a cruel kind of man, but fascinating too. He was to meet me in the bar at nine. When an hour passed and he didn't show, I knew he wasn't coming. So I worked myself into this reckless, go-to-hell frame of mind, and when you came along, well, you seemed like just the right medicine for my wound."

He smiled. "What do you say we limp out and salve our wounds together?"

"On one condition," she replied, aiming a finger. "That you hold onto your—what do you call it?—your Philadelphia bankroll. The party's on me. I make a good salary and I just got my yearly bonus, so I can afford it."

"You're a real sport, Sheila, you really are! You're the first decent girl I've met in a year and a half. No kidding!"

"I'll have to change now," she said in a voice that seemed to quake on the brink of tears, and hurried from the room.

Sheila Marshall, better known in certain limited circles as Maggie McCleskey, pulled on a clean dress and restored her makeup in the mirror. This done, she took a sheet of paper from a drawer, scribbled a few words across it and secured it to a weight which was kept for just such an emergency. At the rear window, she signaled with a pocket flash, then carefully tossed the weight below.

It landed beside a sedan on the shadowy parking apron behind the old, converted house.

The note read: *Pass this one up! I think he's a cop and it could be a trap!*

That was about the only kind of warning you could use to stop big Buck Novak, hiding in the car since she phoned him. He was primed to clobber the next gob of the night with a sap after she led him down the back steps, having told him as prearranged, "My girlfriend gave me the key to her car and said I could borrow it while she's away for the weekend. So, honey, why spend your money on a taxi?"

Buck would lump a cash-heavy sailor to sleep, then drive him down to a deserted area near the bay and heave him out. If he ever did find his way back, Buck, not Maggie, would be waiting in *his* apartment, acting dumb or iron-fisted, as the case required.

Buck was a hard man, no heart at all. But every now and then, Maggie discovered within herself that small, tender spot which tonight the bad-luck sailor had touched. He had, in fact, said one kind thing about her which, however undeserved, had nearly made her cry. For herself, as well as the sailor, she did not want to spoil the illusion.

When they had left the building and were out of sight, she took his arm and fell happily into step. Smiling down at her, Wally told himself that after all, there was, in the city of San Francisco, at least one nice, wholesome, American girl.

DINNER WILL BE COLD

by *Fletcher Flora*

East Elder, the suburban area in which I live, is a place you probably know. Maybe, under another name, it is the place in which you also live. Nothing there is geometrically designed. Everything, however contrived, gives the effect of being natural. Winding roads instead of parallel streets. Rustic fences and country mail boxes. Septic tanks instead of sewers. It costs quite a lot to live there. Somehow, whatever you earn, it takes all of it.

From my office downtown, if I hit the lights right, it was about a fifty minute drive to my home. On this particular Monday evening, having left the office at five-fifteen, I got home a few minutes after six. I went in the back door and through the kitchen into the living room, and there in the living room with a glass in one hand and a cigarette in the other was my wife, Ivy. I could see immediately that she was very worried, and so I knew that nothing had changed since eight o'clock that morning, when I had seen her last, except that maybe it was worse now than it had been then.

"You heard from Carla?" I said.

"No," she said. "Not a word."

"Well," I said, trying to sound casual, "she's a big, beautiful girl now, and she knows what she's doing. You wait and see. She probably just went off for a weekend with someone, that's all."

"I know. That's what you've been saying and saying. She'll be back Monday at the latest, you've kept saying, but now Monday is almost over, and she isn't back, and I'm sick with worry."

There was a pitcher of martinis on a table, and I went over and filled a glass and sat down in a chair.

"I guess one sister has the right to worry about another," I said. "She'll be all right, though. She'll show up in her own good time."

"If she merely went away for a few days, even with a man, why didn't she tell me she was going?"

"Oh, come off, Ivy. Women are sensitive about such things. She might tell you about it afterward, but not before."

"She didn't take a bag. No clothes or toilet articles or anything. Nothing of hers is missing."

"Are you sure?"

"Of course, I'm sure. I've told you over and over."

"She could have bought a bag and a few things in town after she left. Maybe she just didn't want to incite your curiosity."

"I simply don't believe that Carla would have been so deceptive. When she left Friday morning, she said explicitly that she was going to have lunch in town, keep two appointments in the afternoon, and then come home. She said she might be late, but the implication was definitely that she would be back Friday night at the latest."

I had heard all this before. I had heard it repeated at intervals, almost in identical words, all through Saturday and Sunday, and now again on Monday evening. The appointments had been with a doctor and a hairdresser. Ivy had found their names and addresses in an appointment book in Carla's room, but we hadn't contacted them. It was mostly, I guess, because I advised against it. Carla was an attractive girl who knew how to exploit her assets, and I had argued reasonably, I thought, for the weekend somewhere with someone. Although Carla had never done anything like that before, to our knowledge, the idea was not untenable, even to Ivy.

"Well," I said, "what do you want to do?"

"I don't know. I can't think clearly, Ned. I simply don't know."

"How does this strike you? We'll wait until tomorrow. If she doesn't return in the morning, give me a call at the office, and I'll try to look into it."

"Do you think we should wait any longer?"

"Until tomorrow. I don't want to be placed in the position of intruding on Carla's private affairs, if that's all this amounts to."

"All right. I'll try not to worry any more until tomorrow. I already feel a little better, now that we've made a decision."

I had finished my martini, and I wanted another, but I decided I'd better not have it. I got up and put my empty glass on the table beside the pitcher.

"I didn't detect any signs of dinner in the kitchen," I said. "Are we going out?"

"Would you mind terribly? I've been so worried that I couldn't force myself to prepare anything."

"It's all right. We'll go down to the restaurant in the shopping center. What do you say to going about eight? I'd like to go out and saw some wood before we go."

"You go right on and saw your wood, dear. Eight will be fine. I'm sorry to have made things so bad for you. I'll try to relax too."

I went upstairs and changed clothes and came down again. Outside, carrying a bucksaw, I walked down the backyard, which sloped to the bed of a small stream, now dry in a dry summer. Beyond the stream bed, the ground sloped upward rather steeply, and this slope was covered with brush and scrub timber. I owned a couple of acres of the slope, and early in the summer, really late spring, I had cut out some of the trees that were dead or dying. Ever since, in my free time, I had been sawing the trees into lengths for the fireplace when winter came, and I had two large piles of wood beyond the stream at the base of the slope. One pile was of small pieces that were ready for burning, and the other pile was of large chunks that would need splitting. I was almost finished with the sawing and planned to start soon with the splitting. It was hard work, but I enjoyed doing it, and I always felt good when I came up to the house afterward, hot and tired. The palms of my hands were hard. My arms were strong.

I worked steadily for over an hour, and when I got back to the house it was almost eight and getting dark. Ivy was waiting for me in our bedroom, ready to go, and so I showered and dressed quickly, and we drove over to the shopping center restaurant and had a couple of drinks and dinner. It was about ten when we returned, and Ivy went right up to bed, but I had another drink and a cigarette outside in a lawn chair, listening to an owl and some frogs on a pond that the stream behind the house ran into farther along.

In our bedroom, when I went up, Ivy was lying quietly in her twin bed, and I could tell by the precise measurement of her breathing that she was pretending sleep. I undressed in the bathroom and got into bed in the dark. Ivy had not mentioned Carla all evening, and would not mention her now, but I knew that she was lying awake over there in her bed, measuring her breath and staring up into the darkness with wide and worried eyes.

In the morning, after a bad night, I awoke before the alarm sounded and shaved and dressed as quietly as I could. Ivy lay on her side with her back to me, and I didn't know if she were asleep or awake. Dressed and ready to leave, I stopped beside her bed and stood looking down at her, and it was then, for the first time, that she rolled over onto her back and opened her eyes.

"I'm going now," I said. "How are you feeling?"

"Tired," she said. "I didn't sleep much."

"You'll sleep tonight," I said, "after Carla gets back."

"You think she'll come today?"

"She'll come, all right. I have a feeling."

"I hope you're right. I can't stand this uncertainty much longer."

"Don't worry. If she hasn't come by noon, give me a call."

"I'm sorry I don't feel like getting up to fix your breakfast. Will you fix something for yourself?"

"I don't want anything. Just coffee. I'll fix some coffee."

"Good-by, then. Have a good day."

"You, too. Call me if Carla comes, not just if she doesn't. I'll be relieved to know you won't be worried any more."

I leaned over and kissed her on the forehead and went out and downstairs to the kitchen. I made some coffee and drank two cups black and then drove downtown to my office. I was an accountant, and I had been successful enough to employ a pair of junior accountants and a secretary. I wasn't rich, but I was comfortable. I wasn't swamped, but I was busy. I was busy this particular morning, the morning of Tuesday, and I worked straight through until noon, when I went out to lunch. I was back at one, and it was ten minutes later when the telephone rang, and it was Ivy calling. Her voice was dry and taut.

"Carla hasn't come back," she said.

"The day isn't over yet."

"You said this morning, Ned. You said you'd do something if she didn't come this morning."

"All right. I'll see if I can find out anything. Do you have the names and addresses of the hairdresser and doctor there?"

"I remember them. They've been in my mind for three days now."

"Let me have them."

I wrote them down on a memo pad as she repeated them. Then I assured her that I'd call and let her know what I learned, if anything, after I'd talked with the two.

"You have to promise me one thing," she said.

"What's that?"

"If you don't learn anything, you have to go to the police."

"Are you sure you want me to do that?"

"Yes, I'm sure."

"It might be embarrassing in the end. Carla might not like it."

"I don't care. I can't just wait and wait forever without doing anything or knowing anything."

"Have it your own way. After all, she's your sister, and not mine."

"Do you promise to go?"

"I promise."

I hung up and tried to finish the piece of work in hand, about a half hour's job, but it was no use. I gave it up after a few minutes and went out into the street. The hairdresser's professional name was Monsieur Paul, and his shop or salon or parlor or whatever it is properly called was located within easy walking distance. I walked there and went inside and was asked by an enameled girl in a white nylon sheath what she could do for me. I asked to see Monsieur Paul on personal business, and she went away to see if this was possible. While she was gone, I inspected the plush little reception room, and it was obvious that Monsieur Paul was either highly prosperous or deeply mortgaged. I have heard that women prefer men hairdressers, who are, I think, usually called stylists for effect, and it seemed that Monsieur Paul was preferred by his share with more than their share of money. I was prepared to dislike him intensely, and the funny thing was, when he showed, that I didn't. I didn't dislike him at all.

He was young and rather stocky. He had straight brown hair neatly parted and brushed. His smile was candid, or seemed so, and his voice was pleasant. I suspect that his last name was Smith or Brown or Jones. He seemed like a fellow who would enjoy a cold beer, a game of poker, and maybe even sawing wood with a bucksaw.

"How can I help you?" he said.

"I'm hoping you can tell me something about a customer of yours," I said.

"Oh?" His eyebrows climbed a fraction of an inch. "May I ask the customer's name?"

"It's Bridges. Miss Carla Bridges."

"Oh, yes. To be sure. She was in just last Friday."

"That's what I wanted to know. I'm her brother-in-law. My name is Edward Maxwell. My wife, her sister, would like to locate her as soon as possible. Can you tell me what time she was here on Friday? I suppose it would be entered in your appointment book?"

"It is, of course, but I happen to remember exactly. It was immediately after lunch. One o'clock. She had a wash and a set, that's all. She was here only a short while."

"How did she seem?"

"I beg your pardon?"

"I mean, did she seem excited or distressed or in a hurry? Anything like that?"

"I don't recall that she did. Of course, she might have seemed any or all of those things without my being aware of it." Monsieur Paul grinned wryly. "I'm afraid that the intimate rapport between hair stylists and their clients is romantically exaggerated."

"I see." I was convinced, in Monsieur Paul's case, that it really was. "Well, thanks for helping me. You've been most considerate."

"Not at all. I hope that nothing is wrong."

"No. I don't think so."

I thanked him again and went outside, where I paused on the sidewalk to consult the sheet from the memo pad. The doctor's name was Gerald Blaker. His office was out in the Plaza district, too far for walking, and so I hailed a cab, rather than going back for my own car, and rode out there.

Dr. Blaker's reception room was crowded, and I was compelled to assert myself to get a few minutes sandwiched between two patients. Even so, it was a quarter of an hour before I got the sandwich, and then I was permitted to pass through a door into a hall and down to a consulting room, where the doctor was waiting. He was about my age, which placed him in a category I designate as relatively young. He was also about my height, a little on the plus side of average, and he wore his hair clipped short, as I did. Beyond these points of similarity, there were significant differences. He was better looking than I, smoother than I, probably richer than I, and he possessed a subtle quality, which I sensed and could almost smell, of being party to a kind of reciprocity pact with women in general. In brief, Dr. Blaker had that elusive appeal that women of all ages respond to almost instinctively. Reviewing the character of the reception room I had just left, I had an impression of a heavy distaff majority.

Dr. Blaker, however, wore his charm with good grace. He was amiable and earnest, if somewhat abrupt. He asked me how he could help me, and I told him.

"Carla Bridges?" His brow was momentarily corrugated. "I have no patient with that name. If I ever had one, it has been so long ago that I've forgotten."

"It wasn't long ago. She had an appointment here just last Friday."

"You're mistaken. There was no Carla Bridges here last Friday or any other Friday within my memory."

"Are you positive? It may be quite important."

"I'm positive. I'm sorry if you've been misinformed."

"Excuse me, doctor, if I seem persistent, but I must know this definitely. I have a small identification photo of Carla in my wallet. Just head and shoulders. Would you object to looking at it?"

"Not in the least. I'm extremely busy, however, and I'll have to make this interview as brief as possible."

I removed the picture from my wallet and handed it to him. He looked down at it and up quickly at me, returning the picture as part of the same motion. Now in his expression, together with amiable earnestness and the slightest impatience, was a suggestion of wariness. I had a notion that he was swiftly reviewing his professional position relative to confidential communications.

"I believe you said this young lady is your wife's sister?"

"Yes."

"May I ask why you've come here to inquire about her?"

"She's missing. She lives with us, my wife and me, and she hasn't been home since Friday. Naturally, we're concerned. We found a notation of an appointment here Friday afternoon, and I thought you might be able to tell us something helpful."

"Perhaps I can. I don't know. She was here Friday afternoon, all right. I've been seeing her about once a week for perhaps a month, but not as Carla Bridges. She called herself Carla Adams."

"Why should she use an assumed name? Doesn't seem like Carla."

"I'm sure I don't know. It worries me a bit, to tell the truth. Frankly, I was trying to treat her for a nervous condition characterized by periods of depression. I'm not a psychiatrist, but she seemed to feel that I was helping her, and so I continued to see her."

"How was she feeling on Friday?"

"Her condition was fairly good. I gave her a mild tranquilizer. Well, I don't want to violate her confidence, but I suppose I'm justified under the circumstances in revealing that she was involved with a man. Or had been. An unfortunate affair, I gathered."

"Did she tell you who the man was?"

"No."

"Did she make another appointment with you?"

"Yes. For next Friday."

"Did she indicate where she was going when she left here?"

"No, she did not."

I stood up, restoring my wallet to its pocket. He stood also, offering a hand, which I took.

"Thank you for your time, doctor. I know you're busy."

"Don't mention it. Knowing what you have told me, I'm glad that you stopped in. Please let me know if I can be of any help later."

"I'm wondering about amnesia. Is that possible?"

"Possible, but highly improbable. Cases of true amnesia are really quite rare. I rather imagine that you will find the cause of her disappearance to be somewhat more in the area of ordinary experience. An emotional disturbance. There are both precipitating and predisposing factors in

these matters, you know. Different people react differently
to substantially the same circumstances."

"Yes. That's true. Thank you again, doctor."

Hesitating outside to consider what I had learned, I decided that it was enough to be vaguely disturbing, but not
enough to be alarming. There had apparently been an emotional entanglement with a man, a crisis of some sort, and
then the sudden disappearance. The assumptions that could
be made from this were numerous, and there would be little use in anyone's speculating about them on the basis of
what was known. I was reluctant to go to the police, but I
had promised Ivy that I would, and that's where I went. I
went to police headquarters and was escorted by a sergeant, after explaining my mission, to a small bleak room
occupied by a small bleak man.

The man was a lieutenant of detectives, and his name, as
it turned out, was Ferguson. He had a neat still face that
somehow gave the impression of being deliberately withdrawn, its expressions the merest flickering of shadows, as
if they were cast from without by something moving swiftly
between him and the light. His eyes waited and waited in
dark sockets, and they waited there now, lusterless, while I
told him about Carla and what I had learned, which was
little enough, from Paul and Dr. Blaker.

"Girls are always disappearing," he said when I had finished. "Every day there are girls who disappear. Usually
they have a reason that seems adequate to them, even if it
doesn't to anyone else. Usually they show up again when it
suits them."

"It must be hard on their families," I said.

"Yes, it is. It's hard on the families, and the families are
hard on the police. The truth is, there's nothing we can do
about them, even if we can find them, so long as they're of
age. Your sister-in-law, I assume, is."

"Of course. She's twenty-six."

"You see the problem? A girl twenty-six is free to go
where she wants, when she wants. There's no law against
it."

"You think that's all there is to it? You think Carla just
decided all at once to go away?"

"No. Not yet. Anyhow, whatever happened, for whatever reason, there's no reason to think it happened all at

once. Things hardly ever do. Maybe it was coming inside her for a long time. You say this Dr. Blaker said there was a man involved?"

"He said she had been involved with a man. He didn't say the man was involved in her disappearance."

"You take this man. Just for speculation, that is. Maybe he made her so miserable she just went off somewhere alone to get over him. Women do such things sometimes. Maybe they had a fight and made up and went off together. That happens sometimes, too."

"I've already thought of those possibilities. I was hoping that you, as a policeman, could do something more."

"Oh, I'll do something more, all right. But probably not much, and not enough. You can never do enough for someone who's looking for someone who doesn't want to be found."

"What will you do?"

"To begin with, I'll go talk with this hairdresser and this doctor."

"What good will that do? I've already told you everything they had to say."

"Maybe I can get them to say something you couldn't. You never know. It's my business to get information from people, and I may be a little better at it than you are."

"Of course. I'm sorry if I seem to be pressing. I'm concerned, naturally."

"Naturally. I guess I don't seem very sympathetic, but I can't take everything personally."

"I understand that. Will you let me know if you learn anything?"

"I'll let you know if I do or don't. You go on home and try to be patient, and I'll see if I can pick up your sister-in-law's trail. I probably can't, but I'll try. Meanwhile, if she shows up, *you* let *me* know. I don't want to be wasting any time looking for someone who isn't even missing. You got a picture of her that I can borrow?"

I gave him the identification photo, and he took it and looked at it and laid it carefully on his desk.

"She's a looker," he said. "There's usually a man with the lookers."

"I hope you get onto something fast," I said. "My wife is getting pretty difficult to live with."

"I know about wives," he said. "I'll call you."

I had to leave it at that. I left it and him and police headquarters. Back at the building in which my office was located, I decided not even to go inside. One of the juniors would close up at quitting time, and I wanted to go home and get my hands on my bucksaw. It had become a kind of therapy for me, sawing wood. It's hard to explain the way it made me feel.

Traffic was light, the lights were mostly with me, and I made it home in just over forty-five minutes. Ivy was lying down in the bedroom, and I went upstairs and sat on the edge of the bed and told her what I had done and what I had learned.

"It looks like there's a man involved," I said.

"She didn't tell me about any man," Ivy said.

"She must have had a reason," I said. "Maybe he was married."

She lay there on her back with her eyes wide and dry and hot. Instead of feeling reassured, now that the police had been brought into it, she was for that very reason utterly convinced at last that something terrible and irreparable had happened. I tried to take her hand, but she removed it and turned her face away. After a while, I stood up.

"I think I'll go saw some wood," I said.

She didn't answer, and so I changed clothes and went away. I finished sawing up the tree I was working on, which took a couple of hours, a little longer, and when I returned to the house, the telephone was ringing urgently in the downstairs hall, and Ivy was on the stairs coming down to answer it, but I picked it up and answered it myself, while Ivy stood still on the stairs and watched and listened.

"Mr. Maxwell?" It was Ferguson's voice.

"Yes," I said.

"Lieutenant Ferguson here. I think I have some information for you."

"You've worked fast, Lieutenant. What is it?"

"You'd better come down to headquarters."

"Is that necessary? It's an hour's drive."

"You'd better come on down. I'll send a car for you if you like."

"No. No, thanks. I'll drive myself."

"Good. I'll be waiting here for you."

He hung up, and so did I. Ivy hadn't moved on the stairs. Her eyes were feverish and glittering.

"That was Lieutenant Ferguson," I said. "He has some information for us. He wants me to come down to headquarters."

"Something has happened," she said. "Something terrible has happened."

"Probably not. You mustn't let your imagination run away with you."

"Why didn't he tell you over the phone? Why must you go downtown? Why must I be kept waiting and waiting?"

"Listen to me. I'll get back just as soon as I can. Why don't you keep busy at something? Time will pass easier and quicker if you do."

"Why can't I go with you?"

"No. I don't think you'd better. I'll hurry. I'll be back soon."

She continued to stand on the stairs, looking down at me with her feverish eyes, and I had a feeling that she was about to scream. She didn't, though. She made no sound at all, no sound or movement, and I turned and left, not even taking time to change from my old clothes. Driving, I paid no attention to the speed limits, depending on Ferguson to fix any tickets I might get, but I didn't get any, as it happened, and reached the police headquarters in record time. Ferguson was waiting for me where we had talked earlier, a bleak little man in a bleak little room.

"You made good time," he said.

"So did you," I said.

"Yeah. Funny, isn't it? It's almost as if your coming here this afternoon acted as a kind of catalyst. Right away things began to happen."

"Do you know where Carla is?"

"I know." He looked down at his right hand, the fingers folded into the palm. As he looked, he seemed to be filled with wonder at the miracle of such a perfect tool. "She's downstairs. In the morgue."

The words, spoken with deliberate abruptness that may have been his notion of kindness, were like a blow. The room and Ferguson faded for a moment and then returned in an instant to focus.

"Dead?"

He nodded. "I'm sorry."

"I guess I've sort of been expecting it, really. At least I've been prepared for it."

"That's good. It makes things tougher for everyone if there's a lot of fuss."

"You're sure it's Carla? Could there be a mistake?"

"There could be, but I don't think there is. I'm as sure as I can be with only the picture you gave me to judge by. You'll have to identify her, of course, and then we'll know. You think you can take it now, or would you rather wait a while?"

"Now. I couldn't stand waiting."

"All right. Let's go down."

We went down, and I looked, and it was Carla. She had been strangled and had been dead for quite a long time, and she wasn't pretty any more, and would never be again, but it was Carla. I looked at her for a few seconds, pain suddenly like a pulsing knot of muscles above my diaphragm, and then I turned and walked away with Ferguson following. Outside in a hall, I stopped and drew a ragged breath, leaning for a moment against the wall.

"Are you all right?" Ferguson said.

"All right now," I said. "It was a bad sight."

"You're doing fine. It's a big relief, I have to admit, that you're taking it so well. We'd better go back upstairs and talk a few minutes, if you feel up to it."

"I'd like to get home as soon as possible. My wife will be frantic with worry."

"Sure. I understand. We'll just talk a few minutes about a few things, and then you can go on home."

"I don't know how I can possibly break it to her."

"I don't envy you the job. I'd hate to have to tell my wife something like this."

We were going upstairs, and we reached the bleak little room. It was bleaker than ever, starkly naked, under a fluorescent light. Ferguson sat behind his desk, and I sat in a straight chair in front of it so we were facing each other.

"I'd better tell you where she was and how we found her," he said. "She was stuffed into a culvert out in the suburbs. This culvert runs under a narrow dead-end road off one of the main roads. It was just luck that she was found this soon, because there are no houses on the dead-end, and I gather that no one uses it much. A guy just happened along this afternoon and found her. No credit to us. He called headquarters, and I went out with another cop, and there she was.

"You think she was taken there after she was killed?"

"Who knows? Maybe. I'd guess, though, that she was taken there alive by the man who killed her."

"I don't suppose you have any idea who the man is?"

"Not yet. We will." Under the harsh light in the naked room, his bleakness was chilling. "I'm wondering if you can tell me anything more about this hairdresser and this doctor she went to see."

"No. I saw both of them for the first time today."

"That's too bad. It would be helpful to have something more."

"Why? Is there any reason to suspect either of them?"

"No reason to. No reason not to. No reason to consider them at all, as a matter of fact, except I have to begin somewhere, and they were the last two that she saw before disappearing, as far as we know. Besides, it's well known that women talk a lot to hairdressers and doctors. Everyone knows that. She may have told them something they weren't willing to repeat to you. It's a good thing I didn't get a chance to talk with them earlier, as I planned. All I'd have had then was a woman missing. Now I've got a woman murdered. There's a big difference. You'd be surprised how cooperative people can get in a case of murder."

"It's hard to believe that Carla was murdered."

"You'd better believe it. She didn't strangle herself and crawl into that culvert after she was dead."

"Of course not. But I don't understand why. Why would anyone want to murder Carla?"

"Well, from what the doctor told you and you told me, it's pretty sure that a man was involved. These affairs get nasty sometimes. Maybe she became a threat. Maybe she got herself into trouble and was making demands. That's something I want to talk with this doctor about."

"I don't know. My wife and I had no notion of all of anything like that. It's just hard to believe."

"Sometimes things are. Sometimes I have a hard time believing things myself. Well, what I want you to do is tell when you saw your sister-in-law last, how she seemed then, looking back from what you know now, and what time according to your wife, she left home on Friday. After that, you can go on home."

I told him what I could, which was little enough, and then he said I could go, and I did. When I got home, the house was dark, and Ivy was lying in the dark upstairs. I thought she might have fallen asleep from sheer exhaustion, but the instant I opened the door to the bedroom, I heard her stir and sit up on the bed, and I knew that she had been lying there ever since I'd left, waiting and waiting in the darkness of the house and her own fear for me to return. Her voice came to me through that double darkness with a strange intensity.

"Turn on the light," she said.

Still standing by the door, I reached out and pressed the mercury switch on the wall beside me. The bright ceiling light flashed on in silence, and Ivy and I stared at each other across the distance between. She was sitting very erect, her torso shored by its own rigidity, and I thought I could see, although I might have imagined it, the slow dying of the bright and searching light in her eyes. Then she said with a kind of terrible, dull acceptance, "She's dead. I can see in your face that she's dead," and lay down deliberately, as if it required the greatest of caution to contain herself, and turned onto her side with her face away.

I wished she would scream. I wished she would scream or weep or curse or do anything at all but what she did. But she never screamed or wept or cursed. Never once in the days that followed. She lay in bed for two days, and then she got up and dressed and went about her business in the house. She went quietly, rarely speaking, her face like stone and her heart containing its own dull grief. As for me, I spent a lot of time with my therapeutic bucksaw. I finished the sawing of the trees, and then began splitting the big chunks with an axe.

I spoke once with Ferguson when I claimed Carla's body after the autopsy. There had been an affair with a man, all right, and Carla had been in trouble. About two months in trouble. It had been a bad day for her, I guess, when she came, about six months ago, to live with Ivy and me.

"I knew it before the autopsy," Ferguson said. "It was just like I said. When that Dr. Blaker learned his patient had been murdered, he had quite a lot more to say. I don't know why your sister-in-law happened to go to him instead of someone else, but what she wanted at first, he says, was an abortion. He turned her down, but he kept on seeing her because she was in bad shape emotionally. That's what he says, and it may be true. Or it may be true that he had been seeing her long before for other reasons. It's pretty apparent that he and women are not exactly incompatible, and your sister-in-law was an attractive woman. He may have still more to say later than he's already said. We'll see."

"If Dr. Blaker is the man you're looking for, why didn't he simply take care of her. The abortion, I mean. That would have solved their problem."

"I've asked myself that, and I've got an answer that may be right or not. Maybe she didn't want an abortion. Maybe he only said she did. Maybe she wanted Dr. Blaker and thought she had him where she wanted him. He's married, you know. Rich wife in a fancy house. It would have been complicated, I mean. Nasty business."

"Have you talked with Monsieur Paul?"

"I've talked with him. He didn't have much to say, but he said he'd be trying to think of something more."

"What are you going to do now?"

"Now comes the hard part. Being a cop isn't all just sitting and thinking and talking with hairdressers and doctors, you know. Now I've got to try to find the place your sister-in-law and this man were meeting. To do what they were doing, they had to have privacy. Probably that means an apartment or a hotel room or maybe a motel. Anyhow, I've got to try to find the place. Matter of fact, I've already got men on it, but I'll start lending a hand. If there is such a place, we'll find it eventually, and when we do there'll be someone there who will remember seeing your sister-in-law and the man together and be able to give us an identification or at least a description. That's the way it works out."

"There are a lot of places," I said. "It sounds almost impossible."

"Like I said," he said, "it's the hard part."

I took a week away from the office to help bury Carla and stay near Ivy. The funeral was private, with only a few friends and relatives present who were close enough and cared enough. After the funeral, Ivy kept house and cooked and remained withdrawn. I couldn't reach her or console her. I split a lot of firewood. It would take a lot, I thought, ever to warm our house again.

At the end of my week off, Ferguson came to see me, along toward evening, and I was splitting wood when he came. He came down across the back yard and across the dry bed of the stream and sat down on the stump of a tree I had felled.

"That's hard work," he said.

"I get a kind of satisfaction from it," I said.

"That's true about hard work. You may hate to start it, but generally it gives you a kind of satisfaction. Like the hard work I've been doing. I started it and finished it, and now I'm feeling pretty satisfied."

"Did you find the place?"

"I found it. It was a room in a cheap hotel. I don't know why people who are having illicit affairs so often pick cheap hotel rooms to have them in. I guess it's because they *feel* cheap. Or maybe it makes everything seem more daring and exciting. Probably, though, it's because cheap hotels don't worry about such things. Anyhow, I found the place, and there was something odd going on there."

"What's that?"

"Well, this man rented the room once a week for the past four months. He paid for a day in advance, and he always arrived about the middle of the afternoon. He signed the register as Jerome Moore, from Chicago, but that's probably phony. Odd thing was, he apparently never stayed all night. He was always gone next morning, and no one around the hotel could remember ever seeing him there in the evening or night. What does that suggest?"

"I don't know. What?"

"Sure you know, if you'll only think about it. It suggests that this guy wasn't from Chicago at all, or from anywhere but right here in this town. He had to get home for the night, and so did she. *They both had to get home for the night.*"

"Was Carla seen going there?"

"She was seen. I got a couple of identifications from the picture. There was a picture in the paper, too, you know. She came in the afternoon, soon after the guy registered. She was seen going into his room and coming out."

"Did you get a description of this man?"

"Yes. A general one. He was about average height, a

little above. Had dark red hair. Wore heavy horn-rimmed glasses. Doesn't sound much like a lover, to tell the truth."

"Do you think you can find him?"

"I can try. I've *been* trying. As it turned out, that Monsieur Paul, the hairdresser, was more help than anyone else. You'll remember I told you he was trying to think of something more to tell me? Well, he thought of it. It turns out that he sells wigs, and after thinking a while, he remembered that your sister-in-law had bought one from him about four months ago."

"What's so unusual about that? Wigs for women are fashionable now."

"What's unusual is that this wasn't a woman's wig. It was a man's. *A dark red one.*

"You mean Carla bought a wig for her lover to wear as a disguise?"

"That's what it looks like."

"Maybe Paul himself is the man. He could be trying to mislead you."

"I don't think so. In the first place, why should he volunteer the information? In the second place, no one would have needed to buy it for him. He could simply have helped himself. Finally, I had him put on a red wig and horn-rimmed glasses and go to the hotel with me. According to my witnesses, he's not the man. I'm glad, to tell the truth. I sort of like the guy. I never thought I'd like a man hairdresser, but it's a fact that I do. On the other hand, I don't like that Dr. Blaker much, even though everyone is supposed to like doctors. Maybe it's because I was suspicious of his cropped hair. I got the idea that he might have had it cut that way so he could wear a wig over it. It's pretty difficult for a man to wear a wig realistically over long, heavy hair."

"I hope you don't suspect everyone with short hair. I wear my own that way."

"I noticed that. How long you been getting short haircuts, Mr. Maxwell?"

"Quite a while."

"About four months, actually. I found your barber over in the shopping center, and he told me. That was about the time your sister-in-law started meeting her lover at the hotel. About two months after she came here to live."

I lifted my axe and buried the head with a thud in a stump. Not the one Ferguson was sitting on.

"You went to a lot of trouble to find out something I'd have told you myself. What now? Do you want me to put on a red wig and horn-rimmed glasses and go to the hotel with you?"

"I admit I was going to ask you. I took Dr. Blaker over after I took Paul. He objected like the devil, but I convinced him it was the easiest way to clear himself. Anyhow, it was a dry run, and I'm getting hard up for suspects. Would you mind humoring me? I've got the wig and glasses in my car."

"Would it make any difference if I minded or not?"

"I guess it wouldn't, now that you ask. I'm a cop, after all, and sometimes I have to act like one."

"In that case, we may as well get started."

We walked across the dry bed and up across the back yard and around the house to where he had left his car. I turned there and looked back the way we had come. The axe was canting from the stump, and the late light seemed to gather and glisten on the hickory handle. All at once, as I looked, a scrap of poetry came into my head after a long, long absence. It came from the days when I used to read poetry, and it did not come word by word, slowly, but whole and all at once, as if it were printed clearly on my mind:
Long for me the rick will wait,
And long will wait the fold,
And long will stand the empty plate,
And dinner will be cold.

"You can change clothes if you want," Ferguson said.

"I'll just wear these," I said.

"Don't you want to say good-by to your wife?"

"No. I guess I've already said it."

I got into the front seat of the car, and he got in beside me. He apparently wasn't at all worried about what I'd do, and he didn't need to be. We drove down the drive and turned onto the road that would take us downtown.

"We could save time by not trying this wig-and-glasses bit," Ferguson said.

"No," I said. "A man has the right to try."

POACHERS' ISLAND

by Richard Hardwick

The low bluff of St. Lucy Island loomed up in the night ahead of the bateau. Moss Clinton, his eyes cat-sharp in the darkness, stood with one calloused hand braced on the tipped-up outboard, letting his gaze sweep slowly along the shore. Above the faint rim of sandy beach the live oak forest traced a ragged silhouette against bright and brittle stars.

"Yonder's the creek, Sam, off to your right. We didn't miss it more'n fifty yards."

Sam Butler, his huge forearms resting on his knees, grunted. He flexed his hands on the oars and dipped the blades into the black water of the sound. Then he paused and cocked his head.

"You hear that, Moss? Boat comin'."

"Hell, yes, I hear it! Now git this bateau in the creek!"

The big fellow needed no further urging. He laid his massive back into the stroke and the heavy cypress hull shot forward, a swirl of phosphorescence boiling astern.

It was past two o'clock, a couple of hours since dead low water. With an occasional glance over his shoulder, Sam Butler sent the bateau scudding between black mounds of exposed oyster bank. The sound of the engine was louder now, and from beyond the southward curve of the shore the bright stab of a searchlight raked across the sound and along the bluff.

"Senator's goin' to one hell of a lot o' trouble to catch poachers, ain't he, Moss?"

The bateau slipped into the mouth of the creek, threading the narrow channel. The pungent muck banks and tall spartina grass seemed to close in and hover over them on both sides. The searchlight from the boat in the sound swept across the marsh above their heads.

"We just did make it," Sam muttered.

They were safe enough now from the boat out there, which suited Moss just fine. He had learned a hard lesson about St. Lucy Island not many months ago, after Bart Cowan, the Senator's caretaker, had come upon him while Moss was loading the last of three prime deer into his bateau. Poaching, that was what Bart and the circuit judge agreed it was, and Moss helped out on the county roads for sixty days as a result.

Moss hadn't lost any sleep about the name they put on it. To him it amounted to nothing more than poor luck. With St. Lucy the best deer territory in the state, and Moss with a steady, good paying market for venison, the answer was to be more careful in the future.

Fundamentally, Moss Clinton was a law-abiding man. He had no quibble about the Senator owning the island. As far back as most folks remembered, the Parker family had owned St. Lucy. It was just that Moss didn't figure the old boy owned the wildlife, and so he helped himself to that bountiful harvest whenever he took a notion, much to the chagrin of both Senator Parker and Bart Cowan.

"That old tree still there?" grunted Sam Butler. "Damn if I c'n see it!"

Moss was the eyes, Sam the muscle. "It's there. Dead ahead."

The tree, a huge, ancient salt cedar, had toppled from the bluff where the creek had cut back and eroded the high ground at the first turn.

Sam shipped his oars and the bateau glided in among the tangle of limbs. Moss guided through, pulling and pushing on the branches until the boat grounded against the mucky sand at the foot of the bluff.

"They couldn't pick us outta here with a dozen o' them lights," the big man chuckled.

Moss was well aware they wouldn't be seen. The thing troubling him was, "Wonder who the blazes that is out there?"

The sound of the engine told him it was a diesel, coming along slow. The white slash of light swung over the marsh again, paused briefly at the creek mouth on the dark reefs of the oyster bank, then passed on. After a while the faint outline of the boat itself appeared, moving along well clear of the shallows.

"Can you make it out, Moss?"

"Yeah. Looks like one o' them coast guard utility boats." He rubbed a bristled cheek thoughtfully. "Now what's he lookin' for out there?"

Sam knew the coast guard wasn't in the business of tracking poachers, and he breathed easy. "Hell, Moss, he's prob'ly huntin' some o' them fancy yacht folks that's gone and got lost or stuck on a mudbank someplace."

"Don't much figure they'd be lookin' in the trees on the bluff for a boat," Moss replied. (The Senator was an important man. He'd been in Washington longer than most, and some mighty big meetings had taken place on St. Lucy Island over the past thirty or so years. Maybe there was something going on over at the Senator's lodge.)

"You figure something's wrong, Moss?" Sam asked, gazing up at the shadowy form of his partner. "Say . . . the old devil has all the pull in the world. You don't reckon he's fed up with me an' you huntin' out here, do you, and gone and got a gov'ment boat lookin' for us?"

"We ain't big enough fish for that, Sam, just small fry. We ain't much more'n a couple o' thorns in Bart Cowan's hide. Now, if that was Bart or some o' his boys out there, I'd be thinkin' different."

Sam chuckled appreciatively. He turned and crawled across the seat toward the shore. "Let's git movin', then. It's nigh onto three, and sunup's around six."

Moss picked up his old Springfield and Sam his double-barreled 12-gauge, and after burying the anchor in the sand against the incoming tide, they scrambled up the eroded face of the bluff to the forest. The crescent moon, invisible from the creek, hung like a golden scimitar above the distant trees beyond the marsh. Almost directly beneath the moon several pinpoints of light showed nearly half a mile across the bight of the marsh.

Moss lifted the rifle and cupped the scope to his eye. The light to the left would be the floodlight at the end of the Senator's dock. The others would be various lights about the lodge.

"Well, now," he said, steadying the rifle, "what ya make o' this, Sam? There's two guys sittin' out on the end o' the old man's dock."

"So what? Prob'ly fishin'." He opened the breach and dropped a pair of shells into his shotgun. "Come on, Moss, let's get them deer 'fore it gets light. Let's go—"

"Not yet, Sam. I got the feelin' something's goin' on out here. I think we best be sure 'fore we go unlimberin' these guns . . ."

His voice trailed off. Something moving slowly along on the moon track of the eastward stretch of the creek had caught his eye.

"Look yonder," he said, pointing with the rifle barrel. "What's that?"

Sam Butler followed the direction of the gun. After a few seconds he saw what Moss was talking about. "Damn if you ain't right jumpy," he said. "Might be a couple o' minks or coons."

Moss watched the two objects, moving along slightly faster than the tide. Moonlight glinted briefly off one of them and Moss lifted the rifle quickly again and found them in the scope just as they rounded the bend and, out of the moonlight, disappeared in the darkness.

"Sam . . . Sam you're gonna think I'm crazy, but you wanta know what them things was down there! It was *men*—two men in divin' gear!"

"Moss," Sam Butler said evenly, "you ain't sneaked along a bottle o' whiskey 'thout tellin' me, have you? If you ain't, then yeah, I'd say you *was* crazy."

"That's what it was. One of 'em had his face mask pushed back, and just 'fore they rounded the bend he pulled it back down."

"Now come on, Moss," the big fellow said uncertainly. "What would divers be doin' in the creek? It don't make no sense!"

"Hanged if I know what they was doin' down there. All I know is they was *there*."

Sam decided to let it go. "Okay, Moss, if'n you say so. Come on, now, and let's get them deer and get off this island."

"You wait here for me. I'm gonna run over to Pembroke Creek and see what's at the public boat landin'."

"Moss . . . that's more'n two miles over yonder! Be past four o'clock when you got back here! If you're so all-fired spooky about this place tonight, I say let's get on back to the mainland now!"

"The boat landin's closer than the lodge, time you circle clear around the marsh. You just sit tight, and mind you, no shootin' till I get back. Not even if an eight point buck walks up and spits in your eye!"

Moss Clinton knew the forests and savannahs and swamps of St. Lucy Island far better than Bart Cowan or the Senator or anybody else did. He had to, doing all his prowling there at night over a fifteen year span. He was a natural night creature, the same as a possum or coon, or one of the great horned owls that went *hooing* through the night in search of prey.

He moved like a shadow through the forest, padding easily along broad grassy glades beneath the live oaks, through scattered tufts of palmetto scrub, stunted in the eternal shade of the forest floor. He circled a cattail marsh and heard an old 'gator go lunging away through the shallows.

All this was Moss Clinton's world, the rivers, woods, and swamps. The only time he ever left it was when he joined up with the marines more than twenty-five years ago. They sent him off to boot camp and then out to the Pacific islands, which was about the same thing as tossing Br'er Rabbit into the briar patch. Like everything that happened to him, Moss took it all in stride and made a fine accounting of himself. Five years after the war was done, they managed to track him down to his shanty boat on a backwater of the Altamaha and gave him a medal.

He had some of that old feeling this night, that everything wasn't right and something might have to be done about it.

The glimmer of lights filtered through the forest long before he could see the boat dock on Pembroke Creek. He approached warily and settled himself behind a palmetto clump at the edge of the clearing. What he saw backed up his suspicions. There was something big going on. A large yacht and two coast guard boats lay alongside the dock. Three men in civilian clothes stood talking near the dock, each carrying a revolver in a shoulder holster.

It was a good thing they hadn't gone blasting away at deer; they'd have had an army down on them.

As Moss watched, a jeep came bouncing along the crushed shell road from the lodge and three men got out. Changing of the guard, Moss thought, harking back to his service days. The others got in the vehicle and headed back.

No sir, St. Lucy was no place for a couple of river rat

poachers tonight, Moss said to himself as he slithered back into the deep shadows. There'd be other nights. He turned and trotted into the black forest silent as fog, and worked his way back to his partner.

"Whadya see over there, Moss?"

"Enough, Sam. Couple o' more coast guard boats, and men that's got gov'ment wrote all over 'em."

"That's enough for me," Sam Butler said, hauling himself up from where he'd been dozing against a fallen pine. "Let's skedaddle."

Moss sat down on the pine trunk, propping his rifle against it. "I got to thinkin' on the way back here, Sam. Them divers in the creek down there, the navy had fellas like that back when I was in the marines. They'd slip in amongst the Nip beach defenses and blow 'em up so's we could get ashore."

"This ain't no time for tellin' me your war stories." Sam scooped up his shotgun and took the shells out. "It's gonna start gettin' light in another hour, and we don't want Bart Cowan catchin' us out here in daylight."

"I ain't tellin' you no war stories. I'm just tellin' you what I know. I'm stayin' here. You take the bateau and come back for me after dark."

The big fellow blinked. "I hear you right, Moss? You—you say you're stayin' out here?"

"Somethin's wrong. I got a feelin'."

Sam Butler groaned and lowered his huge bulk down again. "I ain't leavin' without you, Moss. And that's a fact."

Soon, beyond the marsh and the distant trees, the sky turned to pearl over the ocean. As the light grew, day creatures began to stir on the marsh. Egrets stalked the shallows of mudbanks. From the wracks of dead spartina, marsh hens cackled like gossips over a back fence.

A faint spiral of smoke lifted above the trees around the lodge. There would be some mighty fine eating going on over there, and Miss Clinton's mouth watered just thinking about it.

He slid the rifle barrel across the pine trunk and settled his eye to the scope. He could make out the long narrow pier that extended into the creek from the lodge grounds.

"Sam . . ."

The big fellow was snoring gently, and Moss reached over and shook him by the shoulder.

"Huh? What'sa matter, Moss?"

"Tide's gettin' about right for trout and reds in the creek. There's some skiffs and that blue fiberglass job o' the Senator's hangin' at the end o' the dock."

Sam grunted and closed his eyes again.

"Most folks around here know the creek's as good a place as there is for trout and reds, wouldn't you say so, Sam? We all know that."

He grunted affirmatively.

"And the Senator allus takes his comp'ny out fishin' on the creek at high water . . ."

He let the rifle swing a bit to the right. The scope gathered sufficient light so that Moss could recognize the familiar form of Bart Cowan dipping live bait out of the tank and dumping it into a pail.

"Yep," he said, "they're fixin' to go out."

"Is that how come we stayed here, Moss? Just so's we could watch the Senator and some o' his big shot buddies go fishin'?"

Moss ignored the question. "The tide musta been floodin' for a couple o' hours when I seen them divers. They coulda come clear through the creek from the ocean in that time."

"That's real interestin'," Sam said. "But how come anybody'd do a fool thing like that?"

"Just what's been botherin' me, Sam," Moss said, half to himself. "They'd have to have a helluva good reason . . ."

There was activity on the high ground at the other end of the dock, and Moss let the scope drift over. He could make out figures moving about beneath the live oaks. Some of them started out onto the dock. He picked the Senator out easily by the flowing mane of white hair. A couple of men moved past him, and then another tall figure appeared.

Moss Clinton's eye blinked rapidly in the scope, and a low whistle escaped his lips. "Big, did I say, Sam? *Man,* this ain't nothing but the *biggest!*" He pushed the rifle toward his partner. "Take a look!"

Sam pulled himself around and put his eye to the scope. It took him a moment to find the target, but when he did he lowered the rifle slowly and stared at Moss, incredulous. "It's . . . its *him!*"

Moss already had the rifle to his shoulder, peering across at the dock. The tall man, a ten-gallon Texas hat perched at a jaunty angle, draped an arm across the Senator's shoulder and they started out toward the boat, side by side.

"That's *it!*" Moss snapped. "That's it, sure as hell! I gotta stop 'em!"

"Wha-what's *it?*" Sam asked suspiciously.

"That's who them divers was after. There ain't but one thing they coulda been doin' in that creek . . ." He chambered a cartridge and slammed the bolt home. Range? Six hundred yards, maybe a little more. He adjusted the scope and slid the rifle across the pine trunk again.

"Moss . . ." Sam said with great uncertainty. "You— you ain't fixin' to shoot that dern thing, are you?"

The crosshairs came to rest on the bow cleat of the Senator's fiberglass boat, and Sam Butler's answer came with the heavy crack of the rifle.

"Great guns, Moss! You're gonna get us killed!"

Moss wasn't listening. He watched the windshield of the boat shatter, two feet left of his target. *Not bad for the range,* he thought. Chambering another cartridge, he let go the second shot.

The sound of his first shot had sent everybody off the dock in no uncertain manner, and now an answering volley came potting across the marsh.

"You crazy nut!" wailed Sam, scuttling down behind the fallen tree. "What're you tryin' to do?"

Slugs whirred past like angry hornets. Moss squeezed off his fourth and fifth shots, and with the last he saw the bow cleat burst loose from the boat's deck.

"That got it! Now, Sam, we'll see if I was right!"

Sam Butler's curiosity was strong enough for him to risk the shots from the lodge. Exposing as little of themselves as they could, the two poachers watched the Senator's baby-blue pride and joy go drifting off on the last of the flood tide. The boat moved away from the line of skiffs, caught an eddy and spun slow and graceful as a ballet dancer.

Then everything flew up and out in a great geyser of water, followed a second or two later by the reverberating thump of the underwater explosion.

Hunks of blue fiberglass were still splashing down in the marsh and creek as Moss heaved a sigh and leaned back against the pine trunk.

"That's what them divers was doin', podner," he said. "Bobby trappin' the Senator's boat." He probed his breast pocket for a cigarette and lit it, trying to ignore the shaking of his hands. "We best leave these guns right here and start hikin' over towards the road." He turned and grinned at Sam Butler. "We wouldn't want to run into no trouble, would we?"

NOBODY TO PLAY WITH

by Irwin Porges

In Mrs. Ellis' bedroom Arthur had first investigated the shelves and drawers. He did this with a caution and finesse based upon experience, lifting folded garments deftly, probing beneath, and then restoring them to their original positions. Boxes were opened, searched, then carefully closed. Arthur had known women to secrete their valuables in the most unlikely places. The jewel box remained but it was locked. He examined it, tested the strength of the lock, and considered. He might be able to force it with a nail file and leave no traces. Bent over the box, the file ready, he had an uneasy sensation. He straightened slowly, then whirled when he heard the creaking noise. Mrs. Ellis stood behind him in the doorway, blocking it.

"I see," she said. Her tone was a mixture of anger and contempt. "I trusted you. I might have known. Your kind is never any good." She walked toward the phone.

"What are you going to do?" Arthur hadn't expected her to return until late that evening. His question was mechanical; he already knew the answer, but he believed that he also knew women of Mrs. Ellis' social status. When she raised the phone, he said, "If you call the police there'll be a scandal. Is that what you want?" He felt confident. Similar scenes had been enacted in the past, the same tactics used and danger had been averted.

Her eyes were coldly amused. "That's your trump card, I suppose. Well, this time it won't work. My social connections are practically nonexistent, and I'm past the age where scandal means anything to me." She began to dial.

Arthur moved closer to her. "You'd better not."

"Why?" She spoke without glancing up at him. "Do you think you can frighten me?"

His hand groped behind him for the metal statuette. Gripping it, he swung suddenly. She tried to raise an arm to block the descending figure, but she was too late. She cried once and crumpled to the floor.

He knelt to gaze at the woman and listen for sounds of breathing. There was none. He stood, his fingers still curled about the statuette. Replacing it on the table, he took his handkerchief and rubbed it thoroughly over the metal surface. While doing this, he looked down at the woman. "Stupid fool!" he said, his voice vibrating with anger. "You made me do it."

He shrugged and began to consider his next steps. The murder was regrettable. He would have preferred that it hadn't happened, but he had no fear. He and the woman were the only ones in the house. She meant nothing to him, as did all of the middle-aged and elderly women he cultivated. He had picked up Mrs. Ellis at a theater several weeks earlier, or it might be said that she had picked him up.

Women, usually widows, divorcees or lonely spinsters, were Arthur's source of livelihood. To a number of them, he had an irresistible appeal. He was not the ordinary type of gigolo who offered accommodation to older women in exchange for money, maintenance and expensive gifts. In fact, Arthur bore no resemblance to the stereotype of the Latin professional lover. He was neither sleek nor dark, wasn't suave, and didn't have glossy black hair or long sideburns. At twenty-five Arthur was small and chubby, only five feet four, with a clear pink complexion and round cheeks. Appearing no more than eighteen or nineteen, he had an aura of innocence, of naivete, which women found charming. He was quite aware of his double attraction, or more accurately of the lure of the two techniques he used so efficiently. For the women who did not respond to the obvious advances, he assumed his act of youthful helplessness, of a need for advice and protection. The women's motherly instincts were at once aroused.

Arthur spent the next fifteen minutes ransacking the house, then filled a cardboard box with valuable bric-a-brac, carried it down to the garage where his car was parked, and placed the items in his trunk. A second load and trip to the garage were required before he was satisfied that he'd taken everything of value. He drove away, certain that nobody had seen him with the woman and that there was no way of tracing him.

As he drove, Arthur reflected about the past few weeks with Mrs. Ellis. The relationship had not been very satisfactory, the woman not very generous. She'd really been quite stingy, he recalled. He felt a surge of resentment. Considering the intimacy of their association, she should have been willing to give him some jewelry as a gift. Other women had done this. Previously, only once in his career had his violence brought a serious aftermath. Several years before there'd been a liaison with a Mrs. Howard—what was her full name, Frances Howard? He had appraised her shrewdly as a woman with a dominating maternal drive and his favorite story, used so often that he had memorized the lines, affected her powerfully.

"Lonely," he said, his voice maneuvered into a boyish pitch. "An only child is a lonely child. You have no idea." He stared blandly beyond her, like one resurrecting ghosts of the past. "I can still see myself . . ." He understood the effect of halting fragments of speech. ". . . sitting on the old wooden steps of the front porch . . . gazing wistfully out . . . really hopelessly . . . never any friends, any playmates . . . nobody, nobody to play with . . . Mother tried, but she was alone . . . and when she died . . ." His voice faded and he made a sudden motion as though jerked back to the present.

The impact upon Mrs. Howard had been greater than he had imagined. With tears in her eyes, she squeezed his hand and the association was launched. She lived alone and welcomed him into her home, pampering him and buying him expensive gifts. The situation seemed ideal, destined to last longer than the others, but as with all of Arthur's alliances, the arguments soon began. The crisis came one evening with a most violent quarrel. A gold watch and an antique vase had vanished. She accused him of taking them. He blustered, shouted, and then in a rage, struck her. She fell heavily, striking her head against the corner of the brick fireplace. He fled, and learned from the papers that she had a skull fracture and was on the critical list. Fortunately, she lived, and the press forgot about it.

Arthur had traveled about in fear and apprehension for weeks, believing she had informed the police and that he was a wanted man. When nothing happened he realized she hadn't talked, and in the passing months he understood that the other middle-aged women could be depended upon to react the same way. He could pursue his activities with little danger. After the affair was over, they were too ashamed—too afraid of scandal and publicity—to chance any public revelations. Since Mrs. Howard, Arthur had threatened and struck a number of women, especially when they were tired of him and he was tired of them.

Now, with no particular destination or plan, Arthur's only precaution was to place as much distance as possible between himself and the Ellis home. The body would be discovered, investigations would follow and, although he was perfectly safe, there was no sense in taking chances. He drove at a leisurely pace, heading westward, and arrived in Los Angeles a few days later. He'd been in the City of Angels before so he knew of a number of small comfortable hotels, residential in nature, where well-to-do women preferred to stay. The clerk at the Wentworth Hotel watched curiously while Arthur registered. Clearly, he was wondering why a young man would choose a quiet, sedate hotel of this type.

"Not much doing here," he said, taking the card and reading the name. "Arthur Lynn, is that it?"

"Yes." Arthur had turned to gaze about the lobby, noting a lounge on one side and a writing room on the other. "That's what I had in mind," he said. "I just wanted to relax for a while, take things easy."

The clerk's face had a gloomy expression. "If you stay around here you'll get plenty of *that*. Most of these women are upstairs and in bed by ten o'clock."

After dinner Arthur struck up an acquaintance with Mrs. Dahl, a plump, pleasant woman in her fifties. After venturing some flattering remarks about her youthful appearance, he observed a speculative light in her eyes, a light he had detected in his encounters with other women. It signified that he had stirred her interest, but shortly afterward the woman's son arrived to take her visiting. Surly and suspicious, he examined Arthur with an unconcealed hostility. Through past experience Arthur had long ago established an inviolable rule: never form relationships with women who have nearby relatives or close attachments. Any designs toward Mrs. Dahl would have to be abandoned.

For several evenings he sat around the lounge or writing room, chatting with a number of women, making acquaintances without any effort at following them up. Nothing appeared very promising until he was introduced to Mrs. Engleman. He had been aware of her glances from the corner where she usually sat, and had noticed that her smile seemed warm and approving. Her appearance was not impressive. She was an elderly woman, thin and rather bony, with unattractive features. However, she was well dressed, and he caught the gleam of an expensive-looking ring and of a jeweled bracelet that clasped her arm.

By the end of the evening they were sitting on a divan together, with Arthur devoting all his attention to her, and she made casual references to her family background. "Engleman," she said. "We're practically pioneers in Los Angeles. Everybody knows the name."

Arthur didn't know the name but there was a sense of familiarity about it. Had he read something in a newspaper or magazine? It was worth investigating. The woman's hints created an enticing possibility—she might be comfortably fixed, with both money and property—and she seemed to be alone.

Arthur met Mrs. Engleman again the next evening in the lounge, after his research in a library. She seemed happy to see him and eager to talk, almost as though she had been waiting for him. He began with oblique attempts to draw her out, but these were hardly necessary. She spoke freely about her family and past happenings. Her grandfather had come to Los Angeles in the 1900s and purchased a tract of land that was now near the downtown area. Her husband, a wealthy realtor, had died five years ago.

"Your children?" Arthur asked.

She shook her head. "There are none. We had a son . . ." She broke off and her face had a tortured look. Then she smiled at him. "I try not to live in the past."

"There was something about your estate," he said. "I believe I read it in the papers."

"Oh, yes." Her chin had a determined set. "The city would like to buy it for a park, but I have no intention of selling. The council even threatened condemnation. I suppose I'm being silly, but I'm keeping it for purely sentimental reasons. I have no need for money. My husband left me more than I'll ever use."

"But you live here at the hotel," said Arthur. "I don't understand—"

"You would if you saw the place and the grounds," she said. "It's enormous. What would I do there by myself? I'd be like a pea rattling around in a huge shell. I've closed it, but I go there to check on things once or twice a week." She was gazing at him in a friendly way. "I should be ashamed. Here I've been rambling on about myself all this time, and I don't know anything about you or your family. You must tell me everything."

While she'd talked, Arthur had been reflecting. Past disappointments had given him a strong sense of caution, but he had to concede that he'd never encountered a more hopeful situation. It was difficult to control a feeling of excitement. Even the question of the best approach seemed answered. Obviously, she was drawn to him, but her interest couldn't be romantic—she wasn't the type. The clue had come from her reference to a son and her tragic attitude. Mrs. Engleman's need was maternal—she wanted someone to mother.

Arthur began to play his cards skillfully. The story of his early home life, of a brutal drunken father who came home to strike him and beat his mother, and of his mother's wasting away—these were spur-of-the-moment improvisations, but in all his career he had never staged a better performance. She leaned toward him, listening, her eyes wide and moist. He stared into the distance, summoning the agonies of his childhood, and slipped into his most tremulous story: "Lonely . . . an only child is a lonely child . . . sitting on the old wooden steps . . . hopeless . . . no friends . . . nobody . . . nobody to play with . . ."

When he finished, allowed for the appropriate minute of silence, and then stirred himself suddenly to return to the world of the present, he could see she was deeply touched. "How terrible," she murmured. "How terrible." He caught the quiver of her throat. She was silent, her gaze intense, as though too overcome to resort to further words.

By the next day, when she brought up the matter of paying a visit to the estate, it seemed only natural that he should hint at a willingness to accompany her. They drove to the area north of the downtown district, a neighborhood that once consisted of large two-story homes with broad, sweeping lawns in front and enormous orchard-like yards in the rear. Some of these still remained, converted into rooming houses, but most had vanished, to be replaced by tiny box-like residences.

She directed him first to follow the outside road that wound about the estate. She pointed and waved to show him the boundaries. Enclosed by a high iron fence and tall hedges, the estate seemed to extend for acres. They parked in the circular driveway, and at the entrance she produced a key ring to open the heavy padlock of the gate.

As they climbed the stairs to the house, she said, "The place will seem sort of hollow and even ghostly. Whatever is left has been covered with sheets."

Inside she opened several windows to allow the light to stream in. The large rooms had an empty appearance. "Much of the stuff has been stored in other buildings," she said. While they walked through the house she commented about a number of objects. She nodded carelessly toward a Chinese vase. "It's a Ming and quite valuable. I should store it in the building in back of the house—most of the valuable items are stored there—but somehow I don't care to bother. Material things have no value to me anymore." She sighed. "Since the tragedy and the closing of the house, I've really had no interests, no pursuits to—"

"Yes, of course," said Arthur. "I understand."

"I honestly haven't the faintest idea of what's left in the house," she said, "and what I've stored away in the back. One of these days I must take inventory." She showed him a jade statue and a painting by Monet.

When they were leaving he watched her take the keys from the table where she had thrown them. "There are all kinds of keys around here," she said. "I've lost track of them too." She pulled open a drawer of the table. "There's an extra set of keys in here someplace."

He went with her to visit the house again several days later, hoping she would open the storeroom in the back and let him see some of her other valuables. He hinted that he might be interested, but she made no response. However, a better opportunity arose when she left him alone while she went about to check the various rooms. He had a very good recollection of the table she had shown him and in the top drawer he found the heavy key ring and thrust it into his pocket.

Arthur arrived at the estate early the next afternoon. He had seen Mrs. Engleman at the hotel and explained to her he had to tend to a business matter. Her next visit to the house would not be for a few days, and he was certain he could do his investigating without any chance of interruption. Actually, Arthur planned to be quite circumspect. The relationship with Mrs. Engleman was progressing well and he had no intention of doing anything to jeopardize it. True, she had no idea of the exact possessions that were lying about the house, and would undoubtedly never miss any small item he might filch but, tempting as it was, there was little sense in pilfering at this stage, when she might soon be giving him valuable presents. Yet he must satisfy his curiosity about the building in the back and its contents.

Once inside the house, he moved through it very quickly to the kitchen where the back door opened to a long flight of stairs. From the foot of the stairs a path led toward a small stucco building. As he drew near it, he noticed that the windows were covered with heavy iron grilles. Several appeared to be fixed permanently so that they remained partially open. He tried to peer inside but could see nothing except the vague shapes of furniture. Adjoining the front door he found another small window, open at the bottom. He began trying the keys on the ring, choosing those that seemed likely to fit. It wasn't until the fourth try that the key slipped into the lock. He turned the knob slowly, leaving the keys dangling. With the door half-open, the light cut through the semi-darkness of the room.

He had just begun to look around when he heard a faint sound behind him. The door had closed and he turned to tug at the knob. He was locked in. Then he heard a woman's laugh.

Mrs. Engleman spoke to him from the front window. "I knew you would take the bait. You couldn't wait to get over here, could you?"

He went to the window and could see her standing there. "What do you mean?" he asked. "Why have you locked me in here?"

"Of course I was certain you'd remember where the keys were," she said. "Then today, when you said something about business, I knew you were coming here."

"All right," he said sullenly. "I was curious and came here to look. I wouldn't have taken anything. I didn't take anything from the house, did I? Now are you going to open the door?"

She appeared not to have heard him. "There was a woman—I know there've been many of them in your life so perhaps you don't even remember the name—Frances Howard. You struck her. She was badly injured. In fact, she never fully recovered—has become a permanent invalid." She moved closer to press her face against the bars. "Frances is my sister. I've been looking for you for a long time. I vowed that if I caught you, the punishment would be short and sudden, but now I have something else in mind, something that's really more appropriate."

She moved away from the bars and he had no idea what she was doing until he heard the click of a switch from outside. Then the room was brightly illumined. He looked about. It was a large room with just a few chairs and a table. The walls were gaily decorated with animals and children. The floor was of some rubberized material.

Returning, she laughed again. "Odd, isn't it? It's a child's playroom. The cupboard on the side is filled with toys. Do you know I wasn't certain it was you until you told me that pathetic story of yours. Frances had mentioned it to me."

Arthur, angry, began to shout. "Let me out of here. You're going to be in serious trouble if you don't."

"It's no use your getting excited," she said. "There's something important you must know. I confess that I told you a big lie. I made you think my son was dead—but, he isn't. He's right there in the building with you."

Arthur started and stared nervously around.

"Oh, you needn't worry. He's in the living quarters in the rear. I must tell you about him, before I press a button to open the door that will let him in. I've taken care of him all his life. He's now about your age, I'd imagine—twenty-five? I was advised to put him in an institution but I couldn't bear the thought. He's retarded and his actions are, shall we say, a little unpredictable at times? But I don't think you need be concerned about violence. He's usually quite docile—unless he's upset or frustrated."

Arthur had thrust his hands through the window opening and his fingers scratched at the bars. "Let me out," he implored. "Let me out."

"You're not listening," she said, "and this is especially

important. Be friendly. Don't do anything to antagonize him."

The door at the other end of the room slid open, and the heavy, ungainly man shuffled into the room. He stood silent, his eyes wide and fearful. He took a step toward Arthur, then moved back hurriedly. His forehead wrinkled as he studied Arthur. Suddenly his face lit up. He went to the cupboard, opened it and pulled out a large rubber ball. He began to chuckle and jump up and down.

"Play," he said. "Play." He bounced the ball awkwardly toward Arthur who allowed it to go past him.

The man ran to pick it up. He faced Arthur and made a growling noise. "Play," he ordered gruffly, and bounced the ball again.

Arthur caught it and returned it.

Mrs. Engleman's voice sounded cheerfully from the window. "He may overdo it at first, but he'll get tired after a while. Within a few weeks I imagine you two will adjust to each other. My son's been terribly lonesome. Remember, he too is an only child. He's never had anybody to play with."

Shortly, the City Council received a very firm letter from Mrs. Engleman indicating she would never sell the estate. If they attempted condemnation proceedings, she assured them that her lawyers would fight the case, if necessary, to the Supreme Court. Under those circumstances, the Council voted unanimously to abandon the entire project—and the Engleman estate remained a private playground.

GALLIVANTIN' WOMAN

by Wenzell Brown

About twice every summer Miss Susie Sloane would come gallivantin' down the mountain a-whoopin' and a-hollerin' at everyone she met on the way. Mostly she'd walk the whole twelve miles from Mount Solomon, 'cause even if someone offered her a lift she warn't a-ridin' in no new-fangled contraption like an autymobile.

She'd be wearin' a sunbonnet and a flouncy, bright-colored cotton skirt such as went out of fashion nigh onto thirty years ago. As for her long yellow curls, they must 'a been a wig 'cause they never changed one mite over the years.

Susie had a voice that would wake a clam, and a laugh you could hear clear to Sebago Lake. The way she'd come prancin' along, a-lookin' at everythin' and doin' a funny little jig step, always gave me a sort o' warm feeling. But there was some in Cripple's Bend was right vexed with Susie and I don't mind admittin' they had reason.

I reckon Susie was just about the nosiest woman in the whole o' Pisquaticook County, or mebbe it was just that she come to town so seldom she plain wanted to see everythin' as was goin' on, which ain't much in Cripple's Bend. She'd been livin' all alone up there on Mount Solomon ever since her daddy died, so it seems like she had a right to bust loose once in a while and get an eyeful to take back to the farm with her.

People around used to complain that Miss Susie warn't never backward about comin' forward, and that was the plain unadulterated truth. She'd march straight into the kitchen o' Gimpy's Diner to watch Mrs. Gimpy makin' flapjacks and then she'd grab a spoon and start stirrin' the batter sayin' as how it needed a pinch more o' bakin' powder or they'd be heavy as lead.

Most local folks would take Miss Susie in good spirits

because they'd all known the loneliness of Maine winters
and what it's like to be snowbound for months at a stretch.
But some of the city crowd who come up here in the summer would get real irked. Like this feller Bingham, who's
supposed to be big shakes in the art world. Seems like one
day he's a-paintin' the lighthouse over to Cushman's Cove
when Susie comes up in back o' him. She stands there for
awhile, her hands on her hips and her head tilted to one
side. Then she snaps, "That ain't right."

Before you could say Jack Spratt, she's swooped up the
pallet and brush and added a few strokes of her own.

Bingham's so mad he almost blows a gasket. He wants
me to arrest Susie and toss her into pokey. When I explain
there ain't no local jail, and anyway Susie didn't mean no
harm, he stamps away, a-huffin' and a-puffin' and a-cussin'
me as a hick sheriff, which is a charge I never did deny.

All the same I have a heart-to-heart talk with Susie, especially after the run-in she has with Mrs. Godwin who's
about the richest woman in town. Susie prances right up to
her on the main street and wants to know if the bloom on
her cheeks is real. Afore Mrs. Godwin can think up an
answer, Susie licks a finger and traces it across her face. I
reckon Mrs. Godwin wouldn't have been so all-fired riled
up if her rouge hadn't smeared and come off all over
Susie's finger.

Talkin' to Susie's about as much use as singin' a lullaby
to a lobster.

"Gracious sakes alive!" she whoops. "Folks around here
is gettin' mighty tetchy. Seems like a gal can't even ask
questions no more without somebody rearin' up on their
hind legs and chewin' her ears off."

I can't help it. I bust out laughin' and the next thing I
know Susie's a-shootin' off across the road to see for herself
if Emmie Coolidge's latest young un is a boy or a girl.

I guess it's plain as the nose on my face that I always
had a soft spot for Miss Susie Sloane, even afore the summer the bank robbers come to town.

There's three of 'em, a trio of hoods as busted loose in a
jailbreak across the state line in Massachusetts. Word had
come through to be on the look-out for 'em, as they might
be workin' their way up to Canada, but there didn't seem
no reason for 'em to show their faces in Cripple's Bend,
seein' as how we're off the beaten track so to speak.

Just to be on the safe side, I take a good squint at the mug shots and memorize the descriptions. The leader seems to be a big ugly feller called Harry Jenks who's been servin' time for woundin' a bank guard in a holdup. His sidekick is a junkie, a wizened excitable hood known as Hoppy Jackson. The third is Lew Abbott. He's hardly more than a boy, and a handsome one at that, but he's got a double murder rap hangin' over him and was headin' for the death house when he made the break.

The bandits hit the Cripple's Bend Savings Bank just about five minutes afore closin' time. Jenks and Hoppy go in, while Abbott stays in the getaway car that's parked down the street a piece, with its motor idlin'.

There ain't hardly a soul around savin' young Tom Nash, the teller, and Lucy Dohm who's secretary to Mert Simon, the president o' the bank. Mert himself is in his office at the rear.

These hoods ain't foolin' none. They're playin' for keeps. Hoppy pulls a revolver on Tom Nash and orders him out from behind his cage. Once he's out, Jenks smashes him along the side of his head with the butt of his gun. Tom slumps to the floor. He's out cold as a mackerel.

Lucy's a-watchin', so scared she can't move. She starts to scream but afore the scream can come out, Jenks claps a hand over her mouth, hustles her to a closet, and shoves her in, warnin' her he'll shoot through the panel if she don't make like a mouse.

They drag Tom out o' sight, pull the blinds, and lock the front door, but they leave the door at the side ajar for a quick getaway, or mebbe because they just plain forget it. Everything goes so fast and smooth, none of the few people moseyin' along the main street notice anything amiss.

Mert Simon's seated at his desk when these two hoods rush into his office, flourishin' their guns. Hoppy sticks his revolver about two inches from Mert's face, but it's Jenks as does the talkin'.

He says, "Open up the vault and do it quick. Try any tricks and we'll blast you."

Mert acts cool as a cucumber. He explains there ain't no vault, just the big wall safe at his back.

Jenks snarls, "Quit yackin' and get busy."

Mert don't panic. He does what they tell him, but he takes it slow and easy. He ain't got no doubt that they mean what they say, but he's safe enough until they get their hands on the money. After that he reckons his chances ain't too good. His best bet is to stall as long as he can, hopin' some act o' providence or dumb luck will save him.

Sure enough, someone does spot that part-open side door. And seein' as how it's Miss Susie Sloane, she has to come prancin' in to satisfy her curiosity. At first she thinks the bank is empty and she goes caperin' and peerin' around. 'Tain't long afore she spies Tom Nash lyin' behind the counter, curled up like he's asleep. About the same time, Lucy Dohm works up enough nerve to start a feeble poundin' on the closet door.

Miss Susie cocks her head to one side. Then she hears voices in Mert Simon's office and she tiptoes down the corridor to listen. Mert's opened up the safe and Hoppy is busy stuffin' all the bills he can find into a duffel bag, while Jenks keeps Mert covered with his gun. Meanwhile, they're arguin' betwixt themselves what had better be done with Mert.

Hoppy says, "If we blast him we got no worries. He can't never put the finger on us."

"Act your age," Jenks answers. "Ain't no sense in shootin' 'less you have to. Tie him up, Hoppy, and let's beat it out of here."

Mert's been wonderin' if he dares to jump for the alarm button beside his desk. The alarm is attached to a klaxon on the roof, and once it goes off, it'll alert the whole town and bring me a-runnin'. But when he hears they're tyin' him up, he decides it ain't worth the risk, particularly as they'll have plenty o' time to gun him down before help can come.

So he slides to the floor the way they tell him to. Hoppy circles his waist a couple o' times with a length o' cord and he's busy bindin' his hands, when Miss Susie marches straight into the room.

If she'd tried to back away or scream, I reckon they would have shot her on the spot. But she ain't scared one bit. She's just curious as all get-out to know what's goin' on. She stands there a-twirlin' the red umbrella she always carries, and watchin' Hoppy who's a-kneelin' in back o' Mert loopin' the knots into place.

Susie drops right down beside him, her lips puckered in

disapproval. "That ain't the way to tie a square knot. Land sakes alive, a man could slip a knot like that in no time flat. Here, let me show you."

Hoppy's so flabbergasted he lets go of the cord.

Susie picks it up and says, "Look. You loop it over like this and tuck the end in here and he's trussed up like a rooster. Now you try it, mister. I'll tell you when you go wrong."

Jenks grates out, "Just leave things the way they are, if you know what's good for you, sister."

Susie tilts back on her haunches, pickin' up her umbrella that's spilled to the floor. Up 'til now she ain't realized that anything was really wrong. It ain't that she's stupid, but she's sort o' lost touch with the world, livin' as she does all alone on the side o' Mount Solomon. Bank robbery is somethin' she just ain't never give a second thought to. Even now it don't cross her mind that these men are really dangerous.

"Don't you get fresh with me, young man," she retorts. "I ain't your sister and I ain't never like to be."

"Shut up," Jenks snarls and covers her with his revolver.

"Don't you use that tone of voice to me and don't you point that thing at me neither," she snaps back, real tart-like.

Jenks stares at her. "Lady, don't you know what this is? It's a .32 automatic that can blow a hole through you the size of a grapefruit."

Susie ain't listenin'. Her eyes have lit on the duffel bag and she yips, "What have you got in there? You're not stealin' from Mr. Simon, are you?"

She stands up and starts for the duffel bag. Jenks yells to Hoppy, "Grab her. Shut her up quick."

Hoppy snatches Susie's arm to swing her around. But he don't know Susie. She may look like a comic Dresden doll, old and fragile, but she ain't nothin' o' the kind. She's worked that farm o' hers for thirty years, sawin' wood, tot-in' water, and tendin' to the livestock.

Susie breaks away, and she's got her umbrella up. She slaps it down hard, right on the top o' Hoppy's head.

He lets out a yell but it's drowned out by another sound. Mert Simon's been edgin' over toward his desk until he can lean forward and press the alarm button with his forehead.

That klaxon is loud enough to deafen you halfway across town.

I'm in Gimpy's cafe, cleanin' up on a platter of fried clams when I hear it. I leap up and race toward the bank, with my gun out.

As I round the corner, Jenks and Hoppy come a-tearin' out of the alley beside the bank, racin' breast to breast. Right behind them comes Susie Sloane, whammin' first at one and then at t'other with her umbrella.

I skid to a stop, my gun pointin', but not darin' to shoot for fear o' pickin' off Miss Susie. While I'm standin' there open-mouthed, bullet whistles by me. 'Taint neither Jenks nor Hoppy, but Lew Abbott, gunnin' me from the getaway car.

Jenks drops the duffel bag and bills tumble out. There's just enough breeze to send 'em skitterin' down the main street.

Hoppy drops to his knees grabbin' at the bills, but Jenks keeps right on runnin'. I see the gun juttin' out o' the window of the getaway car and I fire. At the same time Abbott lets loose a blast. Jenks stops dead in his tracks, then he topples over and slides to the cobblestones. Abbott flings his gun away and steps on the accelerator. The car shoots off down the main street like the devil was on its tail. It screams around a corner, the tires a-burnin' rubber.

I snap off one more shot. The bullet ricochets off a back fender. Then the car's out o' sight.

I look around. I don't have to do much lookin' to see that Jenks is dead as a boiled lobster. In back o' me I hear a groan and spin about. It's Hoppy. He's a-layin' on the ground, holdin' his head in both hands. At first I think he's been shot too. But I'm wrong. Susie's just whammed him over the head so many times that his skull is nigh stove in. He's alive, all right, but there ain't a single ounce of fight left in him. Susie's standin' a-lookin' down at him, her brelly raised high, to get in another whack if he moves.

Hoppy sees me and yells, "Pull her off me. Make her leave me alone."

I go to Susie. She's right pale, and she's got a waxy look to her eyes. At first I think it's just the excitement; then I spot the blood on her sleeve.

She ain't hurt bad, just a flesh wound where a bullet

grazed her arm, but now that it's all over, she faints dead away.

Well, I don't mind tellin' you the next hour or so was mighty hectic. We had to get an ambulance to cart Susie to the hospital along with Tom Nash. As for Hoppy, I send him to get fixed up at the state police barracks over to Barrow.

Mert Simon is still trussed up inside the bank, but I set him free in a couple shakes of a lamb's tail. There ain't nothin' wrong with him, nor with Lucy Dohm neither, though she throws as fine a set of hysterics as I ever did see.

About six miles outside o' Cripple's Bend, Abbott loses control of his car and slams into a tree. The state police pick him up wanderin' along the highway with a concussion. He don't put up no fight at all.

That sort o' wraps things up. O' course we could have tried him and Hoppy for bank robbery, but there don't seem much sense to it with state o' Massachusetts willin' and eager to take 'em off our hands.

Susie Sloane's the heroine o' Cripple's Bend. Soon as people hear what she's done they start flockin' to the hospital, bringin' her fruit and flowers and such. Bein' as how she's Susie, you'd think she'd enjoy all the fuss but that ain't the case at all.

Once she's got a bandage on her arm, wild horses couldn't a-kept her in Cripple's Bend overnight. She says she's got her fill o' the wicked city and she's headin' straight back to Mount Solomon where she can take life easy. Besides that if she don't get back that night, the cow'll be bawling its head off to be milked.

Six years has passed since then and it's a funny thing, in all that time Susie Sloane ain't come gallivantin' down the mountain, not even once. Seems to me like I owe something to Miss Susie. If it hadn't a-been for her, I might have run smack into a brace of bullets, or Mert Simon might have got hisself kilt. So every summer I make the trip up Mount Solomon to see her.

Miss Susie always acts like she's glad for a visit, but there ain't nothin' I can do that'll change her mind about Cripple's Bend.

HARDHEADED COP

by D. S. Halacy, Jr.

Police Sergeant Dave Hackett climbed out of the old sedan and walked slowly toward the kitchen door. At five-thirty it was still hot, and the back of his blouse was soaked with sweat. Even before he opened the door the smell of steak came to him, but it brought no smile.

Margie was at the stove, a faded apron over the maternity smock, turning thick slices of round that spattered in the grease. She smiled and leaned for his kiss.

He knew she was frowning in disappointment as he pulled away too soon, but he didn't stop. In the hall, he slid out of his belt and blouse, hanging them in the closet with the door slightly ajar so they would dry quicker. The gun went on the top shelf where Tina, their three-year-old, couldn't reach it. He loosened his tie and then went back into the kitchen.

"Your beer, oh lord and master," Margie said, making a big gesture of handing him the punctured can. "Sit down and cool off while you tell me all about it; the promotion, I mean."

Her hair was as dark and fine as Dave's was red and coarse; stray strands of it were plastered to her cheek with the humidity. She still looked as young and fresh as the day they were married. Plumper, sure, but her skin was smooth and her eyes shining. Margie seemed at her best when she was producing a baby.

The beer can was wet in his hand, frosted with condensation that promised a cooling drink. But he regarded it dully, not lifting his eyes to his wife's as he parked his solid, five-nine frame on the stepstool. Couldn't she tell from the look of his face how it had gone?

"You're still married to a cop, Mrs. Hackett. Jerry Nelson is the new lieutenant." He drank the beer, half draining the can in one angry gulp before he set it down.

"Dave!" Margie's mouth dropped open and she brushed at the strands of hair in a distracted way. "You have two years more seniority than Nelson. Oh, you're teasing me!" She put down the platter of steak and came to him, both arms going around him.

"Why would I tease you?" he asked. He stood, still holding the beer. "Nelson got the job, is all. Frye was sorry, but I'm not the most popular guy in town, especially after I arrested Councilman Henderson's kid last month."

He thought she was going to cry, but she didn't. Instead, she carried the steak into the tiny dining room. The table was already set, with a centerpiece of carnations from the backyard, and the linen napkins her grandmother had sent them from Ireland. It was supposed to be a very festive occasion.

"Dave, I'm so sorry," she said when she came back.

"You think I'm glad?" He dropped the can in the waste-basket under the sink and slammed the doors shut viciously. "I'll call Frye and tell him to forget about cards tonight."

"We can't do that, Dave," she said gently. "I'm sure he couldn't help what happened."

"I think he could."

"Daddy!" a piercing little voice shrieked from the door-way. "Come swing me!" Tina stood holding the door open for the flies, her jeans muddy and her tee shirt ripped under both arms. She was Margie in miniature, only her name coming from Dave's side of the family.

"Daddy's too tired to swing a great big girl like you!" Margie said briskly. "Besides, it's time to wash up." Tears threatened, but the little girl followed obediently.

Supper was a dandy flop. Tina, trying to liven things up, tipped over her milk, and when Dave impulsively popped her lightly, she wailed and fled to her bedroom. He hated himself and took it out on Margie.

The evening of cards with the Fryes was no better. Wilson Frye was a big redcheeked man in his early forties. He knew everybody in Morriston, and tried with the skill of a wire walker to keep them all happy with his job as police chief. Georgia Frye was a tall, good-natured woman who had taken a real liking to the Hacketts and worshipped Tina. The Fryes were childless.

Margie and Georgia went into the kitchen to fix refreshments when they finished playing pinochle. Frye lit a cigar after Dave refused one, and leaned back on the sofa.

"Margie take it hard?" he asked. Dave dropped the cards into the drawer and slammed it closed.

"No, of course not. She likes being poor," he snapped.

"I'm sorry as the devil, Dave. But Henderson was laying for you."

"Really rubbed my nose in it, didn't you?" Dave asked, still standing. "Nelson has been on the force less time than I have; I know he scores lower on his exams."

"OK. You're the best man I've got, maybe too good. You rub people the wrong way, Dave. And the City Council controls promotions."

"I was hired to do a job. If they want me to do it, there's going to be some rubbing."

"Sure, Dave. But—" Frye broke off as Margie came into the room carrying plates of cake and ice cream. Georgia was back of her with coffee. "That's what we came for, Margie," Frye went on. "Looks delicious!"

Dave managed to stay civil until the company left, much earlier than usual. He and Margie stood on the porch and watched Frye's big sedan move down the block. It was a nice car, seven years nicer than the Hacketts'. And it was paid for.

"Georgia was sorry," Margie said tentatively as they did the dishes.

"So am I," Dave said. "Crime isn't the only thing that doesn't pay." He cracked a glass and swore. "A cop can tell you that."

"It's not like the army, Dave. You can get out anytime."

"For a nickel I'd do that," he retorted bitterly. There was a long, strained silence afterwards. He went to check on Tina in her room, and when he came back from locking the house Margie was in bed, the spread a bulging mound over her. Usually he made some joking comment, but not tonight. In his pajamas, he flipped out the light and got into bed.

"Dad could still use a man in the office," Margie said in the stillness after he kissed her. "He mentioned it today when I talked to him on the phone."

"Right in there for the kill, isn't he?" Dave asked. "Told me so, and all that."

"Five hundred dollars a month," she went on quietly,

ignoring his anger. "And with the town growing like it is, Dad plans to open a branch office in a year or so. You're the only son he's got, Dave."

"What a disappointment that must be," he said sarcastically. But he was mad enough to have cried about it. Five hundred a month for making loans in Tanner Investment Co. was a lot more than four-twenty-five. Civilian suit, and an air-conditioned office too, with his name on the door. No more grief and sweat; no more letdowns like the one he had suffered today.

"Oh, Dave, Dave! I know how much it means to you to be a good police officer. But——"

She didn't finish, and he wondered as he stared at the ceiling how she *could* know what it meant to him. How could anybody know but a hardheaded cop?

In the morning it was cool, and some of the bitterness had faded by the time he got up. Breakfast was quiet, with no mention of last night. Tina, with the cheerfulness of the very young, had forgiven him. He kissed her good-by and left her wrestling her cereal around the table.

Margie walked out to the car with him. She didn't say anything about office jobs, or five hundred dollars a month. All she said was, "I love you," and kissed him hard.

"I love you, too," Dave said guiltily and climbed into the sedan. The starter labored and Margie bit her lip until the motor caught. She was still waving when he turned the corner. Yes, she must love him, all right.

She had stuck it out a long time. First, it had been the Korea business just after they were married. Dave had the idea he should go and he went, though there was a good chance he wouldn't have been called. He still thought it had been the right thing to do.

Then, when he got out he traded a khaki uniform for the blue serge of Morriston's police force. Three-and-a-quarter to start, about what a day laborer got. It was funny, but he'd wanted to be a policeman when he was a kid and never changed his mind.

So these five years hadn't been a picnic. Dave was no diplomat; he knew that. Maybe it was a miracle that he'd made sergeant two years back. People didn't want to be rubbed the wrong way, and that's where the diplomats came in; Nelson, for instance. There were times when it was easier to turn the other way, to wink and let something slide. Not that Nelson wasn't OK. Only Dave Hackett wasn't built that way.

Even after he had rationalized the kick in the teeth about the promotion he thought was his, it was tough on Margie. Pride wore thin when all your friends had nice things and you had nothing but that pride. Dave's face had tightened again by the time he parked back of the station, half an hour before his men would come on duty.

Jerry Nelson looked up from his new desk, self-conscious in the gabardine suit. He was a lean, good-looking guy, handy with the paperwork. He was a good press agent, too. "Show us cops doing favors for people instead of arresting them," Frye was always saying, and Nelson had that knack. Pictures in the papers, the ice cream routine for lost kids, and all the rest of it. And the unwritten agreement with the town to ease up when laws went against the grain too much.

"Morning, Dave. Look, fella—" Nelson was embarrassed.

"Relax," Dave told him. "I've had my cry, forget it. Just take it easy, boy. And congratulations." It nearly stuck in his throat, but he said it and felt better afterwards.

He checked the reports of the previous two shifts. There was nothing important to brief his patrolmen on. He sent them out with a curt word or two; four men, four cruisers. It was bad, but what could you do? Instead of the desirable 1.7 men per thousand population, Morriston had a budget that allowed for just one man. So two men to a car, even at night, was a luxury to dream about. It was dangerous, more ways than one. A cop could get roughed up. And he could get accused of rape when he went in to pick up a female suspect. It was the officer's word against somebody's. No witness.

The town was way behind, and yet a lot of the citizens thought there were too many cops now. Some of the Council thought that, and it was the Council that did the hiring, instead of an impartial merit system.

It's not the army, he reminded himself, and climbed into the cruiser. At least the day shift wasn't so bad, except for traffic. He began crisscrossing the town in random fashion. It was quiet, and he was glad for that. At ten-fifteen he picked up a hitchhiker, a boy about fifteen, and brought him in to the station to put a scare into him.

"Ride the bus next time, son," Dave said when he let the boy go, after reading him the statute. "You can afford fifteen cents."

"Big man," the boy said in a surly voice. But Dave figured he'd quit thumbing for a while. Three weeks ago four teenagers had bummed a ride, stolen the car, and robbed and beat the driver. A month before that, a drunk had picked up two sixteen-year-old girls who got tired of walking the mile from school home. They regretted it. But the town forgot things like that in a hurry.

The Chief came into the office as Dave was leaving, prosperous-looking in gray suit and felt hat. Frye made his six hundred a month, and got invited to Rotary and Lions now and then for a free meal to pad the growing bulge under his belt. But even at that, he wasn't too happy in Morriston. It was a strain, and he would have liked something better. Frye hadn't been born in the town. That was the difference between liking people and loving them.

"How goes it, Dave?" he asked, breaking cigar ash into a tray on the dispatcher's desk.

"Fine," Dave said. "Not a single murder this morning."

"No hard feelings?"

Dave shrugged. "Like Margie said, it isn't the army."

"You go at it like it was," Frye told him, a doleful look on his face. "Your own personal war, Dave."

"I'll see you," Dave said, and went outside and climbed into the cruiser.

It was plenty hot now as he started down Main, and he could feel sweat soaking the back of his shirt. He drove mechanically, taking in everything. He shooed a double-parker from in front of the supermarket, and then spotted a jammed signal light at Seventh, backing up a line of cars. He called for a repair truck, parked, and got out to direct traffic until the maintenance crew showed up.

At twelve-thirty he should have been heading home for lunch. It was a shame he didn't, because then he wouldn't have blundered into trouble.

Dave thought the driver was drunk from the way the coupe weaved onto Main. The car was doing over fifty when the driver saw the flasher and heard the siren. The coupe screeched to a halt, and the driver was out of the seat and yelling before the cruiser stopped.

"My kid—his hand's cut almost off! I have to get to

Mercy fast, buddy!" His eyes were glazed and wide, and Dave sprinted around him to the coupe. A boy about twelve years old was holding a rag tight around his left hand, blood dripping from it onto his clothes and the seat. He was pale and scared, starting to cry when he saw Dave. Nasty, but the kid wasn't going to bleed to death in a matter of minutes.

"I'll give you an escort," Dave told the father, and raced for the cruiser. He left the flasher on, touched the siren occasionally. The limit along Main was twenty-five, and traffic was heavy in the middle of the day. It was seven blocks to the hospital; they could make it easily in about two minutes.

The father must have decided that thirty-five wasn't fast enough. With a shriek of rubber, the coupe tore past Dave like he was backing up. It slammed through the red light at Wembley, barely missed a truck loaded with cases of pop. Dave toed the gas and hit the siren. He should have loaded them both into the cruiser.

The coupe made a green light, and took another red at sixty. There was one more light before the hospital, and blind luck couldn't hold out. The cruiser came abreast at last, and it was more than the weather making Dave sweat as he forced the coupe to the curb, a block or so short of the hospital. In the intersection, a gas truck and trailer pulled across Main; it would have been a sitting duck for the coupe and its wild driver. Dave swore under his breath as he climbed out. He was shaken and not ready for what happened next.

"Damn you!" the panicky father raged. Effectively blocked, he was getting out in a hurry. He swung as soon as he was free of the seat. The blow was wild and missed, but Dave was off balance. He stumbled and fell sidewise against the fender of the coupe. The driver ran around the back of the car, jerked open the door and got the boy out. Swinging him up, he set out at a trot for the hospital.

There was a muttering crowd by the time Dave had taken the license and checked the registration on the coupe. One or two people had seen enough of what they wanted to see, and puffed the thing out of all proportion. Somebody shouted angrily as Dave got back into the cruiser to drive on to the hospital, and he shook his head wearily.

The boy was all right. There would be some bad scars, and he was missing the tip of his little finger, but, at least, he wasn't smashed up. The father was still livid, declaring he had seen no truck and trailer, and that Dave was a poor excuse for a cop.

"You'll hear about this, buddy!" he promised. "You'll hear plenty!"

"Will you sign this citation?" Dave asked, holding the book out to him. "Either that, or I take you down to the judge right now, Mr. Marshall." That worked.

There was a green sedan, with a press sticker on the windshield, parked in front of the station when Dave reported in after lunch. Inside, the dispatcher frowned.

"You'd better go see the Chief," he told Dave. "He ain't happy, Sarge."

Frye looked up when Dave came in. There were two men sitting across the desk from him. Dave had tangled with the skinny one before, a reporter named Blaze. The other was a photographer.

"The boys tell me there was a mix-up down at the hospital, Dave," Frye said evenly. "What's the story?"

As briefly and accurately as he could, Dave told him what had happened, including the wild swing. The reporter snorted.

"Kid bleeding to death and you write his old man a traffic ticket," he said indignantly. "I'd have done worse than just swing at you if it had been me, Hackett."

"You try it, friend!" Dave snapped hotly, his face twisting in anger. The photographer picked that moment to snap his picture.

"Take it easy," Frye said calmly. "Both of you. You did write him up then, Dave?"

"Here it is," Dave said. There were two counts, a 693 and a 701, with the notation that the driver failed to cooperate with the officer.

"I didn't mention the assault," Dave said coldly. "He was pretty upset."

"Real decent of you!" Blaze said, smiling thinly. "You got any kids, Hackett? How do you think you'd act under the same circumstances? Kid with his hand cut half off and—"

"A minute or two wasn't going to make any difference,"

Dave retorted. He wanted to smash his fist into the sharp face. "I checked with the doctor, and the kid was all right."

"You could tell by just looking at him in the car, I suppose?" Blaze taunted. "Why didn't you escort him to the hospital the way you would for some visiting movie star? You—"

"All right, Blaze," Frye said, getting up. "That's enough, I believe, especially for the papers."

"It's plenty," the reporter said triumphantly. "Thanks, Hackett, thanks a lot."

"Spell it right," Dave shouted after him. "That's two t's!"

"They'll go after you now, Dave," Frye said flatly.

"OK. What was I supposed to do; let that guy pile up? He would have it, if I hadn't stopped him. You're not suggesting I tear up this ticket, maybe?"

"Of course not! You know me better than that. But it looks like we can't win in this town. That's all, Dave."

Blaze spelled the name right, even to the initials. It made the front page, along with the picture taken in Frye's office. Contrasted cleverly with one of the Marshall kid in his hospital bed, it made Dave out a raging maniac. The reporter's slanted piece would make readers think the boy was near death when Dave stopped his father.

Margie saw it, but she didn't say anything. Her father wasn't so tactful. "OK, Dave," he said on the phone, "give it up, boy, and come in with me."

The worst of the whole thing was the holdup across town just about the time Dave made his arrest; a successful holdup, in which a lone bandit got away with nearly five hundred dollars from a supermarket safe. The editor of the Sentinel made capital of that, with a "Where Were The Police?" spread on the editorial page telling where at least one of the police was: asininely ticketing a man trying to save the life of his injured son!

In a day or so the letter-to-the-editor column picked it up. One reader mentioned Margie and her condition. "Let us hope this rule-crazed officer will not meet with a similar situation!" It was a field day for the righteously indignant, and Dave decided he was a fool for not accepting his father-in-law's office job.

There was coolness among his tract neighbors, not that they had ever been especially friendly. A cop on the block was apparently a painful thing. Margie cried about it when

Dave wasn't home, and he was thankful that Tina was too young to know what was going on when the kids on the block hooted at her.

Margie laughed off the letters, but it worried Dave. It wouldn't be long until the baby arrived. Tina had been no trouble, and the doctor accused Margie of being disgustingly healthy, but you never knew. What would he do when the chips were down, really down?

A citizens' committee paid the fine for Marshall, and made him a martyr to police stupidity. Henderson, the councilman whose toes Dave had stepped on, smiled smugly next time they met. The paper kept hammering away at Dave and the police department in general. Even Frye, with his knack for getting along, got his share of lumps. It seemed to bother him for a couple of days, then suddenly the Chief looked years younger. He called Dave in and showed him the reason.

"You know I've been sweating it out," he said, leaning back in his chair. "My contract is about up, and I was on pretty thin ice in Morriston. Well, this came today. Read it, Dave."

It was an offer of a job as chief of police in Rockford, up in the north of the state. The salary was seventy-five more a month; and it was a better town, a town with much less pressure. When Dave finished and looked at his boss, Frye jolted him.

"I told you you were the best man I had, Dave. Now, I'll prove it. I'll need an assistant, and I can pick my own. Come with me. Lieutenant up there makes five hundred. And Margie would get a pension if anything happened to you."

"You're kidding," Dave said thinly. "Or else I'm hearing things."

"You heard me right. Look, maybe I could have fought Henderson and won on your promotion, but I was praying this thing would work out. Maybe I'm a heel, Dave. Maybe I'm just selfish. You don't owe this town anything. It's not the army; you told me that yourself."

There was a folded copy of the Sentinel on the desk, with a headline, COUNCIL PUTS HEAT ON FRYE. What did Dave owe people like that? He remembered Rockford. It was a nice town, two hundred miles from the temptation of an office job with Tanner Investments. The pay was good, too. But slowly Dave shook his head.

"Thanks, Wilse," he said earnestly. "But no. I guess I'm a knuckleheaded cop with a one-track mind. I'll stick here."

"Afraid of being called a quitter?" Frye asked, taking back the letter and folding it carefully. "That it, Dave?"

"Yeah. Afraid of being called a quitter by Dave Hackett. This is my town; it's where I belong."

Frye said with an odd, resigned look, "It's nice to have known an idealist. Lots of luck, Dave. You may need it, when the new Chief takes over."

The realization worried Dave. For all Frye's shortcomings, the big guy had backed him up. He had been a pretty good boss, and he had been a friend. How could Dave buck the Council and an unknown quantity in the Chief's seat? He would find out shortly.

"Thanks for the offer," he said finally. "And good luck to you. I guess Georgia is happy about it."

"I don't know how she'll get along without Tina," Frye said. "Better think it over."

Dave went home for lunch, dreading telling Margie about the job he had turned down. But he told her, quickly, before she could say anything.

"You married a nut," he finished up. "There's still time for me to tell—"

"I want you to do what's right," she said, and then bit her lip hard and shut her eyes. "Now maybe you'd better take me to the hospital. Dr. Skinner missed the time a little bit."

They dropped Tina off with Margie's mother. Back in the cruiser, Dave looked at his wife's pained face, and it was a temptation to floor the accelerator and touch the siren. But it wasn't the insinuating letter in the paper that made him drive a safe speed to Mercy.

Just before they reached the hospital the radio sputtered. The dispatcher's voice was tense as he read the APB. Robbery and a shooting, the bandit taking along a girl clerk as hostage. It was a supermarket holdup, and a bell rang in Dave's mind as he wheeled into the hospital. The last holdup had been a supermarket too.

Margie's eyes were shut and Dave swore softly. Of all the times for bedlam to break loose! Reaching for the mike, he called in, telling the dispatcher he had an emergency of his own. Five minutes later, the nurses shooed him out of the labor room so they could get Margie ready.

When they let him go back in, the doctor still wasn't at the hospital and Dave was tense. Margie saw it and smiled up at him as she reached for his hand.

"You'd better get back to work, Sergeant Hackett," she said so softly he wondered if the drugs were already working on her. "Go catch your robber."

"To hell with that!" Dave said, squeezing her hand. "I'll wait right here." Tina had been born with Dave fighting a fire at the paint plant. This time he would be with his wife, where he belonged.

"Even the nurses are better at bringing babies than you are, darling," Margie whispered, her lips moving in a weak smile. "Go on, Dave. I want you to." So he went, and as he ran down the steps out front, Dr. Skinner was running up. He waved pleasantly.

"Sorry I'm late," he said. "I'll make it a boy this time."

"Take care of my wife, Doc. I'll try to beat the baby back here."

Whipping open the car door, he called in to find out how things were shaping up. Instead of the dispatcher, he heard Jerry Nelson's voice. The new lieutenant didn't sound sure of himself.

"This is Lieutenant Nelson, Dave. Our boy fooled us. He got through our inner block, and I'm afraid we've lost him. We've called the state highway patrol; they'll pick him up south of here."

"He took the river road, then?" Dave asked, getting the cruiser rolling. "I'm at Mercy, and I'll try to cut him off."

"Be careful, Dave. This guy is dangerous; probably killed one man and he's got the girl with him. Maybe you'd better—"

"We can do our own laundry," Dave said and hung up the mike. He swung out onto the dirt road and opened the cruiser up. It would have been nice to have another man along.

He was out in the country now, the road dropping towards the river. It joined Highway 95 at the bridge and, by a miracle, he might intercept the bandit. If not, it would be a while before a highway patrol car did the job. A lot could happen in that time. He fought the cruiser around a rutted curve and the bridge came in sight. His dust would show a long way off, but that was a chance he would have to take.

Braking hard, he slid into the cover of the trees on this side of the bridge. If the holdup man was desperate, it wouldn't hurt a bit to have the element of surprise in Dave's favor. He reached for the mike to call in, barely getting the message out when he saw the oncoming car. Moving the gear selector to low range, he waited until the black sedan was on the bridge and then gunned out to block the near end of it.

The driver had no choice. He rode the brakes all the way down, to within ten feet of the cruiser, both hands on the wheel fighting a skid. Dave would have felt foolish if this was just a citizen, but he had no reason for apology. Gun drawn, he was out of the police car and waiting when the driver dropped his right hand from the wheel.

There was a hard, glassy look in the man's eyes, and a wide, panicky one in the girl's. It was worry about hitting her that slowed Dave's aim, and the automatic in the bandit's whipping hand fired first. The noise of it seemed to tear at Dave's shoulder, and then his gun smashed back. The girl's thin scream echoed the shots, and the man in the sedan was looking down, open-mouthed, at the red stain on his shirt front. Dave blinked back the gray fog and handcuffed his man to the wheel. Then he had to hang onto the car for support. He was still hanging on when Frye and Nelson screeched up back of the car.

"You crazy fool!" the Chief said, and he sounded mad. "I went by your place after lunch and found out you took Margie to the hospital. Now I find you out here bleeding like a stuck hog."

"How about waiting until they patch me up to chew me out?" Dave suggested as they helped him into Frye's car.

"OK. But I've got something to tell you before your hero picture comes out in the Sentinel," Frye said, and he had a baffled grin on his red face, "just so you'll know that isn't the reason you got the job. The Council just OK'd my recommendation for the new Chief, Dave. I'm afraid you're in."

"This is a fine time to joke!" Dave said, fighting the fog again. "I can see my pal, Henderson, voting for me."

"Henderson is only one man. Three or four of the others don't go along with all he says, Dave. I guess maybe they woke up, at last. Guilty consciences, or something. Anyway, that's what I stopped by your place to tell you."

When Dave could see again, they were helping him out of the car. Funny how weak a slug in the shoulder could make you, but he wouldn't let them put him on a stretcher. Not yet, anyway. With Frye on one side and an intern on the other, they proceeded along the hall. A door opened and a man backed out of a ward. His face seemed familiar and he colored when he looked at Dave. It was Marshall, the guy whose kid cut his hand.

"Look, Hackett," he said in an embarrassed voice, "I'm sorry as the devil. I thought it over, and—I'm a dumb clown. You want to take a poke at me? When you're OK, I mean? My kid's fine, but if I'd clobbered that truck—"

"Skip it," Dave said, wondering why he felt so good. "You could come see me, and I'll give you a cigar."

He insisted on seeing the baby then. Frye twisted somebody's arm, and a nurse brought out a red-faced little scrap with red fuzz for hair. Dr. Skinner had earned his money; it was a boy.

Margie was in a ward, a screen around the bed, and they left him alone with her for a minute or two. She was half asleep, but he talked to her and she mumbled back, things that didn't make any sense, but it made him feel good all the way down to his toes. It was nice having a wife who was proud of a hardheaded cop. He hoped being Chief wouldn't change any of that.

TIME TO KILL

A Novelette by Dick Ellis

The crack of dawn was still echoing across the slate-gray waters of Schooler Lake when someone began pounding on our cabin's front door. I got out of bed and yawned my way to the door and opened it.

The kid standing there glared wildly at me and yelled, "She's dead, Mr. Gates! She's layin' up there dead—"

"Who's dead?" I asked.

"That Blair woman, from Monroe. I just found her!"

"Where?"

The kid, an oversized teen-ager named Tommy McKay, who worked at the general store a couple of miles down the lake, pointed shakily toward the wooded ridge behind my cabin.

"Up yonder at the Osterman place," he said. "She—she's got a knife in her back. I figured you'd know what to do, you bein' the county attorney and all."

"Just a minute," I said, and went back to the bedroom to put on some clothes.

My wife was awake now, propped up on her elbows on the bed. She asked, "What's going on?"

I relayed what McKay had told me. Martha threw her legs over the edge of the bed and sat up, looking startled.

"Helen Blair—dead?" she said incredulously. "Why, I saw her yesterday afternoon; she and Zelda Ross drove by. You were still out on the lake, fishing."

"Yeah. Where're my shoes?"

"In the front room, I think. But what *happened* to Helen? They told me that Zelda wasn't going to stay. She just drove Helen out from town, then was going right back. Was Helen alone up there?"

"Honey, I don't know," I told her.

As I turned to the bedroom door, more or less dressed in

jeans and a shirt, I found the McKay kid standing there, gawking past me at my wife's bare legs.

I gave him an ungentle shove and said, "Let's go."

Minutes later, panting from the hurried climb up the ridge, I followed McKay into the Osterman cabin—three rooms and bath—and on through to the bathroom.

Helen Blair was dead, all right.

She was floating facedown in the half-filled bathtub, her long blonde hair fanned out over the surface of the water. She wore only a sodden terry-cloth robe. From between her shoulder blades protruded the hilt of a hunting knife.

I bet over and touched the back of her neck; the skin was cool, as was the water in the tub. I lifted her floating left hand and felt for a pulse that was long since gone. I noticed she was wearing a watch; the crystal was smashed, the hands stopped at 11:37.

Behind me, McKay said, "Just like I told you, Mr. Gates. Like to scared me to death when I seen her in there."

"How did you happen to find her?"

"She—Miss Blair—called the store last night. Told the boss she was up here for the weekend, and didn't have no food for breakfast. Asked him to have me deliver a load of stuff first thing this mornin'. So—so I did. When I got here, nobody answered my knock, but the door was open. I came on in and—there she was."

"What did you do then?" I asked.

"Dropped the sack of groceries here in the hall, and run like hell down the hill to your place. I knew you and Mrs. Gates was out here at the lake."

I glanced around the bathroom. On a chair near the tub was a frilly nightgown and a neatly folded towel. Lined up on the counter of the built-in lavatory were an unopened box of dusting powder, a spray bottle of cologne, and other jars and bottles.

Evidently Helen Blair had been preparing for a leisurely bath late last night, when whatever happened—happened.

I found a phone in the cabin's front room and called the sheriff's office in Monroe. The sheriff himself answered the phone.

"Nice of you to think of us workin' people, while you're loungin' around out there with your fishin' pole," he said in jest.

Then I told him the reason for my call and he cut the comedy. I hung up and turned to take a good look at Tommy McKay. He'd seemed nervous and frightened enough before; now his square-jawed, freckled face was so pale I thought he was going to faint.

"Take it easy," I said. "You've done fine so far."

"I—I got to get out of here, get some air," he croaked, and stumbled out the front door into the early sunshine. He hunkered down on the front steps, cradling his head on his arms.

Sheriff Ed Carson covered the ten miles of highway and backwoods roads between Monroe and Schooler Lake in not much more than ten minutes. His two deputies and the county coroner, Dr. Pearce, weren't far behind.

It was still several minutes short of eight o'clock that mid-September Saturday morning when Dr. Pearce finished his examination of the body and came out of the bathroom.

Sheriff Carson and I were talking in the hallway.

A fast once-over of the small cabin had turned up nothing in the way of clues. It appeared that Helen Blair had spent a quiet evening reading in the bedroom. The bed was rumpled, a table beside it held an ashtray crowded with cigarette butts, an empty glass and a twisted candy wrapper; also a book titled *Black Midnight*. Very appropriate.

The living room, furnished with several comfortable easy chairs, a floor lamp or two, and a huge radio-stereo set, didn't show any signs of having been occupied. In the kitchen, where we had taken the groceries that McKay had dropped in the hall, we had found nothing beyond a half-full bottle of good Scotch and a six-pack of canned soft drinks in the refrigerator.

The cabin's back door was bolted on the inside. All the windows were down and locked. The wooden front door and the screen door were both intact, with no trace of their having been jimmied open. Yet McKay had found them unlocked.

Now Carson said, "What've you got, Doc?"

The coroner frowned. In his usual querulous voice, he snapped, "What do you want from me? The woman's dead, and that's all there is to it. Stabbed once with that hunting knife—six-inch blade. Penetrated the heart."

"When did she die?" I asked.

The doctor, a small, pigeon-breasted man with a halo of reddish hair around a bald, egg-shaped head, looked at me without favor. "You saw that watch on her arm," he said. "It was busted when she fell into the tub, I reckon. Stopped at eleven-thirty-something."

"Uh-huh, but what do *you* think?" the sheriff put in.

"Well, when was she last seen alive?"

"We don't know," I said.

"Then I don't know when she died," the doctor countered. "No, now—you fellers don't need to give me those go-to-hell looks! Her being in that tub full of water bollixed up things. I'd guess she died somewhere within an hour or two of midnight, either way. So maybe the watch—"

"Never mind the watch," I said. "We'd rather have medical evidence."

"Well, you're not going to get it, keeping me standing here," Dr. Pearce growled. "Let me get her into town to the morgue for autopsy, and maybe I can tell you more."

The sheriff asked, "Was there any sign she'd been in a fight?"

"Nope. Way I see it, she was standing in there by the tub, probably just about to take off her robe and hop in, when the killer come up behind her and let her have it," Pearce said.

"Looks that way," Carson agreed, but with some hesitation.

"She fell into the tub, and that was that," Pearce went on. "Thing is, a body in water don't cool off at the same rate as a body lying on the ground somewhere. Fact, if it's floating in water hotter than normal body temperature, it don't cool off a'tall . . . and in ice water, of course, it cools a lot faster."

"Well—"

"Sheriff?" boomed a heavy voice from the front of the hall; Deputy Buck Mullins lumbered toward us, his shoulders almost scraping the walls on either side. "Listen, Dr. Osterman and some woman showed up. They're out here raisin' hell 'cause I won't let 'em come into the cabin."

Sheriff Ed Carson let out a sigh that ruffled the shaggy lower fringe of his pepper-and-salt moustache. "All right, I'll talk to them," he said. Then, to the coroner: "You can take her on into town when you're ready."

Carson and Deputy Mullins headed for the doorway that

connected with the living room. As I started to follow, Dr. Pearce grasped my sleeve.

"What's Osterman got to do with this?" he asked.

"This is his cabin, for one thing," I said. "He and Helen Blair were supposed to get married in a few weeks."

"Good match," Pearce growled. "From what I've heard, they deserved each other."

With a vigorous nod and a snort, the doctor bustled toward the front door. I followed more slowly, reflecting on what I knew of Helen Blair.

She and my wife had been friends since their school days, but I knew Helen only casually.

She was an extremely well-built, good-looking blonde, somewhere in her thirties, with a husky voice and a rather dramatic manner that didn't especially grab me, though a lot of men didn't share my view.

She had returned to Monroe a couple of years before, after several years in New York, where she had run through a couple of husbands and come away with their scalps and respectable chunks of their bank accounts. She had opened a more or less exclusive ladies' dress shop in Monroe's tiny business district, and reportedly had done very well.

Also, by report, she had spent her spare time playing around with the town's eligible males—and a few not so eligible.

Then she'd hooked up with Dr. Paul Osterman. He is a surgeon, two or three years younger than Helen, with something of a reputation of his own for after-hours fun and games.

Before long the *Monroe Gazette* was announcing their engagement, and plans for a mid-October wedding.

As I entered the living room I heard voices coming from the tree-shaded yard beyond the open front door. A baritone I recognized as that of Dr. Paul Osterman said, "I've always thought this area should be patrolled regularly, Sheriff. Now see—"

"We do the best we can," the sheriff said.

Then suddenly a woman's voice cried, "I should have stayed with her—I should have stayed!"

Reaching the front door and pushing open the screen, I saw that the last speaker was a chubby woman crammed into a white uniform. A nurse's cap was set askew atop her lank brown hair. I knew her slightly: Zelda Ross, a nurse at County Memorial, where Dr. Osterman was a resident surgeon. Now she spotted me and her slightly bloodshot blue eyes took on a blaze of anger.

"And you, Mr. County Attorney, where were *you* last night while some—some maniac was cutting Helen to pieces?"

I said, "I'm sorry, Miss Ross, but I don't—"

"She's not herself, Gates," broke in Osterman, giving me a bleak smile. "Such an incredible thing to happen—to Helen, of all people."

Dr. Pearce was returning, shepherding along two ambulance attendants carrying a wicker stretcher between them.

Osterman went on: "May I see Helen, Sheriff?"

The sheriff nodded. "Mebbe you'd look around the cabin, too, while you're in there. Check to see if anything is missin'."

Osterman nodded and followed the other men inside.

That left Zelda Ross, Carson and myself. Carson said, "Miss Ross was about to tell me how she drove Miss Blair out here yesterday afternoon."

"I was?" Zelda said, and rubbed the back of a shaky hand across her forehead. If she had weighed twenty pounds less, and had taken a little more care with her appearance, she would've been an attractive woman. Now she blinked once or twice, and said, "I haven't had any sleep—Paul called me just as I was going to bed half an hour ago, and said he'd heard—I'd just barely got home from the hospital—"

"Yes. But about yesterday," I said.

"We—we left town somewhere after five. Paul planned to drive Helen out here but he got tied up at the hospital and asked me to bring her. Helen didn't drive."

"Go on, Miss Ross," Carson said, as she hesitated.

"Oh. We got here shortly before six. We saw your wife, Mr. Gates, and stopped to talk to her for a minute. Then came on up here. I—I only stayed long enough to get Helen settled in. I had the night duty at the hospital so I had to be back by seven."

"What time did you start back?"

"I don't know exactly—six-fifteen, something like that."

Zelda's plump face twisted. "She asked me to stay the night with her . . . I could easily have got someone to take my shift at the hospital, but—but I didn't."

"Yes. Did Miss Blair seem at all upset or worried about anything?" I asked.

Zelda was shaking her head. "Not at all. She was looking forward to some peace and quiet out here. Of course, Paul was to come out Sunday—tomorrow—and spend the day, then they'd drive back to town tomorrow night."

Zelda paused, then burst out, "If only I had stayed! Helen would be alive this morning—"

"Or you might be dead, along with her," I broke in.

She gawked at me; evidently that idea had not occurred to her. Then she breathed, "Oh, that's—"

There was a stir at the cabin door. The ambulance attendants appeared, carrying the now-laden stretcher. Pearce was right behind them as they crossed the yard to the waiting ambulance. The doctor called, "I'll be in touch!"

A moment later, Osterman came out, his lean, handsome face set in a scowl. He said, "Nothing is missing that I can see. That knife—the knife used on Helen—it was mine. I kept it in a drawer in the kitchen. Whoever did this used *my knife*—" He broke off with an angry shrug.

"When did you last see Miss Blair alive?" Carson asked.

"What? Oh. Yesterday afternoon. She was bubbling over with high spirits. Didn't even mind when I had to stay in town, and Zelda here drove her to the lake. She was a good sport."

I happened to be looking at the nurse as Osterman spoke. I noticed her eyes narrow and her full lips compress at the tone of Osterman's voice as he carelessly said the last.

Dr. Osterman had a slightly patronizing way about him that was enough to grate on anyone's nerves, but he was supposed to be an excellent doctor and I knew, from having served on two or three civic-improvement committees with him, he didn't mind hard work.

Now he was saying, thoughtfully, "I have to go along with Pearce. It's going to be hard to get a time of death by the body-temperature route. If we can find out when Helen ate last, we can get some idea from the state of digestion in her stomach and small intestine—"

"For heaven's sake, Paul," Zelda Ross said. She suddenly

looked ill and turned away, saying over her shoulder, "I'll wait for you in the car."

Osterman looked after her with a puzzled expression. Then he shrugged well-tailored shoulders and said, "Women."

Carson said, "Uh-huh. As far as you know, Miss Blair wasn't upset about anything? Worried?"

"Far from it." Osterman stared speculatively into space, while the tip of his tongue moved back and forth along the narrow, bristly moustache that decorated his upper lip. Then he nodded and said, "I'd better tell you something. Helen and I were married last week over in Jacksonville. No one knew about it but the two of us, and the justice of the peace who performed the ceremony."

I said, "But I thought—"

"The big church wedding next month? We were still going to have that, but—well, the truth is, Helen was not at all what you might think, from the idle gossip around town. She wanted that marriage certificate in her hot little hand, so . . ."

"But why keep the wedding a secret?"

"Her idea," Osterman said, with a wry smile. "I think she figured the shindig next month would make a bigger social splash if it weren't known we'd already tied the knot beforehand. Anyway, that's how it was."

The sheriff nodded slowly. "You know of any relatives she had anywhere? Someone we should notify of her death?"

"There aren't any. She was all alone, as far as blood kin goes," Osterman said. Now his hazel eyes narrowed as he looked past me at someone approaching along the ridge. "Isn't that Frank Ivy coming? That damn busybody!"

Turning, I saw a skinny middle-aged man hurrying toward us, an outsize bathrobe flapping about the legs of the striped pajamas he wore. A large, motherly-looking woman was some distance behind him.

"What the hell is all this?" the skinny man bawled.

His name was Ivy; he ran a department store in Monroe. The woman following him was his wife, Sarah.

"What the hell's it to you?" Osterman retorted.

Ivy ignored the young doctor. To Carson he said, "By damn, I *knew* something was going on over here last night!"

"Your deputy, Mr. Avery, was by our place a few minutes ago," Mrs. Ivy said, joining us. "He told us what happened—"

"Lights blazing, radio blaring fit to wake the dead," Ivy broke in. "I'm not surprised that Blair woman's ways finally caught up with her!"

Dr. Osterman scowled at the older man, and said quietly, "I told you last week, Ivy, what I'd do if I heard any more of your talk about Helen." As he spoke, the doctor took a step forward, his hands doubling into fists.

Ivy retreated, putting his wife's comfortable bulk between himself and Osterman. "Ha," he snorted then, "I'm not scared of you."

The sheriff said mildly, "Calm down, Doctor. Mr. Ivy, just what did you see last night?"

"Why, they had a big party going over here."

"Now, Frank," his wife said. Then, to Carson: "Actually, we just noticed that the lights were on in the front room during the evening. And once the radio did come on loud, but only for a few minutes. Then they turned it down. That's all."

"What about the motorcycle?" Ivy cried. "Roaring up and down, stopping and starting right over here. Went on for half the night!"

"Now, Frank," sighed Mrs. Ivy. "We heard the motorcycle after we'd gone to bed, sometime past eleven. It did go back and forth along the lane a few times, but then it went away. Frank got up and looked out the window, and—"

"I'd have come over here and raised hell about all the racket, but Sarah wouldn't let me," Ivy inserted.

His wife gave him an indulgent smile.

Dr. Osterman was looking thoughtful. "You know, there is a bunch of kids from town who come out here on their motorbikes. Hasn't been so bad since school started, but during the summer they caused a lot of trouble." He glanced at the sheriff and added, "Of course, you didn't do anything about it."

"Now, come on," I put in. "Sheriff Carson has himself and two full-time deputies to cover a territory as big as the state of Rhode Island—"

"Okay, okay." Osterman shrugged. "What I was thinking, if a couple of those punks were out here last night, they might have discovered that Helen was here alone."

"Alone? Her?" snapped Ivy. "Had half the men in the county after her. Alone—ha!"

Again I thought the doctor was going to take a swing at Ivy but the sheriff served as peacemaker. He said, "Doctor, there's nothin' you can do out here. I'm sure you got business in town."

Dr. Osterman hesitated, then gave a curt nod. "You know where to find me. Either at the hospital or at my place. There is one last thing, Sheriff. You should take a very large grain of salt with anything this—this man might tell you. The fact is, Helen's shop had taken away a lot of his store's business. That's the reason for his—"

"That's a lie," Ivy cried. "Hell, I've never said a thing about the woman that wasn't common knowledge!"

Osterman turned on his heel and walked to the big black car in which Zelda Ross was sitting. He got into it and drove away along the sandy lane that ran the length of the ridge before dipping down to join the road that led out to the highway.

Sarah Ivy folded her arms across her ample middle, and said, "Frank and the doctor don't get along too well."

"I kind of got that idea," Carson said solemnly. "About what time did you notice the lights on over here, and the radio playin'?"

"The lights were on all evening—"

"They went off sometime between eleven-thirty and midnight," Ivy put in. "They was on when that racket with the motorcycle started. And I noticed the cabin here was dark when I glanced this way right at midnight, just before I went back to bed."

"And the radio?"

"That was earlier—around nine-thirty, maybe."

"Did you actually see anyone?" I asked.

Mrs. Ivy shook her head; after a moment Ivy reluctantly did the same. Then he burst out, "One thing, at least—that woman got what she deserved!"

"Frank," said his wife, this time sharply, "we'd better get back. Breakfast is on the stove."

A moment later the pair retraced their steps along the ridge, moving through the dappling of sun and shade caused by the pines, toward their cabin about fifty yards distant and half-concealed by intervening trees.

Now we spotted Carson's second deputy, Jack Avery,

toiling up the ridge. He had been checking the other cabins in the area of the Osterman place. There were about half a dozen of these spaced irregularly along the top of the ridge—the Ivy cabin being the nearest—and on the slope facing the lake. More cabins, including mine, were along the shore some distance below.

Avery reached us, shaking his head mournfully. He was even taller and thinner than the sheriff, with a narrow face and heavy-lidded eyes that made him look as if he might topple over asleep any moment.

He said, "That was a dry haul. Ain't but a few people out here this weekend. And none of them seen anything last night, except an old couple named Ivy."

"They was just over here," Carson said. He turned to stare thoughtfully at the weather-beaten front wall of the cabin a few feet away. "What really happened in there?"

I didn't have an answer. Neither did Avery, nor did Buck Mullins, when he turned up a few minutes later. Carson had sent him down to the general store to ask the owner about the call from Helen Blair last night.

"Just like that McKay kid told you all," Mullins said. "She phoned around eight-thirty, nine o'clock, wantin' some eats delivered first thing this mornin'."

"How was Tommy doing?" I asked the big deputy. "He looked like he was ready for the hospital when he left here a while ago."

Mullins shrugged massive shouders. "He must've perked up some. The old feller who runs the store said Tommy came in and told him what had happened, then asked for the day off. Then he changed his clothes and headed for town. He lives with his married sister in Monroe, when he ain't stayin' at a room he's got fixed up over the store out here."

Soon after that Carson and Avery left for town. For the time being Deputy Mullins was to stay at the lake, giving the Osterman cabin another going over and generally keeping an eye on things. I plodded down the steep ridge and along the shore to my cabin.

I found that my wife had already packed the car with the meager gear we had brought out yesterday afternoon.

"Another weekend shot to hell," I said glumly, as Martha and I drove along the shore road to the general store, then turned onto the graveled road that led to the highway.

Martha gave me an irritable glance and said, "I doubt if Helen got herself murdered just to keep you from enjoying your fishing."

I grunted. "How did Helen seem when you saw her?"

"You mean yesterday? I told you, she and Zelda Ross just stopped for a minute. Helen seemed to be in a good mood. Said she was going to spend the evening reading and relaxing, and get to bed early."

"Yeah. You didn't get the notion she might've been expecting to receive any visitors?" I asked.

"No. In fact, she made it clear she'd be alone—and wanted it that way. She did say she'd come down this morning to keep me company while you were out on the lake."

We rode in silence for a while. The woods that flanked the road were just beginning to put on their autumn colors. We reached the blacktop highway and turned north.

I said, "It's all so damn neat—up to a point."

I didn't realize I'd spoken aloud until Martha said, "What's so damn neat?"

"Just about everything we saw and heard this morning makes it look like Helen really did what she told you she was going to do—read and laze around the cabin. About eleven she ran a bath and got undressed. And just as she was about to take off her robe and step into the tub a little past eleven-thirty, the killer came into the bathroom and stabbed her in the back. She fell forward into the tub of water, breaking her watch against the side of the tub as she did. Then the killer turned out the lights and left."

Martha was frowning at me. "So? It makes sense to me. There's been trouble before with prowlers out there at the lake—you know the stories we've heard."

I nodded. "But any casual prowler who had the nerve to enter an occupied cabin would bring a weapon with him. Helen was killed with a knife belonging to Dr. Osterman."

"For heaven's sake," Martha said impatiently. "He probably stumbled on the knife while he was sneaking around inside the cabin. Since Helen was in the bedroom with the water running, she wouldn't hear him."

"Maybe. But while he was stumbling on the knife, why didn't he stumble on Helen's purse? It was on the bedroom dresser in plain sight—with something over fifty dollars in it. It hadn't been touched. Neither had the diamond ring Helen was wearing."

"Well . . . perhaps he wasn't interested in robbery. Helen was an awfully attractive woman."

"Yes. But she hadn't been touched, either—except for the knife in her back."

"He panicked when he saw what he'd done, and ran—"

"Taking the time to turn out all the lights in the place as he went. Some panic."

Now the seedy outskirts of Monroe loomed up ahead. I glanced at my watch: nine-fifteen. Just about two hours since Tommy McKay had pounded on the door of our cabin at the lake.

Martha was saying, "What do *you* think happened?"

"I think Helen had a visitor, someone she was expecting. But what happened then, I haven't even got a good guess."

I dropped Martha at our place, stopping long enough myself to shave and put on fresh clothes, and have a cup of coffee. Then I drove downtown. Since it was a Saturday, the streets in what passed for the business district around the courthouse square were fairly crowded.

I turned into the alley that bisected the square itself, and parked in the lot between the brick jail and the ancient heap of stone that was the Pokochobee County courthouse.

I went in the back door and along the echoing ground-floor corridor to the sheriff's office. I found Carson in his private cubbyhole, sitting back in his swivel chair with his dusty brogans propped up on his desk. He looked half asleep.

"I'm glad the voters can't see this," I told him. "The biggest murder case in years, and all you can think to do is sit here twiddling your thumbs."

The sheriff stretched, yawned, and gestured me to a chair. "Set and twiddle with me, for a spell . . . No, I'm waitin' for the McKay boy. He phoned from his sister's place a while ago, said there was somethin' he kind of forgot to tell us this mornin'. And he figured he'd better tell it now."

"You think he—"

"Let's wait till he gets here, and ask him."

"There's one thing I just remembered," I said slowly. "He drives a pickup belonging to the store during his work-

ing hours. But I've seen him around the lake in the evenings, riding a motorcycle."

At that moment Deputy Avery shuffled in from the big
outer office, carrying a clipboard stuffed with notes.

He gave me a mournful nod, and said to Carson, "I been
on that phone so long both my ears is ringin'. Course, they
do that anyway."

"Uh-huh. What've you got?"

"Looks like Dr. Osterman and that nurse, Zelda Ross,
was tellin' the truth about last night. The doctor was in and
out of the hospital till ten o'clock. At that time he started
an emergency operation that lasted till after midnight.
After that he went to a room in the residential quarters and
got a few hours' sleep. He could've fitted in a fast trip to
the lake before ten, or after midnight, but—"

"But it ain't too likely," Carson nodded.

"The Ross gal got to work at seven last night, and was
on duty till seven this mornin'. She couldn't have gone to
the bathroom durin' that time without half the nurses on
duty with her knowin' about it. There ain't no doubt about
it, she was at the hospital all night."

"All right. You talked to Helen Blair's lawyer?"

"Yeah, old Judge Fancher. She was evidently pretty
well-fixed. The judge hemmed and hawed, and finally allowed that her estate would amount to more than half a
million bucks. She never made a will, and don't seem to
have no kinfolks, so the whole bundle will go to Osterman—if him and her was really married like he told
you."

Carson nodded his gray-thatched head. "I'd bet they
were. Osterman don't strike me as the type to tell you
a outright lie, not if he knowed you could easily check on
it."

"Outside of that, the judge wasn't no help. As far as he
knew, Helen didn't have any enemies—except mebbe old
Frank Ivy—and that was just business. Seems Miss Blair's
dress shop was cuttin' pretty heavy into Ivy's sales at his
department store."

I leaned forward in my chair and tapped ashes from my
cigarette into a grimy ashtray on Carson's desk. I said,
"Maybe we should give that guy some thought."

"Mebbe," the sheriff agreed, and added, "but that wife of
his would have to be in it with the old coot."

Avery shifted glumly from one size twelve to the other, and went on: "I called a few people here and there that I thought might have some dirt, but no luck. Seems like since Dr. Osterman and Helen started goin' together, six, seven months ago, they both've been out of circulation, otherwise. Before that, Helen dated several of the town gents, but nothin' very heavy, in spite of all the talk. Osterman, he done his share of woman-chasin'. Ran through all the nurses in the hospital, even Zelda Ross for a while; she was a lot thinner then. But there don't seem to be anyone around with hard feelin's toward either Helen or the Doc."

I offered, "Don't forget Frank Ivy."

The sheriff shook his head. "Can you really see old Frank and his wife pussyfootin' over to that cabin last night, and puttin' a knife in Helen Blair's back? For one thing, I doubt she'd even let them step foot in the cabin, Lon."

"They—or he—could've found the door unlocked."

"Or she might have left the screen door unhooked, and they had a key to the wooden door," Avery said helpfully. "Course, so might half the rest of the people in the county. Door opens with a plain old skeleton key. There's a bolt on it, but—"

"But it wasn't bolted. Unless the girl undid it to let in a visitor," the sheriff said.

"Or simply forgot to lock the door altogether, and some stray nut walked in," I added. "Anything's possible."

Avery said sadly, "The truth is, all we're doin' is goin' around in circles—"

Carson interrupted him by leaning forward over the desk, his gaze going past me to the open door connecting with the outer office. He called, "In here, son."

Twisting around in my chair, I saw Tommy McKay coming slowly toward us, looking as if he were on his way to the gas chamber. He entered the little private office. He looked around at me, at Deputy Avery, then at Carson.

He gulped, and burst out, "It was just that I was afraid you all would think *I* killed that woman! I didn't—I swear I didn't go near her! Honest, I didn't have no idea she was dead till I went in there this mornin', just like I told Mr. Gates here."

Carson said mildly, "All right, son. For the moment, let's agree that you was just ridin' around on your motorcycle last night, and just happened to be near the Osterman cabin. Then what?"

The teen-ager's pug-nosed face grew redder. For a moment I thought he was going to break his fingers, the way he was twisting them together behind his back, as he stood there facing Carson across the desk.

"It all sounds so durn dumb," he said. "Heck, I knew all the time that that—that Miss Blair didn't really want me to come over. I was kind of livin' a daydream or somethin'. Oh, hell! I went up there last night and dragged back and forth along the lane on my cycle. I thought maybe she'd hear the noise and come out to see what was goin' on, and—and invite me to come in . . . But she didn't."

"What gave you the idea she might?" I asked.

"Her callin' the store," the kid said. "You know? I thought she was kind of hintin' she wanted me to—to come over. Durn it, I told you it was dumb!"

"What happened?"

"Well, I dragged back and forth in front of the cabin. I knew she was still up, the lights was on in the front room and all. Finally I went on past and parked my cycle, and walked back." Tommy twisted his fingers some more, and went on: "Thing is, the shade wasn't all the way down at one of the front windows. I went across the yard and looked in. The front room was empty, so I went on around the cabin, but none of the other rooms had lights on."

"Uh-huh," the sheriff said. "Why don't you set down?"

McKay blinked at him dazedly, then shook his head. "I'm all right. Anyways, I hung around there outside the lighted window in the front room. Hopin' she'd come in, you know? I never done anything like that before—that's the truth. But that Miss Blair . . . I don't give a damn *how* old she was. She made the girls I run around with look sick." He stopped, wiped his sweaty face on his shirt sleeve, then croaked, "You all mind if I sit down?"

Avery silently pushed a chair forward.

When the kid was perched on the edge of the seat, Carson asked, "She wasn't in the livin' room at all?"

"No, sir. Fact, I got the feelin' the cabin was empty. There weren't a sound. Nothin'. It was kind of weird."

"What time was this, Tommy?" I put in.

"I don't know, Mr. Gates. Around eleven-thirty, I guess. Maybe a little later than that. Anyway, I stayed crouched down there at the window, hopin' to—to see her. Maybe in her nightgown or maybe—you know . . ."

He paused, stared down at his hands, now knotting themselves together in his lap, then said, "That's when it happened. No warnin' or nothin'. Like to scared me out of my socks."

"What was that?"

"All at once the light in there went out. Without no one in the room to *turn* it out, that I could see. It was a big floor lamp settin' next to an easy chair. I thought maybe somebody had been crouchin' down behind the chair where I couldn't see 'em, and had jerked the lamp cord out of its wall socket. I sort of froze up for a minute, waitin' to hear somebody come bustin' out of the cabin and around the corner to grab me—but nothin' happened."

"You didn't hear anything at all?"

"No, sir. That was the creepiest part of it, just that dead silence. When I could move, I took off along to where I'd left my cycle, and beat it back to the store and up to my room. And—that's all. This mornin' was just like I told you." He glanced timidly at Carson. "You goin' to jail me?"

"Let me think about it a while," Carson told him. "What made you decide to come in?"

"This mornin' after what happened, I went to see my sister. She lives here in town. She could tell I was worried, and kept after me till I told her. Then she said I'd better come tell you, no matter what you done to me."

"Uh-huh. You always do what your sister tells you?"

"Most times. She's smarter than me."

Carson nodded thoughtfully. "You better go on home, then. And stay away from other people's windows at night."

"Don't worry!" the kid said decidedly, and was gone.

After a long moment, Deputy Avery said, "How about that? The killer is not only unknown, but unvisible as well."

The sheriff leaned back in his swivel chair, clasped his gnarled hands behind his head and stared up at the dingy plaster ceiling. He muttered, "Now, I wonder . . ."

Abruptly he sat forward, and picked up his phone. He got the operator and had her connect him with Osterman's cabin at the lake. After several rings he got an answer.

"Buck? This is me," he said. "You're in the front room there, ain't you? Yeah. You see an easy chair with a floor lamp beside it? Near that big radio set. Uh-huh. Go see if the lamp cord is plugged into the wall. No, I ain't funnin'!"

There was a pause. The sheriff's craggy face was set in lines of tense expectancy. I watched him curiously.

Then he said into the phone, "Yeah? Uh-huh."

An unlikely smile appeared under his bushy moustache. The phone conversation continued, the sheriff's end being the asking of cryptic questions about makes and models, and was something a twelve- or twenty-four-hour thinga-majig?

Then Carson hung up, squinted at the notes he'd scribbled, and said, "There ain't but one or two places in town that carry this kind of thing. Comin', Lon?"

We found what Carson was looking for at Frank Ivy's department store. A clerk in the electrical appliances section read the make and model numbers Carson had gotten from Buck Mullins. He rummaged around on one of the laden shelves, took down a smallish box, and said, "Here we are."

Inside the box was another box, this one made of metal. Set into it were what appeared to be four clocks.

"This here is a good item," the clerk beamed.

I suddenly saw the light. "A timer!"

"Yes, sir," agreed the clerk. "You plug it into your wall outlet. Then you can plug two separate items into the timer. See? The two top dials are the 'on' dials. The bottom two are when you want things to go off. The two sides are independent. Have a lamp, say, come on at dark and go off a couple hours later, while on the other side you could have your TV or radio."

"Uh-huh," the sheriff said. "You keep records on who buys these things?"

"No, unless it's a charge purchase, of course. Why?"

"Mebbe you could remember if you sold one of them to Dr. Paul Osterman in the last—"

"Oh, yes. He bought one early last summer."

While this was going on, I was studying the timing device. I saw that each of the clock faces was calibrated not from one to twelve, but one to twenty-four.

"So whatever you had plugged into it would come on at twenty-four hour intervals," I said.

"Right," the clerk agreed, giving me a doting smile. "People use them in their homes when, say, they're going on vacation, or going to be away on business."

"Thanks a lot," Carson said.

When we were on the street again, I asked, "Did Mullins tell you if the timer in the cabin out there is still hooked up?"

"Yep. It is," the sheriff said. "And plugged into it is that lamp, set to turn on at 8:30 tonight, off again at 11:45. And that radio—it's due at 9:30 till 9:45. Just long enough to get attention directed toward the cabin, for somebody to see the lights was on there."

We reached the county car and got into it.

"The killer didn't have a chance to get back out there and disconnect the thing before Tommy McKay found Helen's body this morning," I said. "He still hasn't had a chance."

"But he'll just about have to make a try 'fore this evenin'," Carson said. "Else those things'll be turnin' on."

"And there goes his alibi," I added.

The sheriff backed the car out from the curb, and aimed it toward the courthouse.

There, we found Avery once more on the phone. When he'd finished, he gave us a gloomy nod, and said, "You was right, Sheriff. Accordin' to the phone company records, there wasn't any call from the Osterman place at eight-thirty last night. Or any other time last night."

I stared at him. "Helen called the store out there—"

"Somebody *sayin'* they was Helen Blair called the store, but not from that phone," Avery sighed. "Howsomever, there *is* a record of a toll call from a public booth at County Memorial Hospital to the store at the lake. At eight-forty last evenin', to be exact."

Suddenly the phone rang and the sheriff took the call. It was Dr. Pearce. Carson listened intently a few moments, said, "Yeah. That helps. Thanks."

"Well?" I said, as he turned slowly from the phone.

"Doc changed his mind a bit about the time of death," Carson said. "Now he allows that the woman could've been killed anytime after four or five o'clock in the afternoon, providin' her body was put into a tub of very hot water right afterwards—and left there."

I said, "That sort of opens the door, doesn't it?"

"Yeah. Doc told me somethin' else. He figures from the body's stomach contents that Helen had a meal roughly two hours before she died. What say we do a little checkin' at the cafes around here?"

Leaving Avery looking, for once, as if he might last out the day on his feet, the sheriff and I made a tour of the restaurants in Monroe's business district. No luck. Then we stopped at a ramshackle diner on a side street; it was lousy in appearance, but had the best hamburgers in the county.

Helen Blair had been there yesterday afternoon.

"Sure, Miss Blair come in around four, four-thirty," the diner manager told us. "Lovely woman. One of my best customers, she was. Yesterday she had her usual snack— two cheeseburgers and a double order of fries. Eat like a horse, and all it done to her figure was make it better." He shook his head admiringly.

Again in the county car, the sheriff said, "Want to ride out to the lake with me?"

I didn't bother to answer that. Minutes later we were barreling down the highway south of town. I said, "Helen could've had another meal later on."

"We didn't find no traces of it at the cabin," Carson reminded me. "Only that one empty candy wrapper."

"Yeah. But it could still be either Osterman—or Zelda Ross. Which one? Or someone else altogether?"

Carson took his eyes from the road long enough to glance at me. "Remember the first thing Miss Ross did when she seen you this morning?"

"Yelled at me," I said. "Wanted to know where I was when Helen got—'cut to pieces,' I think was the way she put it."

"Uh-huh. Only, up till then, I don't think anybody had mentioned in her hearin' that Helen was stabbed to death."

I whistled softly. "But she would've had to kill Helen as soon as they reached the cabin," I said. "Then rushed around there setting the scene: the bathroom, the cigarette butts and book in the bedroom, placing that timer in the front room—"

"All that wouldn't take more'n a few minutes, actually," Carson said. "She'd been out to Osterman's place in the past; she could easy have known about that timer, and how to work it. Bein' a nurse, she'd also likely know how to stick a knife in somebody's back and hit the heart first try. That takes some doin' if you don't know where to aim."

"All right," I agreed. "But Osterman would also know all that—even better. And he had half a million bucks to gain by Helen's death. What'd Zelda have to gain?"

Carson shook his head. "Thing is, I can see her callin' that store last night, and pretendin' to be Helen Blair. But I can't see Osterman, with that deep voice he's got, foolin' anybody about him bein' a woman. Even over the telephone."

"Maybe the two of them were in it together."

"You think so?"

It was my turn to shake my head. "No, I don't. Not for a minute."

"Neither do I."

It was a few minutes before noon when we reached the lake. As we drove up the ridge and along to the Osterman cabin, I saw that there were a good many people on the lake or fishing along the shore. I wondered if Zelda Ross was among them, keeping a covert eye on the cabin on the hill and hoping against hope that she'd have a chance to get in there unobserved before evening.

At the cabin, Mullins lumbered out to meet us.

"I stood inside there, just like you told me," he greeted the sheriff. "Nobody's tried to get in."

"Good. How about you drive your car down yonder and park it out of sight," Carson said. "Then come back and do the same with my jalopy."

Deputy Mullins massaged his forehead, then brightened. "Oh, I get it. You want folks to think we've pulled out and left the cabin empty."

"That's it," Carson said.

Inside the cabin, it was dim as a cave after the bright noon sun outside. When Mullins returned, the sheriff locked the front door, removed the key, and the three of us sat down to wait.

"This could be a fool's errand," I said, after half an hour or so. "Zelda may not have the nerve to try, or she might hope that if and when we caught onto the timing device, we'd blame it on Osterman."

The sheriff was lying back in an easy chair, with his ancient gray hat tipped forward over his eyes. He muttered, "Mebbe. But I'm bettin' she comes."

"But what was the motive, jealousy?" I said. "If that was it, why wait all these months? And why put on this act of being such good friends with Helen all this time?"

Mullins rumbled, casually, "What if Miss Ross just found out yesterday that the doctor and Helen Blair had gone and got married?"

I stared. "Yeah. Buck, I owe you an apology."

"Huh?"

"I keep making the mistake of thinking that you're as dumb as you look."

The sheriff sat up abruptly, waving a hand for silence.

There came the soft *thunk* of a car door closing outside. Footsteps. Then, after a long minute, the rattle of a key in the door lock.

Quickly we moved into the hallway beyond the living room.

Then the door opened, and Zelda Ross slipped in, shut the door and leaned back against it. Taking a deep breath, she crossed the room, and her bulky form knelt down at the wall behind the radio-stereo set.

"That's enough, Miss Ross," said Carson, stepping out of the shadowy hallway.

Zelda stayed as she was for a few seconds. Then she slowly straightened and turned to face us. Her chubby face was pale and her eyes darted from one to the other of us.

"I had—something I forgot—oh, to hell with it. I wasn't cut out to be a murderer." She tried a shaky smile. "I haven't got the figure for it."

After Carson had placed her under arrest, and after she had waived her right to have an attorney present, we asked a few questions, enough to make it clear things had happened much as we thought, even to the motive.

"On the way out here, that—that woman told me they were married," she said huskily. "It was just too much. Throwing it in my face like that . . . She knew how I felt about Paul. All this time, I expected—hoped—that he'd get tired of Helen and come back to me. She was such a shallow woman, always talking about how she could eat anything and not gain a pound . . ."

Zelda suddenly put her hands to her face and moaned softly, but she made no resistance as Carson took her elbow and guided her toward the open door.

Then she hesitated, dropping her hands to look up into the sheriff's face, and said, "Do you think we could stop somewhere on the way into town? I'm dying for something to eat."

MURDER OUT OF A HAT

by Henry Slesar

"Don't tell me what I can or can't do! How many other exams have you been cribbing?"

"None, Professor, I swear it!"

"I wonder if the Dean will believe that."

"Please, Professor!"

Jarvis shuffled to the blackboard and began wiping off chalk marks with furious concentration. Then he turned.

"I won't report you, Hatch. Not to the dean. It's too early in the semester to get a student into trouble."

"Gee, that's swell of you—"

"But I don't intend to let your dishonesty go unpunished. So I'm writing to your father tonight."

"To my father? What for?"

"I find that I'm often not as persuasive as a parent," Jarvis said acidly. "So I intend to enlist some support in your discipline. That will be all, Mr. Hatch."

Jarvis started for the door; Perry's hand clutched at his sleeve. "Professor, wait a minute! You don't understand about my father. I mean, about what he's like—"

"I hope he's very, very strict."

"He'll murder me! He'll cut off my allowance!"

Jarvis pulled his shabby sleeve away, and marched out of the classroom in solemn, immovable righteousness.

Dino was waiting at the General's statue when Perry emerged onto the campus. Dino had a close-cropped head round as a melon, and an expression almost as blank. Perry, a good-looking boy with a sullen mouth, was even more sullen when Dino inquired about the interview.

"The old crumb," Perry muttered. "He says he's going to write my old man. Boy, I can see the fireworks now."

"Gee, that's tough, man."

"What's he always pickin' on me for? What makes him so mean?"

Dino chuckled. "You know what they say about him, Perry. About what a terror his wife is. Man, he's the original henpecked husband, you know that."

"Yeah, I'll bet that's it, all right. That old shrew gives him hell every night, and he takes it out on us."

"Remember what happened last year? When she chased him out of the house, and he had a bunk at the Reo Hotel?" Dino chuckled. "Man, that was a ball. Remember how everybody razzed him in class the next day?"

"Well, I hope she makes him suffer tonight—"

"No such luck," Dino said. "She's not home. She went off to visit her sister or somebody a couple of months ago, and she's not back yet."

"That's too bad," Perry grunted. "Now I got *nothing* to look forward to. Except getting my allowance cut off."

"Gee," Dino said, genuinely concerned, "maybe if you went to see the professor—"

"What good would that do?"

"Well, maybe if you swallowed your pride, apologized—"

"You really think that might work?"

"You'll probably have to crawl a little. But that's better than losing your allowance, right? Go on, see the old boy tonight. I'll come with you, if you want."

"You mean it?"

"Sure," Dino said, clapping his back. "Let's get a hamburger and you can rehearse your speech. Er, by the way, can you pick up the check? I'm tapped out."

At night, the university was the smallest of small towns, the tiny residences at its perimeter darkened early. Professor Jarvis' house was no more than a bungalow, with a small lawn in front and neighbors flanking him on both sides. As Perry and Dino approached, they saw a yellow light illuminating his study. They could discern, through the large front window, the book-crammed room, the desk covered with papers, reference works, and general bric-a-brac. A skeleton was strung in one corner, an anatomical chart hung crookedly in another, a motheaten moose head above the mantelpiece looked down forlornly. They saw it all from the street, but no professor.

"Well, come on," Dino whispered. "You goin' in or ain't you?"

Perry halted, chewing his lip. "Aw, what's the use? You know the old guy. He'll just bawl me out again."

"You're chicken," Dino said tauntingly. "That's what's the matter with you."

"It's not that. Besides, I don't even *see* him."

"He's there, all right. Come on, will ya?"

There was a scraping noise near the house; it startled them both, and they moved into the shadows guiltily.

"What was that?"

"How should I know?" Dino complained. "Will you go to the door, for Pete's sake?"

"I think he's coming out—"

"The noise came from the back. Probably a cat."

Perry moved cautiously around to the back of the professor's home, with Dino grumbling behind him. When he saw the stream of yellow light spill into the back yard, he pulled Dino aside and flattened himself against the siding. There was the shuffle of footsteps, and both recognized the heavy tread of Professor Jarvis on the back steps. The next sound was a metallic clang, and Perry peeked cautiously around the corner and saw the old man lifting the cover of a trash can. It was a simple, homey action, but the object that was being relegated to the trash pile was unusual: it was a large round cardboard box, still prettily tied with a pink ribbon. Jarvis shoved it into the container, and pressed the lid down. Then he shuffled back to the house, and closed the door.

"Did you see that?" Perry whispered.

"See what? He was just throwing out some junk."

"In a box? With a ribbon on it?"

"Okay, so he's neat."

Perry snorted, and pulled Dino's arm. "Come on," he said. "Let's take a peek at it."

"Aw, look, Perry—"

"Come on!"

They tiptoed to the back of the house. Perry, delicate-fingered, lifted the trash can lid, and Dino pulled the round box from the top of the pile. Then Perry replaced the cover noiselessly, and they headed down the street again.

They didn't examine the contents until they were a good six blocks from the residential area. They ducked into a dorm hallway, and Perry placed the box on top of a radiator. But before he attacked the pink ribbon, he paused and looked at Dino with a numb expression.

"Wait a minute," he whispered, "I just thought of something."

"What?"

"You say the professor's wife's been gone a long time?"

"Yeah. Why?"

Perry wiped his hands on his trousers, staring at the box. "Dino, maybe you'll think I'm nuts—"

"I do already."

"I'm serious. You know how his wife treated him. What if—I mean, isn't it possible that the old guy finally got up nerve to—*do* something about her?"

"Like what? Hey! What's eating you, Perry?" Then he followed Perry's eyes to the box. "Oh, my God," he said. "For Pete's sake, Perry, you don't mean that—"

"It happens, doesn't it? I mean, guys are always knocking off their wives. He *said* she was visiting her sister, but that doesn't make it true."

"You don't think that box has—"

"We better open it," Perry said grimly.

"Not me! Oh, no, not me!" Dino said. "You tried to scare me, buddy, you succeeded. You want to open that—that thing—you go right ahead. But I'm not touching it!"

Perry laughed. "Don't be a jerk. It's probably just some old orange peels."

"Well, you open it then. Go on."

Perry put his hand on the bow, but hesitated.

"Go ahead!" Dino said. "You started this, pal. You finish it."

Perry slid the ribbon off the box. Then, cautiously, with Dino moving back two steps in preparation for grisly surprises, he lifted the lid.

It was a hat box, for reposing in it, still nestled in tissue, looking fresh from the milliner's, was a perky little straw hat, gaily decorated across its front with a spray of artificial flowers.

"It's a hat," Perry said blankly. "Just a hat."

"For the love of Pete," Dino breathed.

"Only what's he throwing it out for? I mean, it looks new."

"Maybe he doesn't like it."

"Yeah, but I'll bet his wife does. Yet he throws out a brand-new hat, just like that."

"Well, his wife can't complain. She ain't here."

"That's just the point," Perry said. "She's not here. So he can do anything he wants." He grabbed his friend by the bulky collar of his sweater. "Don't you see it, Dino? He threw it out because he didn't want it anymore—because *she* won't be needing it?"

"You're crazy, Perry!"

"It's the truth! Can't you see it? He *did* get rid of her. Now he's getting rid of her things. Little by little. Piece by piece—"

"He wouldn't have the guts—"

"How do you know? He's been pushed, buddy, he's been pushed hard! And he pushed back! The hat proves it!"

"But what about her body? Where's her body?"

"Who knows? Maybe he buried it. Maybe he burned it. Maybe he even—" His eyes glowed with excitement. "Listen, if anybody would know how to dispose of a body, it would be Jarvis. I mean, it's his business, it's his life, this biology stuff. He's probably dissolved her in quicklime—"

"Cut it out!" Dino squirmed. "You're giving me the shivers."

"And that old crock was going to write my father! About *me!*" He laughed wildly. "And all the time, he's a killer, a murderer! And he was going to complain about *me!*" He shoved Dino ahead of him. "Come on, buddy—"

"Where we going?"

"To the cops! That's where!"

Lieutenant Jack Roman sat quietly, solemnly, and attentively, and didn't take the liberty of smiling until the eager, tumbling speech of the hot-eyed youngster seemed finally over. Then he tapped the hatbox with his fingernail and said:

"And because of *this*, you want me to accuse a man of killing his wife?"

"I *know* it sounds nuts," Perry said. "I know it isn't any kind of *proof*. But if you'd just ask around, I mean about what kind of home life Jarvis and his wife had—you probably wouldn't find it so hard to believe."

Roman filled a pipe slowly. "Tell you the truth, boys, I know that part already. I don't think there's anybody in

town who doesn't. But fights and bickering and stuff like
that—well, murder isn't the usual outcome."

"Then where did Mrs. Jarvis go, huh?"

Roman shrugged. "We didn't check her movements; no
need to. If Jarvis said she went to see her sister, that's probably where she went. And as for the hat—well, maybe she
told him to throw it out. Maybe she was tired of it."

Perry slumped in the wooden chair, and looked at Dino.
Dino hoisted his plump shoulders and spread his palms
outward. Roman smiled again, this time sympathetically.

"It's not that I don't appreciate this, boys. But you see
how it is. Of course, if you really want to set your minds at
rest, we could always call Mrs. Jarvis at her sister's
house . . ."

"You think we could?" Perry said eagerly, hating to see
the victory slip away. "Could we call her tonight?"

"Well, it's a little late . . ."

"It's only nine o'clock!"

Roman smiled, and picked up the telephone.

"Phyllis?" he said to the operator. "You know Professor
Jarvis' wife, I think her name's Margaret? She's gone over
to visit her sister in Peggotville, but I don't know her sister's name . . ." He covered the mouthpiece and winked at
the boys. "Phyllis knows everybody and everything . . ."
Then he returned to the receiver. "What's that? . . . Yes. I
guess that must be it, Beattie. Would you give Mrs. Beattie
a ring? Thanks, Phyllis."

He hung up, drummed on the desk until the phone jan-
gled. Then he picked it up.

"Mrs. Beattie? Sorry to disturb you, Mrs. Beattie, but I
was just wondering if Mrs. Jarvis was with you at the moment? It's nothing important, but—" He stood up, taking
the telephone with him. "What's that, Mrs. Beattie? . . .
Well, no, I thought she was there . . . Yes, I guess I
must be mistaken . . . No, no message . . ."

He dropped the receiver back, but kept his eyes on it,
biting his lower lip.

"What's the matter?" Perry said. "Isn't she there?"

"No," Roman said softly. "She was never there. Her sister hasn't seen her in over a year."

Dino whistled, and Roman picked up the hatbox.

"Maybe it wouldn't hurt," he said casually, "to talk to
Professor Jarvis. Just for a few minutes . . ."

"Can we come along?"

"You can wait for me outside," Roman said. "But keep those imaginations under control; we don't know anything for a fact. Understand?"

"Sure," Perry Hatch said, with a small, triumphant grin in Dino's direction.

The lieutenant drove them back to the professor's house, but when he stepped out of the car, the hatbox in his hand, he commanded Perry and Dino to remain quietly in the back seat.

"You wait here," he said sternly, "and hold down the conversation. If I need you for any reason, I'll call you."

"Yes, sir," Perry said obediently.

The obedience was a ruse; as soon as Roman gained admittance to the house, he stepped out of the car and beckoned Dino after him. When his friend protested, he whispered. "I'm not waiting in the car. I want to hear what happens."

"You're asking for trouble," Dino said.

"Who's chicken now?" Perry grinned.

He tiptoed towards the front window; there was a thick hedge beneath it, high enough for concealment. Crouching, he moved among the branches, ignoring the prickly twigs. When he finally heard noises in the study, they were too faint for clarity; then the occupants of the room must have moved, because he heard plainly the husky, querulous sound of Professor Jarvis' voice.

"I don't understand this, Lieutenant," he said. "Why this sudden interest in my wife?"

"Just curiosity," Roman said. "You see, it isn't every day that someone throws out a brand-new hat." He laughed lightly. "Nice-looking hat, too. You should see some of the horrors my wife brings home."

There was a pause. Then Jarvis said, "Would you mind telling me how you got this hat, Lieutenant?"

"For the moment, Professor, I'd rather not say."

"I threw this hat out not more than an hour ago. Since when do the police investigate trash cans?"

"Just tell me *why* you were throwing it out. Doesn't your wife care for it anymore? As I said, it looks brand new."

"It *is* new. But I just don't want it around."

"Wouldn't your wife have some objection?"

There was a creak as the Professor sat down in the wooden chair behind his desk.

"I'm beginning to find a strange implication in all this, Lieutenant. Are you trying to—accuse me of something?"

"No, just trying to gather some facts. For instance, I understand your wife went to visit her sister. In Peggotville, I believe. Am I right?"

The pause was longer.

"No," Jarvis said flatly. "As a matter of fact, there's no truth to that story."

"But you *did* tell people that's where she was?"

"Yes, I did. It was simpler than the truth."

"And what is the truth, Professor?"

Jarvis sighed.

"I suppose it's all right to tell you," he said. "I'm sure there's some kind of professional ethics in the police department which will respect my confidence. The truth is, Lieutenant, that my wife and I are subject to frequent and often violent quarrels. We had one about two months ago, and as a result—well, she walked out on me. I don't know where she went, and frankly, I don't care. That's all there is to it."

"And you haven't heard from her in all this time? I see." But there was skepticism in Roman's voice. "And there's nobody you can contact, no relative or friend?"

"Her sister was her only living relative, and they were not on amicable terms. As for friends—" He snorted. "Margaret didn't like people."

"Then you don't have any actual *proof* that your wife walked out on you? No note, no telegram, no letter?"

"Nothing at all." He made a sound of annoyance. "Now really, Lieutenant, I wish you'd get to the point. If you have an accusation to make—"

"I'm not accusing you of anything."

"Not even making little guesses? Tiny speculations?" He laughed. "Oh, you've got a policeman's brain, all right. I can see the little wheels turning in your head. Why, you really think I might have—done away with Margaret."

"I didn't say that," Roman answered gravely.

"But that's what you're thinking, isn't it?" Now he laughed loudly, in the simulation of huge enjoyment. "Why, this is absolutely delicious! You actually suspect me of murder, don't you? You think I'm some kind of Crippen, or Landru? Perhaps you think I chopped her into hamburger and served her at the school cafeteria."

"I don't think murder's funny," Roman said stiffly.

"Then it *is* homicide you're thinking about?"

"If you want, Professor, I'll be blunt. If there's even the slightest possibility, it's my duty to investigate it. I don't doubt you're telling the truth, but you'll have to admit that you had sufficient motive for such a crime. And your recent actions . . ."

"Yes, I suppose I *have* been acting like a skulking scoundrel, haven't I? Telling lies about my wife's whereabouts, throwing out hats . . ." He chuckled. "But tell me how you think I might have done it, Lieutenant? Just from your professional point of view?"

"Well . . ." Roman cleared his throat. "Just as a thought, Professor, it strikes me that you might be the ideal sort of person to dispose of a body intelligently. I mean, with your knowledge of biology, body chemistry . . ."

"Ah! So you think my special training equips me. Interesting! All right, then. And how, for instance, might I have done the deed? Buried her, perhaps? I don't own a car, you know, and I couldn't very well carry Margaret on my back. Sneaked out onto the lawn and buried her? Dear, dear, I'm afraid my neighbors would have found the spectacle amusing—"

"There are other ways."

"Perhaps I burned the body? I'm afraid that won't do, Lieutenant. My oil burner wouldn't accommodate the dear woman. Or maybe you think I dissected her, and mailed the remnants all over the country? If you check with the post office, you'll find that I rarely send so much as a postcard. Of course, if you'd like to search the house, you have my permission . . ."

Roman wasn't enjoying himself; the edge of his voice was sharper. "There are other ways, Professor, for instance—"

"Quicklime? My, Lieutenant, I'm afraid you weren't much of a chemistry student. Despite what you may have heard, quicklime won't destroy a body; in fact, it actually preserves it. Oh, there are some powerful acids, of course, but do you realize the difficulty of their use? A truly corrosive acid wouldn't destroy only the body; it would also eat away the container—such as a bathtub, for instance." He chuckled dryly. "No, Lieutenant, I might achieve partial destruction of a body, but not complete, total disintegration. I'm afraid I'm not that clever."

"Professor, I think you're laughing at me—"

"Do you think so? Yes, I suppose I am." Then his voice softened. "I'm sorry. I didn't intend to make light of it. I suppose it's my own guilt . . ."

"Guilt?"

"Of course," Jarvis said wearily. "Do you think I haven't wished Margaret dead a thousand times? Wished that nagging tongue was stilled forever? But the human animal is a complicated beast, unfortunately. Because in my own tormented fashion, Lieutenant, I still love my wife. I love her, isn't that incredible? And if she walked in that door now, I'd beg her to stay with me . . ."

There was a moment of silence. Then Roman said:

"Professor, I want to apologize."

"What?"

"I'm sorry. But when those kids came in with the hatbox—"

"Kids?"

"Students of yours. One of them's named Hatch—he was coming to see you tonight when he saw you throw it away. But I wouldn't take it out on him, if I were you."

Jarvis smiled sadly. "Take it out on him? No, Lieutenant, I should apologize to Mr. Hatch—to all my students. I know I've been criminally harsh to them lately; you can understand why. But you can tell Mr. Hatch that he has nothing to worry about, not even his—indiscretion in class this afternoon."

"That's very fine of you, Professor." Roman stood up. "If there's anything I can do, to help find your wife—"

"I'm afraid finding her isn't the answer. Finding her won't make her want to return."

"Well, you can count on my help, if you need it."

"Thank you," the old man said gently.

They were going to the door; Perry scrambled out of hiding and made a dive for the automobile at the curb; he was just climbing into the rear seat, when Roman came out of the house and walked briskly towards them.

He opened the car door, and jerked his thumb.

"All right," he said. "Out."

"What happened?" Dino said, wide-eyed. "Did you learn anything, Lieutenant?"

"I learned something, all right. I learned not to listen to a couple of nutty kids."

"But, Lieutenant—" Perry protested.

"Get out of there before I throw you out," Roman growled. "And the next time you decide to rob a trash can, you better not let me know about it!"

Professor Jarvis remained at his desk for another after the lieutenant took his leave. Then he looked at his pocket watch, clucked, and wound it carefully. He stood up, a shaggy, bent figure, and headed for his bedroom.

Then he remembered the hatbox that was still on his desk. He returned, and picked it up. On his way to the trash can, he paused at the end of the room and stopped before the skeleton hanging on silken black threads. It was an admirable skeleton, finely joined, and in superb, almost new condition. He placed the flowered hat on the skull.

"Good night, Margaret," he said pleasantly, and shuffled out of the room.

THE ELECTRIC GIRL CAPER

by Edward D. Hoch

Her name was Madge August, or at least that was the name she'd taken at the age of seventeen when she got her first job dancing in a topless bar downtown. It was a pretty good name, and it stuck. She'd wanted to break into show business ever since a boy in high school told her she looked like Marilyn Monroe, and if topless dancing in a cheap bar was a route to success, she was more than willing to follow it.

Now, eight years after the topless bar, Madge August was not yet the toast of Broadway or of Hollywood. Instead, she was the Electric Girl at the state fair, a position which brought her one hundred fifty dollars a week. All she did was sit in a chair eight times a day while the suckers paid their money to see sparks leap from her fingertips. She'd hoped for something better by her mid-twenties, something better than sideshow atmosphere and one-night stands with crusty carnival workers.

The man who employed her was named Tommy Small, though it appeared nowhere on the outside of the tent. She received the top—and only—billing: *See the Electric Girl! She Makes the Sparks Fly! You Won't Believe Your Eyes! See Her! Touch Her! IF YOU DARE!* At most shows, every single one of the men dared.

This night, at the end of a hot Labor Day weekend when the entire fair was drooping just a bit, she sat in her chair and stared out over the audience and prepared to be electrocuted for the last time. Tommy Small adjusted the wires, pulled the switch, and shouted, "There she is, ladies and gentlemen! Thousands of volts of electricity are passing through this girl's lovely body at this very moment!"

There was a low murmur from the crowd, as always, and Tommy hurried on. "Let me prove it to you! Electric Girl—raise your right arm!" Madge August obeyed him without a word and he placed a long blue mercury arc tube against her skin. The tube lighted instantly, and a gasp ran through the crowd.

"Another test," he said, attaching a piece of cotton to the end of a wire. He dipped it into a bottle of gasoline and then touched her hand with it. She always hated this part, and had to control herself to keep from yanking her hand back when the cotton burst into flame. Finally Tommy came to the climax of the act, when the audience was invited to file past Madge and touch her hand. There were always a few who went for her spangled breasts instead, but the result was the same—a sharp shock, with sparks leaping from her body to theirs.

This night, though, one man was different. She'd noticed him in the crowd during Tommy's spiel, standing near the back, but with a well-groomed casual air that one rarely saw at a state fair. He was more the country club or stock-exchange type, and her contact with that sort was limited. Later, when he came forward to touch her hand and feel the spark of electricity, he didn't jump like the others, or make some bawdy comment. Instead, their eyes met as if they shared some private secret. She would remember this man, and perhaps that was what he wanted.

After Tommy Small closed the tent show and paid her the money she'd earned, Madge hurried across the hard-trodden earth toward the parking lot where she'd left her car. As she reached it a shape materialized out of the darkness at her side, and a hand closed gently over hers. "What the hell!" she gasped, ready to scream.

"Don't be frightened. I want to talk to you." His voice was soft and calm, and even in the dark she recognized the well-groomed man from the last show.

"I saw you inside," she said. "You were watching me."

"Wasn't I supposed to?" he asked with a grin. "You're quite pretty in that spangled costume."

"What do you want?" she asked, though she thought she knew.

"The fair is closed. If you're unemployed, I could offer you a temporary job. Can we go someplace and discuss it?"

"All right." Why not, she decided, there'd been a lot worse-looking guys than this in her life.

He was driving a rented car, and he led the way to a nearby bar that had enjoyed a boom during the week of the fair. She parked her dented VW next to his car and they went in together. He steered her to a booth in the back and ordered a couple of drinks.

"My name is Byrd," he said with a smile. "Ulysses S. Byrd. I'd like to hire you for a few days' work, doing pretty much what you did at the fair."

"How much?"

"What did Tommy Small pay you?"

She was surprised he knew Tommy's name. "Two hundred a week," she said, adding fifty to the true amount.

He nodded. "How about ten times that for half the work? Two thousand dollars for three days."

"Sure," she replied, trying not to seem too eager. Maybe this guy Byrd wasn't an ordinary trick at all. Maybe he had a legitimate occupation. Maybe he was even in show business.

"First you'll have to explain how this Electric Girl gimmick operates, so I can get the necessary equipment."

"That's easy. My chair is on a little platform, and hidden underneath is something called a Tesla coil or Tesla transformer. It produces high voltages of high-frequency alternating current, but the current is low in amperage and lacks any destructive power. A wire runs from the transformer up the hollow chair leg and attaches to a metal plate in the arm of the chair. When I press the plate with my arm, current flows through me but I hardly feel it. The mercury arc lamp lights because it's designed for high frequency. An ordinary incandescent bulb wouldn't work." She didn't fully understand the explanation she gave, but that was how Tommy Small had explained it to her. It worked, so she didn't ask questions.

The man named Byrd listened closely, making a few notes on a paper napkin. "No problem," he assured her. "I figured it was something like that."

"Tommy's always hard up for money. With the fair closed, you could probably rent his equipment."

"Good idea," Byrd agreed.

"Just what does this work involve?"

He signaled for another round of drinks and began to tell her what would be expected.

The next day he made the arrangements with Tommy Small, and phoned her by noon to tell her everything was set. "Meet me at the Southview shopping plaza at two this afternoon," he instructed.

"I'll be there."

When she pulled her car into a parking space at the shopping center, she saw that Byrd was already there waiting. She locked her own car and hurried over to his. "Here I am!"

"Get in—and fasten your seat belt."

As he started the car she glanced sideways at him and said, "I've been asking around about you, Byrd."

"I hope you didn't tell anyone about our little venture."

"No, no! I just asked a couple of friends if they'd ever heard of you."

"So?"

"You've got quite a reputation. The Early Byrd, they call you."

"Sometimes," he admitted. He slowed to turn in a side street.

"They say you're a con man, but not the ordinary sort."

"We'd better talk later," he advised. "This is the street, and her car should be coming along any minute now."

"This part scares hell out of me."

"Relax." They sat and waited a few moments in silence with the car's motor running. Then suddenly Byrd said, "Here she comes—hang on!"

A tan sedan with a black top had turned into the street, and Byrd shot his own car forward to meet it. The front fenders came together with a crunch. Madge was thrown forward as the seat belt tugged at her middle. "God, Byrd!"

"You all right?"

"I think so."

He didn't wait to see. He released his own belt and hopped from the car, running over to the tan sedan. "Are you all right?" he asked the woman behind the wheel.

Madge wanted to get out too, but he'd instructed her to stay in the car. She sat still and listened.

"I think so," the woman said, getting out to inspect the damage to her car. "I didn't even see you coming." She glanced in Madge's direction. "Is your passenger all right?"

"It's my wife—are you sure you're not hurt?" he called.

"I don't think so." On cue Madge unstrapped herself and got out, holding onto the car a bit unsteadily. "I'm just a little shaken."

"My home is just down the street," the woman said. "Do you want to bring her in and call a doctor?"

"I'll be all right," Madge insisted. "If I could just sit down. . ."

"Could we trouble you?" Byrd asked. "While she's getting herself together we can exchange insurance information."

Byrd helped straighten the woman's fender so she could drive the car into her driveway down the street. The house was large and old, shielded from the street by a row of hedges. In a middle-glass neighborhood, it gave the impression of special status. The inside was modestly furnished, but with a few touches—a lighted oil painting, a bar—that hinted at recent affluence.

And piled high on two card tables against one wall were booklets, folders, envelopes. "A political campaign?" Madge asked innocently.

The woman smiled. "No, that's the fan club. I really should introduce myself, I suppose. I'm Florence Pregger, president of the Hard Starr fan club."

"Hard Starr?" Madge oozed as instructed. "He's my favorite rock singer! I have all his albums!"

Florence Pregger smiled. "Then you should join the fan club."

"What do you do? Could I actually get to meet him?"

Through it all Byrd kept a tolerant smile on his face, like a loving husband humoring his immature wife. Florence Pregger produced pamphlets and autographed photos and even a brief authorized biography of the 23-year-old recording and concert star. Madge pored through it all with interest, seeing mostly a long-haired youth with an electric guitar and skin-tight spangled pants, bare-chested, looking like a performer in some sort of male burlesque house. It was not her idea of show business, but she kept up her act.

"He's performing here in town this weekend," Florence Pregger said. "The entire club is going."

"Oh—could I go too? Or are they mostly teen-agers?"

"Do I look like a teen-ager, honey? We have women of all ages, and a few men too. My husband Sloane helps me run it." She produced a pile of mimeographed sheets. "I'm just getting out this month's newsletter to members. Look at some of these reviews for Hard's new album! *They're* by male reviewers!"

"Oh, I wish I could meet him!" Madge gushed. "It must have been fate that brought me to this house!"

A car had pulled up in the driveway and they could see a husky man heading for the door. "That's Sloane," the woman explained. "I'm glad you'll have a chance to meet him."

Sloane Pregger was a hard-eyed man with a deep voice and a bone-crushing handshake. Madge saw Byrd wince a bit and withdraw his hand as the big man said, "Glad to meet you. What's this about an accident?"

Byrd gave his explanation of how it had happened, while Madge continued to look through the fan-club newsletters. "Guess what, Sloane!" his wife said finally. "The Sparrows are fans of Hard Starr!"

It took Madge an instant to react to the name. Then she remembered that Byrd had introduced them as John and Mary Sparrow, the name on his faked driver's license.

"*Are* you?" Sloane Pregger said. "Then you must join the club!"

"How much does it cost?" Byrd asked.

"Only ten dollars a year, and that includes a free Hard Starr album, an autographed photo, a subscription to our monthly newsletter, and discount tickets to any local concerts by Hard. Last year he played here twice."

Madge had discovered another box on the car table. "What about these scarves and charm bracelets?"

"Oh, we sell a number of Hard Starr items to club members, all priced quite reasonably."

"Could we come back again?" Byrd asked. "I know my wife loves to talk about Starr." He reached for his wallet. "And of course we'll want to join. In fact, give us two tickets to this weekend's concert while we're at it."

"Oh, John!" Madge squealed, feeling like an idiot.

When they were alone in Byrd's car, Madge asked, "You're going to rob those people, aren't you?"

"I've never robbed anyone in my life. I'm simply going to take what they give me—what they urge upon me, in fact."

"They don't seem like bad people."

"They're not, really. No worse than me, I suppose. In this life, Madge, everybody has a con game. Theirs happens to be the fan club, taking ten bucks at a time from a bunch of kids, and then selling them a lot of junk besides. And Hard Starr has his own con too, earning close to a million dollars a year from records and concerts and television. People pay to see him take off his shirt and to hear deafening amplified music. He and the Preggers work their con and I work mine."

"I don't know," she said, staring through the windshield. "It still seems wrong."

"You're getting two thousand dollars. Isn't that enough?"

"Oh, of course it's enough! I even lied to you about how much Tommy was paying me! But. . ."

"Don't think about it so much," he advised. "Come on, we have to talk about Friday."

And there was much to talk about. The first part of Byrd's plan had gone well, but Friday would be tricky. Madge could think of a dozen things that might go wrong, starting with the obvious fact that Hard Starr simply might not find her attractive. Byrd laughed when she voiced this objection. "Don't worry about that," he assured her.

"But he has all those groupies hanging around him."

"All the more reason why he'll go for you."

"And what about the rest of it?"

Byrd smiled. "You leave that to me. You just act your part."

"I always wanted to be in show business," she mused.

"Well, now you are! In fact, Friday you'll be on stage."

Byrd was busy Friday afternoon, and when Madge met him in front of the Memorial Auditorium he wore a broad grin. "It went like clockwork," he told her. "There are so many electricians working in there, nobody noticed one more."

"I'm still worried."

"You were worried at the accident. You were probably worried every night during Tommy's act."

"I was," she admitted.

"Did you phone Florence Pregger?"

"Yes. I did it just like you said. She promised we could meet Starr before the show."

The Preggers arrived promptly at six-thirty, and Sloane Pregger took charge at once. "You know this is most unusual. We rarely get to see Hard ourselves, and we never take other fans backstage. I had to call and clear it with him." Pregger gave Byrd a little smirk. "Of course when I told him what a charming little wife you had, he was all for meeting you."

A few fans had already taken up positions by the back door of the auditorium, but the guard let the Preggers and their guests enter. Obviously they were expected.

"I'm so excited," Madge babbled.

"You never thought you'd really meet him," Byrd said.

"He's a great guy," Pregger assured them. "You'll love him."

They passed through an outer phalanx of business managers and assorted hangers-on before finally being ushered into the presence of Hard Starr himself. He rose from his dressing-room table and eyed Madge with open admiration through eyes just the least bit glassy. "Well! This is really something!"

"Mary Sparrow, and her husband John," Florence introduced them. "Mary is a great fan of yours."

Hard Starr leaned against his chair. "Sparrow. A real cute little bird, huh?" He chuckled and tossed the long hair from his eyes, and Madge realized that he was high on something. Had Byrd counted on that? she wondered.

"So pleased to meet you," she mumbled.

He grinned foolishly and gave her hand a little squeeze. "I'll dedicate a song to you tonight."

"Your manager says you've got another sellout," Pregger said. "Our fan club took twenty percent of the seats."

"And don't think I don't appreciate it," Starr said, but his eyes hadn't left Madge's face. He might have been thanking them for her rather than the ticket sales.

She managed to glance at Byrd and saw his barely discernible nod. "I'd love to see your guitar," she said.

"Sorry, pet," Starr said, "it's already on stage, hooked up to the juice."

She had to admit he was handsome close up, and the drugged look in his eyes gave him a sleepy sensuality that young girls especially might find hard to resist. "Couldn't I see it anyway?" she pleaded. "I'd love to be on stage with you and pretend we were performing together."

"We could pretend lots more than that," he said, grabbing her hand. "Come on!"

Byrd lingered behind, and Madge heard him say to the Preggers, "Look at her! She's having the time of her life!"

The auditorium stage was in darkness except for an up-right worklight that glowed at one side. The guitars and drums for Hard Starr and his backup trio were all in place, wired to the amplifiers that would soon deaden or delight the ears of the paying customers. "Wonderful!" Madge said, running her fingers gently over Starr's guitar.

"Here! Let me show you!" He flipped a switch and be-gan grinding out a familiar melody. Byrd and the Preggers were watching from the side of the stage, and a couple of stagehands worked above, securing some flats of scenery.

Madge threw back her head and gave a few bumps and grinds in time to the music, to Starr's obvious satisfaction. After a few moments he put down his guitar and came to join her.

"Here, baby," he said, and that was when she made her move.

She moved against him, with his body partly shielding her movements from the Preggers. Then suddenly she moved backward, pulling him along. She broke free, seemed to trip over a cable, and went down in a shower of sparks. She screamed once, turned over and lay still.

"My God!" Byrd shouted, running across the stage ahead of the others. "What happened?"

"I. . .I don't know," Hard Starr said, holding onto his forehead as if he couldn't believe it.

Byrd felt for Madge's pulse and sparks shot to his finger-tips. "She's been electrocuted! She's on a live wire!"

"Do something!" Sloane Pregger shouted. His wife screamed, and now stagehands and musicians came run-ning from the wings.

Moving quickly as the sparks continued to play about Madge's limp body, Byrd grabbed at the nearest stagehand. "Kill the power out here! All of it!"

The lights went out and instantly the sparks stopped their crazy dance. The men pulled Madge free of the entan-gling wires and then as the lights went back on Byrd rushed to her side, pushing Starr away. "Haven't you done enough already?" he growled.

"I just. . ."

"Somebody call an ambulance!" Florence Pregger shouted.

Byrd knelt to feel her pulse. "She's alive, but just

barely." He rose to direct his full fury at Starr. "Damn it, what were you trying to do to her?"

Starr's business manager had appeared from somewhere. "We've got a show to put on! What's happening here?"

"There'll be no show tonight," Byrd told him. "My wife may die, and if she does Hard Starr killed her!"

"No! I . . ."

The Preggers were in on it too now. "This auditorium's sold out! You can't cancel the show now. Think of the fans!"

"Think of the money!" Byrd snorted cynically. "Here—someone has to get her breathing again." He dropped down next to Marge and began administering mouth-to-mouth resuscitation.

He was still at it ten minutes later when the ambulance arrived. As Madge was being lifted onto the stretcher, Byrd resumed his attack. "I'm holding you personally responsible," he told Starr. "I'm suing you for one million dollars!"

"On what grounds?" his manager stormed.

"He was attempting a sexual assault on my wife when the accident occurred. And there can't be any doubt that his equipment and wiring were faulty."

"I been all over it," one of the stagehands grumbled. "I can't find what caused it."

They were still arguing when the attendants carried Madge out to the waiting ambulance.

The doctor was just completing his examination when Byrd appeared in the doorway of the emergency-room cubicle. He straightened up with a smile. "Your wife will be all right, sir. She's a very lucky girl, from what I hear."

"She's all right?"

"Oh, she complains of a little pain, and there are some visual hallucinations, but that's normal after electric shock. It'll pass. The important thing is that her vital signs—heart, breathing, pulse, blood pressure—are all normal. There's not even any sign of skin burns. I think she was mostly frightened when it happened."

"Then she can go home?"

"Perhaps we should keep her overnight, just for observation. She can leave in the morning."

When the doctor had left them alone, Byrd gave Madge's hand a squeeze. "Need I tell you you were great?"

Madge hunched herself into a more comfortable position. "Too great, I guess. I don't want to spend the night in this place."

"You have to. The Preggers will surely phone about your condition. If you were out of the hospital they might tell Starr to stop payment on his check."

"Check?"

Byrd smiled. "He just insisted I take money for your hospital expenses and everything."

"How much money?"

"Twenty thousand."

"You're kidding!"

"I guess I was causing such a scene they thought the show would be cancelled. When the paying customers began lining up outside, they came around quickly enough. I signed a release absolving them of further damages. The check is made out to you, and when you sign the endorsement on the back you'll be releasing them from further claims too."

"But twenty thousand dollars!"

"I was hoping for at least twenty-five, but I didn't want to press my luck. And you'll get the two thousand, just like I promised."

"What about the Tesla coil?"

"You hit the metal plate perfectly when you fell. After I had them kill the power, I simply unplugged it and stuffed wires, coil and metal plate under my coat. When I followed you to the ambulance I dumped the whole thing in a trash barrel, then went back and retrieved it later. Tommy can use it in his act again."

"You're really something, Byrd!" she said with admiration. "What time will you cash the check?"

"They have Saturday banking hours here. I'll be there when the place opens tomorrow. They don't call me the Early Byrd for nothing."

A GOOD HEAD FOR MURDER

by Charles W. Runyon

She drove down the twisting Mexican road, while he dozed beside her and listened to the music from Uruapan. She struck the brake suddenly, throwing him forward against the dash. He saw the animal leave the glow of the headlights and slink into the thorny brush at the side of the road.

She gasped. "*Did you see that dog?* It couldn't possibly have been carrying—"

"It was," said Gordon Phelps, lighting his pipe. "A human head. I wonder whose it could've been?"

"Gordon! How can you just . . . just . . ."

"Sit here? I don't know what else to do. What does one do in a situation like this?"

"Well—follow it!"

Her shrill voice trembled on the edge of panic. Gordon felt an icy calm weighting him down in his seat. Had he been alone he might have given way to the sharp teeth of hysteria which nibbled at his mind—but he always reacted contrary to Ann.

"Through a trackless waste of mesquite? Ann, they don't call this 'Little Hell' for nothing. It's totally uninhabited."

"*Somebody* lives here . . . or did."

"Yes, I suppose you could call the head evidence of human habitation. And where you find one person you might find another. Which is sort of what I'm afraid of."

"What do you mean?"

"The person who, uh, severed the head could be . . ." he waved his hand at the dust-covered bushes which bulged out into the graveled track, "lurking, you know . . ."

"Oh!" She tromped the accelerator. The car threw up its nose and jumped forward, paused, made another jackrabbit leap—and died.

"You forgot to shift into low," said Gordon.

"Oh! This darned . . . old . . . *heap*." Keys jingled as she turned the switch. The starter groaned. The car inched forward in a series of tiny lurches.

"The clutch," Gordon said. "You didn't push your clutch in. This rental car doesn't have an automatic shift, you know."

"I *know*. Please don't talk while I'm driving."

Gordon opened his mouth, then closed it as the engine caught. Tires grated on loose gravel, the rear end skewed leftward as the car moved forward with agonizing slowness. A thorny branch clawed at the front fender, smacked the windshield, and scree-eee-eeched along the side of the car. Gordon shuddered as the sound blazed a track of fire up his spinal ganglia. After eight years of teaching he'd never gotten used to fingernails on a blackboard.

The front wheels found the packed tracks and the vehicle picked up speed, pumping fine gray dust up through the floorboards. Gordon leaned forward in the seat, his spine rigid as a steel rod. The headlights swept along the bank of thorns as the car swiveled around a right-angle turn. Shattered twigs tickety-ticked against metal as she raced up the steep slope, skewed around another curve, then dipped down into a valley.

"If we hadn't had that flat back there . . ." Her voice trailed off.

"We'd have been to the coast. I know. But we had it, and we aren't . . . and if you don't stop taking those curves so fast, we never will be."

"If they'd just put up little warning signs . . ."

"They'd bankrupt the country. This road is nothing but curves. Look out for that rock!"

He held his breath as she swerved to straddle a rubber-streaked gray boulder. A metallic thump sounded from below and rumbled the length of the car. He let his eyes drift to the oil gauge. The needle held steady. At least the oil pan had survived.

But now something dragged behind, clattering against the gravel.

"Tail pipe," he muttered.

"What?"

The clatter ceased. He decided not to look back to see what had fallen off. The car still moved, so it hadn't been a vital part.

"Why don't you let me drive?"

"You said your eyes were tired."

"That was before—watch it!"

He hunched his shoulders as a stubby tree limb loomed out of the dusty foliage. It passed over the roof of the car with less than an inch to spare. With the heel of his palm he wiped the dust off the side window and looked out. The aerial bent backward at a 45-degree angle.

"Slow down. Nobody's after us."

The car slowed slightly. "But good heavens, Gordon, a human head . . . a dog carries a human head across the road in front of us and we don't even . . . I mean, I'm beginning to feel awfully wrong about this."

"You want to go back?"

She paused. "Do you?"

"There's no place to turn around."

"You're so good at rationalizing, Gordon."

He leaned back and fingered a kitchen match out of his watch pocket, scraped his thumbnail across the head and held the flame to his pipe. In the rearview mirror he saw nothing but a billowing fog of dust, tinted red by the tail-lights. It had trailed them for the last two hundred miles.

The taste of the fragrant smoke relaxed him slightly. "Call it rationalizing, if you will. The local people, I understand, are rather primitive. Used to settling quarrels in the quickest way, with machetes. This may be one of those cases. Best for the local authorities to handle, if there are any."

"And if there aren't?"

He forced down a rising annoyance. "All right, let's say we went back, and I managed to find the head. What would we do, carry it all the way to the beach? Turn it in at the hotel and say, Here's a little item we picked up along the road? We'd be hung up with the authorities for the entire vacation—maybe longer."

"I wasn't thinking about the head. I meant . . . the rest of the body."

Gordon muttered, "Wouldn't do him much good without his head."

"I don't think it was a 'him,' Gordon."

"Come now. It was all coated with dust. You couldn't have gotten any impression of gender."

"It had long hair . . ."

"That's an indication of nothing these days."

". . . And an earring, one of those jade pendants, with a loop of copper wire running through it."

"You're fantasizing, my dear."

"I *know* what I saw. I think it was a white woman."

"With how many freckles across the bridge of her nose?"

"I don't feel particularly humorous, Gordon."

"I don't either—but are we going back? We aren't, because we can't turn around, and we'd never find the spot anyway. We've crossed fifty valleys, and they're all exactly alike. Anyway, I'm not sure we've got enough gas for it. I don't know what kind of mileage we're getting in this car."

"You told me once that if I had more than one excuse I didn't have any."

"Okay, I don't have any excuse. But we're not going back!" He bit down hard on the stem of his pipe, and fumbled another match out of his pocket. "When we get to the hotel, we'll make discreet inquiries. If any disappearances have been reported, we'll tell about the head. Otherwise, silence is golden. Agreed?"

"What if it just happened? There won't be any report, will there?"

"Just let me do the talking when we get to the hotel. Will you do that?"

"I don't see how I could do otherwise, since I don't speak the language."

Gordon knew it was the best he could expect. She liked to keep her options open, so that if he were proved wrong, she could always say she had reservations.

What the hell do we look like, a couple of Indians? Part of an old joke, burlesque-vintage, a man and a woman go into the hotel and ask for a room, and the clerk asks if they have reservations . . .

Thinking too much . . . Too hard . . . Trying to keep his mind off the horror in the road. He now wished he'd stopped—gone back and picked up the bloody thing, looked into its eyes and said, *Cynthia, who did this to you, my dear?*

Ann would never have understood. She would not even have *wanted* to understand. New to the hard line of reality, home-school-church-and-family, all life as constricted as a baseball diamond, touch all the bases and when you cross home plate God is there to shake your hand . . .

Then he had to admit that he had chosen *her,* out of a vast pool of available females (so it seemed in retrospect) because she'd always turned in neat papers and was never late to class. Whereas he was sloppy and dilatory. Contrasts always hooked him. Black-white. Antonym-synonym. She was tall, willowy, ash-blonde; he was stocky and black-haired. He'd visualized a balanced marriage, or at worst a seesaw of authority, but his aimless hedonism stood no chance against her patient logic. In all life's choices he saw a high road and a low road, but she always picked the one closest to earth. Take his degree in education: *"You'll have the summers for your beachcombing and there's the sabbatical every seven years . . ."* But summers had been occupied in fixing up the house, and the first sabbatical was spent building the cabin on the lake. He began to wonder if he hadn't let the wine stand too long in the glass . . .

A new rattle had developed somewhere in the left rear. He listened to it a moment, decided it was one of the fender mountings and not something which would collapse and leave them stranded in this godforsaken country. It was hot, stuffy inside the car, but he could not open the windows because of the dust. Still it sifted in, fine as talc, around the windows and door. He could feel it coating the inside of his nostrils, crusting his lips with the dry burning taste of alkali. He closed his eyes and tried to visualize the hotel on the beach which Norval had described, the green lawns, the spacious swimming pool, the sun-drenched balconies, and the low, low rates. But he kept thinking of the head and how clean the cut had been, right below the Adam's apple . . .

The car jolted, bounced, came down with a crunch that jarred his teeth. Dust billowed up from the floor. Looking out, he saw that they were crossing a dry wash, one of dozens they'd negotiated during the last seven hours.

"Gordon . . ."

He turned and saw her round glasses reflecting the glow of the headlights. Behind them her eyes were wide and staring.

"What's the matter?" he asked.

"I saw a foot sticking out from under a bush back there."

His heart lurched, then went on beating faster. "Where?"

"When we crossed that creek bed."

"Why didn't you stop?"

"I don't know."

"You probably saw a tree root."

"I saw a *foot*!"

"Oh, hell! What's the point of arguing? Stop the car and back up."

"I *can't*! I can't even back up our own car, let alone this dilapidated wreck."

"You want me to do it?"

"I just want to get to the end of this trip, Gordon. I don't want to back up or turn around or anything. I just want to get *off . . . this . . . road*!"

Then why did you tell me about the foot? he thought, but he said nothing. She'd sounded like a little girl on the brink of a tantrum, refusing to go into the dark spooky bedroom. He wasn't too calm himself. The foliage pressed in toward the center of the road, making him feel hemmed in. Forward visibility was less than twenty yards. He held his breath as they rounded a curve, half-expecting to see an Aztec priest with a stained obsidian knife, ripping the pulsing heart out of a naked torso . . . an eerie thought . . .

He stiffened as the engine coughed, sputtered, then settled into a strained growl as it carried them up the steep ridge. His eyes slid to the gas gauge. The needle sat on empty. That settled the question of backing up. It might even settle the question of going forward, though he had a feeling there was more in the tank than the gauge showed. The steep pitch of the hill would drain everything to the rear . . .

He breathed a sigh of relief as the car topped the ridge and tipped down into another ravine. The gas gauge edged off the peg and stopped at one-eighth full.

After a minute she spoke. "You were probably right. That was only a gnarled tree root back there."

Immediately he felt wary. "I see. And the head?"

"Oh . . . a coconut."

"Why not a pumpkin? Ichabod Crane thought he saw a head, but it was only a pumpkin."

She said nothing for several heartbeats. "Pumpkins don't grow here."

"Neither do coconuts."

"Well, they have trucks, you know. It could have fallen off a truck."

"And where did it get that hair?"

"Coconuts have hair—sort of."

"And jade earrings?"

"Oh, Gordon, for heaven's sake. Are we going to spend our whole vacation chewing over this thing?"

"It might be the lesser of two evils."

"What do you mean by that?"

"Nothing." He stuck his pipe in his mouth and clamped his teeth on the bit. Her protest that she had *not* seen a foot was proof to Gordon that she had seen it—and was now so shaken that she wanted to back out of the whole reality sequence.

As for his comment about the lesser evil—he meant that he'd be only too happy to sit in a safe, comfortable hotel and mull over this intriguing mystery. The thing he dreaded most was a sudden *denouement*. He had a feeling that the head had been only a preliminary, like the first rumble of thunder which presages the downpour . . .

Coming to another one of those miserable gullies. Beyond the scoured basalt bedrock he saw what looked like a crooked branch, off one of those slick white-barked eucalyptus trees that grew in the arroyos. He *hoped* it was that. Even as the car bounded across the wash, he ground his pipe between his teeth and silently prayed that the sharp bend in the middle was only an accident of growth and not an articulated elbow . . . that those curved appendages were only blunt-ended rootlets which happened to total five in number . . .

She had to swerve to miss the object, and in that moment he saw it clearly, coated with a white film of road dust.

Gordon drew a deep breath, then let it out slowly. He felt an odd relaxation of tension; he identified it as the end of self-deception, the closure of doubt, the presence of a certainly which could be . . . *must* be dealt with. No more speculation, no more games with reality . . .

"Stop the car, Ann."

Instead she speeded up. He glanced over and saw her sitting rigid behind the wheel, looking neither right nor left, the mouth set in a tight, downcurving line . . .

"Ann . . ." He touched her forearm lightly, felt the hard rigidity of muscle. He reached down and turned off the switch. The engine died, but she didn't seem aware of

it. She pumped the accelerator until the car shuddered to a
halt in the middle of the roadway.

"Ann, we've got to go back."

"No!" She made a grab for the keys; he caught her wrist
and took her hand in his, stroking it until the tight hard
knot of her fist unclenched, and her hand lay trembling in
his . . .

"Ann, that was definitely a human arm. You saw it too,
didn't you?"

"Yes." Her voice sounded small and weak.

"Well, then . . . ?"

"You were right the first time, Gordon. I think we'd better not get involved."

"I was *wrong* the first time. We *are* involved. I don't like
it, but we are. Now, wait—before you argue, think. How
many cars pass along this road? One, two, three per night?
Those people back at the station, the ones who patched our
tire, *they* know we came this way. There's no turning off
this road. It leads straight from the crossroads to the hotel
on the beach. So what if somebody comes along behind us
and picks up that arm? Assuming the most elementary investigation, they'll find out we were the last ones along this
road. And they'll ask us, Did you see an arm lying beside
the road? Why didn't you pick it up? Why didn't you report it?"

He spoke with calm emphasis, as if he were lecturing to
his class. In fact, he felt utterly detached, as if he were
standing on a cool, windy mountaintop and looking down
upon a roiling, writhing mass of humanity.

"You could go back and kick it into the brush," she said.

"Then we'd be concealing evidence of a crime."

"How do you know it was a crime?"

"I doubt that it's legal to go around dismembering
corpses in Mexico."

"So? Who would know?"

"We would know."

"My conscience can handle it."

"It's not a matter of conscience. It's . . ." His mind
groped for words to explain his feeling that this was one of
life's watersheds, where one stream opens into a broad
green valley, and the other narrows to a canyon filled with
thorns and venomous reptiles. He was determined that this

time she would not force him into the low road, no matter how logical and self-preservative it might be.

"It's a question of responsibility," he said finally.

"Is it *our* responsibility?"

"I'm afraid it is."

"I don't agree. It's not our country, these aren't our people, we don't even speak the lang—"

He reached across her and punched in the light button. She gasped as sudden darkness pressed in upon them.

"Gordon, what are you doing?"

"Trust me, Ann." He opened the glove compartment and took out the flashlight. He opened the door and stepped out, pausing to let his eyes acclimate to the darkness. Above him on the ridge, a gnarled tree lifted its tufted fingers against the faint blue glow of the skyline. The stars were incredibly bright, as though a white-hot furnace leaked light through a velvet curtain. He walked to the back of the car and looked down the pale strip of gravel. Nothing moved. He listened until his body ached with the effort, but heard nothing. Was that normal? Hadn't he read somewhere that the absence of night-sounds signified a lurking predator?

He lifted the trunk lid, careful to make no sound. The dim yellow beam of his flashlight revealed a dusty burlap bag and a lug wrench. He closed the trunk gently and walked around to her window. She rolled down the glass and he handed her the lug wrench.

"Keep this in your hand, just in case."

Her cold damp fingers touched his. He took her hand and squeezed it, waited until the answering squeeze came, faint at first, then a tight, desperate clutch.

"Let's go on, Gordon."

Gently he disengaged her hand. "Roll up the window and lock the doors. I'll be right back."

His footsteps on the gravel sounded loud—obscene, like someone eating potato chips at a funeral. Strange to retrace on foot the distance covered in a car. He seemed to have walked a long time. Had he passed the arm? No, the road still sloped downward; he hadn't yet reached the dry wash. He thought of returning to the car and backing it down the road. He didn't like all this space separating him from Ann. She was already terrified, here in the midst of desolation, in a foreign land, in total darkness . . .

You're not yodeling for joy yourself, Phelps.

The arm had a curious sheen in the red-yellow light. The hand—frozen in a grasping reflex—tripped his brain into visions of a grunting, gasping death-struggle. Could there be blood and tissue under the fingernails, a shred of fabric which would lead to the murderer?

Let the police worry about that.

He reached down to pick it up, then straightened and listened. From beyond the ridge came the growl of a laboring engine. Headlight beams fanned across the sky—and his car sat blocking the road. Something had to be done.

For a second he stood wavering. Run back and leave the arm lying there? No, have to pick it up . . .

He threw the burlap over the arm and grasped it gingerly between his fingers. He shut off his flashlight and started at a fast trot back to the car. He felt a vague surprise at how heavy the arm felt, but then he'd never carried an unattached human arm before.

The truck crested the ridge. Twin lights dipped down and shone through the car, silhouetting Ann's head behind the wheel. He broke into a run, jerked open the car door, and tossed the burlap bundle onto the floor behind the seat.

"Scoot over, quick!"

She slid over and he thrust himself behind the wheel. The approaching headlights dazzled him. He groped, found the switch. The engine coughed and died. Damn rental car. Why couldn't he have driven his own? Couldn't be sure of finding gas, better fly to Guadalajara and hire a car, that's what Norval had said . . .

Curse you, Norval.

The engine caught, and he jerked on the lights. The oncoming lights neither dimmed nor swerved, but came on like a pair of blinding suns. They stopped so close he could feel the heat against his face, burning his eyes.

"They've got the road blocked," said Ann. Her tone was the same one she used to tell him there was a raveling on his sleeve.

He shifted into reverse and twisted his head to look out the back window. He saw nothing but two spinning green discs on a sheet of coruscating purple. He was blind as a mole. Without backup lights he'd surely blunder into the brush . . .

The truck was red and riding high on heavy-duty shocks.

A square chrome grill glittered above a baby-blue bumper which carried the words: EL TORO DEL CAMINO. Bull-of-the-road. A symbol of aggression which seemed borne out by the man who stepped down from the cab. He looked . . . not tall, but thick and broad as an oak stump. He wore grease-stained khaki pants and a once-white undershirt which now bore finger paintings of oil on dust. A dusty red bandanna hung around his thick neck. His stubbled cheeks spread in a wide grin, and Gordon thought of the Mexican bandit in *Treasure of Sierra Madre* . . .

"Hand me that lug wrench," he said, holding out his hand. He felt the bar smack his palm and reflected that his best defense would be a savage merciless attack. Yet he knew his civilized reflexes would make him hesitant and clumsy . . .

"He's got a gun," said Ann, in the same flat tone she'd used before.

Gordon saw it as the driver turned to speak to someone up in the cab—ugly blue-steel death-dealer clipped to his belt above the rear pocket.

The man hitched up his pants and started toward their car.

Gordon said, "Don't talk. I'll try to bluff our way past him."

The driver stood grinning outside the window, his face only inches from the glass. Waving his hands and dipping his shoulders, he ripped off twenty seconds of rapid Spanish.

"Did you understand him?" asked Ann.

"Too fast. He's using some local dialect." Gordon pushed out the side-vent and spoke through the narrow gap: *"No entiendo."*

"Muñeca?" The man waited, his brows lifted in question. *"Muñeca?"*

Gordon shook his head. "No understand. *Americano.*"

"Ah . . . *Americano!*" The man bent down and pressed his nose against the window. "*Sí, Americano.*" He stepped back, lifted his hand and waggled his fingers, then trotted around behind the truck.

"Was he waving good-by?" asked Ann.

"I think he wants us to wait."

"He isn't giving us any choice."

Gordon watched the driver come out from behind the

truck with a grotesquely truncated object under his arm. Ann gasped as he held it up in front of the headlights. Gordon saw the naked, headless, limbless female torso and thought: *This can't be real, we've driven off the world and dropped into a nightmare* . . .

The smooth breasts had no nipples, the round tummy lacked a navel, and the space between the truncated thighs was only a smooth mound of plastic . . .

"Gordon, is that a . . . *mannequin?*"

He couldn't speak, but let his breath out in a long sigh. Only then did he realize how tense he'd been. His muscles went limp, his spine wilted into its normal curvature.

He felt utterly ludicrous. The driver stood in the headlights' glare, demonstrating by signs how the dummy had shaken apart in his truck, and how the parts had tumbled out one by one. Gordon reached behind the seat and seized the arm wrapped in burlap . . .

He froze as the driver came back to his window.

"Ha visto alguna parte? La cabeza? Cabeza?" He held his hands to his temples and rocked his head from side to side.

"Cabeza—he wants to know about the head," said Ann.

"I know. Keep quiet." Gordon put his mouth to the vent. "A dog got it. Dog. What's the word for dog? Perro. Perro."

The driver tilted his head and looked puzzled.

"Rowf! Rowf!" barked Gordon.

"Ah . . . perro, si. Gracias. Muchisimas gracias!"

The driver grinned and saluted, then ran back and climbed into his truck. A minute later the engine roared, and the big vehicle backed into the crackling brush. The driver waved his hand as Gordon drove past.

Neither spoke until they crested the ridge. The road stretched straight ahead, with neither hill nor curve breaking its slow descent to the coastal plain. Moonlight glittered on the crinkled sea. Off to the right he saw splotches of light which marked the hotel complex. He heard a choking sound beside him and turned to Ann.

"Are you laughing or crying?"

"Both," she said.

"You think I was silly?"

"No. You were awfully brave—even if the danger wasn't real. And you were right about stopping. Can you imagine what would have happened if we'd just kept driving? All our lives we'd have been haunted . . ." She talked without stopping for breath—her way of releasing tension. ". . . And what paranoid assumptions we made! That all unexplained deaths are a result of murder, that all foreigners are hostile. There's only one thing I don't understand."

"What's that?"

"Why didn't you give the nice man back his arm?"

Gordon reached behind the seat and groped for the burlap-wrapped bundle.

"There's another assumption we make about foreigners," he said. "That even though they're shrewd, they haven't the intelligence to pull off a really cool subterfuge. Like carrying around a dummy in order to recover a lost corpse."

He gripped the arm just below the elbow, avoiding the cold sticky end which had shocked him so much the last time.

"This one's real," he said.

Later he realized he shouldn't have laid it in her lap—but he wasn't thinking straight at the time.

ROUNDHOUSE

by Frank Sisk

I like a shot of vodka before breakfast, and after. It makes my morning. On this particular blue Monday I'd had the first and was just throwing the lip over the second when the phone began to ring.

I answered it by saying "Pilgrim Investigations" because the apartment phone is an extension of the one in the office when the office is empty.

"May I please speak to Mr. Pilgrim?" said a masculine voice with an authoritative quality.

"Speaking," I said.

"My name is Fortunato," the voice said. "Leonard Fortunato. I'm certain we've never met."

We may never have met but the name was vaguely familiar. "And now you'd like to remedy the situation," the second shot of vodka said.

"Yes. I'd like to have a half hour of your time today if that's at all possible."

"Name the time, Mister Fortunato, and we'll see what can be worked out."

"How about two this afternoon?"

"It's a date."

"Then I'll be expecting you."

"I see. You want me to come to *your* office."

"I'd prefer it that way. It's a quite delicate problem and I wouldn't want to be seen entering the premises of a private detective, if you'll forgive my saying so, Mr. Pilgrim. I'm with Dreisch Chemicals in the Emerson Building. Nine hundred Pearl Street. Just ask for me at the receptionist's desk."

"All right, sir. Two o'clock."

"One other thing, Mr. Pilgrim. To humor my somewhat absurd desire for secrecy in this matter, would you be good enough to present yourself under an assumed name?"

"A man named Jones will keep the appointment," I said, and hung up. Now, where had I heard of Leonard Fortunato before, and just recently?

Dreisch Chemicals occupies the entire tenth floor of the Emerson Building. When I stepped off the elevator at exactly two minutes before two I stepped into a large, bright reception room, the principal ornaments of which were murals in the geometric manner of Kandinsky and, behind a semi-circular desk, a very pretty young lady with long straight hair two shades of orange.

"Mr. Jones to see Mr. Fortunato," I told her.

She batted her long false lashes cordially and pressed one of a battery of buttons on top of the desk. She spoke briefly, almost inaudibly, into a panel invisible at least to me, and then said, "Miss Fabian is coming for you in a minute, sir. Why don't you take a seat?"

Instead, I studied the murals. One reminded me of a series of telephone wires stretched from a saw-toothed horizon to a globular bowl containing either square fish or colored confetti. Before I could determine which, Miss Fabian arrived. She was also a pretty young lady, as most of them seem to me these days, but the eyelashes were her own and her hair, short and glossy black, was probably the color with which she was born.

"This way, Mr. Jones," she said.

We proceeded through a wide door to the right of the reception room and down a hushed corridor richly carpeted in electric blue. The doors on either side were paneled with opaque glass and lettered in black with an identification of the contents. At the end of the corridor, where it angled right and left, we came upon L. E. FORTUNATO, *Executive Vice-President*. Miss Fabian opened the door and stood aside to let me enter. I was in a nice clean outer office, obviously Miss Fabian's, and facing another door which bore in smaller letters Fortunato's name again, but not his title.

Miss Fabian went briskly to this door, tapped it once with a dainty knuckle and then turned the knob.

I guess I expected L. E. Fortunato, executive vice-president, to be at least my age and perhaps a few years older. I was rather surprised to find a man in his early thirties—thirty-three at the most. He rose from behind a gleaming blonde Danish-style desk and walked quickly around it to shake hands. Of medium height, slender, tanned, he wore his pinstripe silk suit with the assured air of professional model posing as a modern young executive keeping cool amid the heat of big decisions. His concession to closing the slight generation gap was a set of neatly-trimmed dark sideburns that ended an inch below the ears.

"It's good of you to come on such short notice," he said, with a smile of dismissal in Miss Fabian's direction.

I heard the door shut behind me. "The month of May is never my busiest. Spring fever seems to keep people somnolent and out of trouble."

He gave a short mirthless laugh. "Apt, very apt. In my case, however, not true."

"What kind of case is your case, sir?"

"Be seated and I'll tell you."

I sat in a blonde Danish chair, refused a proffered cigar and began to wait.

Fortunato went back behind the desk. "I suppose you recall the disastrous explosion in that roundhouse over in East Riverton five weeks ago."

"Who doesn't?" Suddenly I recalled more than that. I recalled, now, why Fortunato's name had been dimly familiar. "Three young bomb makers blown to smithereens."

"Well, at least two of them were young. We know that because they have been positively identified by the police. That third one, though, they're not sure of. Even after five weeks, nobody in authority can say whether the unidentified victim was young or old, black or white, male or female."

"Do you still think it was your nephew?"

Fortunato gave me an approving smile. "You do your homework, don't you, Mr. Pilgrim?"

"It's just coming back to me—the newspaper accounts. A few days after the other boys were identified, you came forward with the idea that the third victim might possibly be your nephew. I can't remember his name."

"Gerald Davies."

"Oh, yes. And do you still think number three is Gerald Davies?"

"Yes, I do. But I want to be certain. That's why I've called you in."

"I'm no magician, Mr. Fortunato. If the police lab can't say for sure, I don't think there's much I can do."

"You may be right, but I want you to try a different approach. The police, you see, are trying to ascertain who the victim *is*. I want you to ascertain who the victim *isn't*."

"Spin that once again."

"If it isn't Gerald, I want to know as soon as possible."

"You have some doubts, then?"

"Not really. It's just something the police mentioned to me yesterday. Gerald was over six feet tall, and one of the shinbones found in the wreckage indicates the unidentified victim was about six inches shorter than that."

"That sounds kind of conclusive."

"Without qualification, yes. But the police do a lot of qualifying. For instance, two other shinbones are so fragmented and pulverized that it's not absolutely certain which belong to whom. The report says as much. The whole thing is like a jigsaw puzzle, with guesses, more or less, about a lot of missing pieces."

"You think I can find a missing piece or two?"

"I think you can establish whether or not Gerald entered that roundhouse sometime prior to the explosion."

"I'm sure the police have covered that."

"More or less, but they lacked one piece of information which may have hampered them a little."

"Such as?"

"Gerald phoned me an hour before the explosion."

"About what?"

"A very personal matter, not at all relevant to what happened later. That's why I thought it better not to mention this to the police. They dig like firemen break windows— often unnecessarily."

"Do you happen to know where he phoned you from?"

"I do. The Meridian Motor Lodge, out on Brunswick Turnpike."

"Was he registered?"

"I checked back later—after the roundhouse tragedy was reported—and learned that he had been, and had checked out without paying his bill."

"This is what the cops don't know."

"That's right, Mr. Pilgrim. Now, what I want to know is this: do these few facts give you enough of a lead to ascertain beyond a reasonable doubt whether or not Gerald entered the roundhouse?"

"Could be. But let me tell you what I'd like to know. I'd

like to know why you're making an association between
Gerald Davies and these hapless bomb makers in the first
place."

Fortunato smiled sadly. "The two victims who have been
positively identified were close friends of Gerald."

"I see. Another point now, Mr. Fortunato. As the kid's
uncle you have every right to be interested, but what about
his parents? Or doesn't he have any?"

"His mother—my older sister, that is—is alive and well
and unhappily remarried in Queensport. His father was
killed in the Korean war when Gerald was just a child."

"What's his mother's new name?"

"Harrington. Mrs. Ames Harrington. Are you going to
undertake this job, Mr. Pilgrim?"

"I'm going to give it a whirl."

"You'll need some money, then. What are the usual arrangements?"

I mentioned the current rate. He wrote out a very fast
check for a week's supply of money and expenses.

My first stop would normally have been the Meridian
Motor Lodge, but police headquarters was en route, so I
stopped there and renewed an old acquaintance with Captain Thomas McFate, chief of the homicide division.

"This is primarily a bomb-squad case," he told me.
"We're interested in certain aspects of it, though. Here are
some pictures of the scene, inside and out, taken an hour
after the dynamite let go."

From the outside shots, the heavy stone walls of the old
roundhouse didn't appear much affected except for a few
gaping cracks in the mortar. The huge wooden double
doors, however, had been blown out and now hung fragmented on their hinges, and there was a large ragged
wound in the tin roof. In the foreground stood a yellow
sports car of foreign make, with a peace symbol painted on
the door facing the camera.

"Whose car?" I asked.

"It belonged to one of the boys," McFate said. "To his
father, actually. Bobby Resnick was only twenty, not old
enough to hold a car title in this state."

"Bobby Resnick. And who was the other you've positively identified, Tom?"

"John Purvis."

I looked at the inside shots. The long-range ones depicted nothing but a kind of gray shambles of things that once must have been benches, shelves, railroad track and girders. The close-ups were grisly— several fingers, a knee-cap, part of a jawbone.

"Hell of a way to go," I said.

"Yeah, and with so much to live for. Both the Purvis and the Resnick families are fairly rich. When I think of the poor kids growing up in the slums, ready to knife you for a dollar, fighting day and night just to survive, I wonder what these rich college boys hope to prove by tossing a bomb into a dean's office. Makes no sense to me at all, but of course I'm considered over the hill by these vocal long-hairs."

"You and me both, Tom. The third victim, now—you've got no idea who it might be?"

"The lab came up with an idea this morning. They're beginning to think it was a girl," McFate said.

"A girl? And nobody's put in a claim for a missing daughter?"

"That's right. A poor kid we'd probably have heard about, but the rich ones have their own dough, their own wheels, their own pads, and the old folks know from nothing. We're beginning to think this poor little bag of bones is another rich one. Some sweet day her mother or father may look up from whatever is holding their attention right now and realize she is missing."

"It's a hell of a world, Tom."

"I'd sell it cheap today, Jake."

"Well, my boy Gerald Davies must still be walking around on it. That ought to ease his uncle's mind."

"Don't be too sure of that."

"What do you mean?"

"On the few occasions when Fortunato came visiting he didn't strike me as burdened with grief. Urgent curiosity was more like it. Each time we told him we couldn't be sure the remains of the third party was his missing nephew, he seemed more disappointed than not."

I mulled this odd item of information over during the drive out to the Meridian Motor Lodge. The place was fairly new and its sign advertised a heated swimming pool, sauna bath and putting green. I asked the pretty white-haired lady at the desk to put me in touch with the manager. She buzzed for him, and a tall young man with a Fu

Manchu mustache and sideburns that nearly met on his chin emerged from a room behind the key rack. He said his name was Finch. I told him mine and my business with regard to Gerald Davies.

Finch raised a skeptical eyebrow. "You want to pay his bill, no doubt."

"I might at that. What did he leave behind?"

"A few scanty articles of travel, as I recall." He turned to the white-haired lady. "Leah, is Mister Davies' bag in the storage room?"

"Unless it's been claimed."

"I'm almost certain it hasn't, but we'll check." He took a key from the rack and came out from behind the desk. The door to the storage room was the first in the left corridor off the lobby. Inside, there were at least a dozen assorted pieces of luggage, indicating that Gerald wasn't the only deadbeat on the Meridian's books, and we found what we wanted almost at once—a zippered affair of blue canvas with the initials *G D* hand-lettered in black. It was the sort of thing you were more likely to take to a gym than to a hotel.

"It's all yours," Finch said, "inasmuch as you represent the family. But first you must settle the bill."

"And how much is your bill?"

"Leah can tell us."

Back at the desk, Leah consulted a file and told us the bill was $22.90.

"A brief stay," I said.

"One night," Leah said.

"When did he check in?" I asked.

Leah glanced at the registration card still in her hand. "April twenty-nine at two-fifty in the afternoon."

That was the day before the roundhouse explosion. "Did you notice whether he had any visitors?"

Finch snorted. "Five weeks ago. Are you kidding? With the turnover we have here—"

"A girl visited him the next morning," Leah broke in. "I remember it particularly because the young man asked our permission to let her use the pool."

"And you said no," I said, with a smile at Finch.

"We said yes," Leah said. "Mr. Donnelly was in charge that day."

"And is that the last you saw of either of them?"

"Yes," Leah said.

I gave her a twenty and a ten in return for some change, a receipt, and Gerald's gym bag.

I drove to the office and checked with the answering service. Nothing on the line that couldn't flap for another day. Besides, it was already getting on toward six. I like a shot of vodka before dinner. I took a good one from the bottle in my one-bottle liquor cabinet. Then I began to examine the contents of the gym bag.

A few pairs of socks, a pink tee shirt, plaid boxer shorts, swimming trunks, a tube of toothpaste squeezed in the middle and a toothbrush with sad bristles, a comb, and a red jeweler's box of the size that often contains a desk set comprised the lot.

I opened the red box. Inside, rather elaborately cushioned in cottony down, was a cigarette lighter of brushed gold with the red script initials *gd* centered. A small ivory card lay beside it with the typewritten message: *Happy Birthday.*

Lifting the lighter from its cotton bed, I studied it with the infallible eye of an old connoisseur, my own of course. Worth all of a hundred dollars. Quite a pleasing gift for a kid—if he smoked. A lot of the young ones these days didn't smoke—at least nothing so conventional as tobacco. But whether Gerald smoked or not, why hadn't he taken this fine lighter along with him? It was eminently portable, and quite hockable.

I returned the lighter to its box. A tiny smear of oil remained on the tip of my forefinger. Automatically, I raised finger to nose. We old connoisseurs are great for sniffing. Lighter fluid? Definitely not. I touched fingertip to tongue. The taste was sweet at first and then unexpectedly hot.

After that, the lighter in its cotton bed commanded my highest respect. With care I replaced the cover. With greater care I returned the box to the gym bag. With the greatest care I skinned the zipper shut.

An hour later, on the outskirts of Queensport, I found just the spot I was looking for—a small, fenced-in grave-yard which, judging from the tilted headstones, hadn't been used since 1866. (*Josiah Lee 1815–66 Pace.*) There, under a mulch of many years' leaves, I concealed the gym bag most carefully.

A telephone book in the Queensport Pharmacy informed

ne that Ames Harrington, Gerald's stepfather, resided at 3 Greenbriar Lane. The teen-age girl behind the soda fountain told me how to get there.

Dusk was muffling the countryside as I reached the Harrington home. Situated a hundred yards back from the narrow town road, it seemed in the last light to be constructed largely of glass placed at eccentric angles on warp-beams of blonde wood. The door knocker was a brass monkey, palms over eyes, which saw no evil.

The door was opened by a small raven-haired woman with dreamy brown eyes. She held a half-empty highball glass. On her rather full lips was the start of a smile that said neither yes nor no.

"My name is Pilgrim," I said. "Are you Mrs. Harrington?"

"Yes," she replied, "but I'm not buying anything."

"I'm not selling anything."

"So?"

"I'm doing a chore for your brother. It concerns your son Gerald."

She took a thoughtful sip from the glass. "In that case, come in."

The living room was furnished with angular chairs and black glass tabletops and conical flowerpots. I sat on what might have been an upholstered trapezoid. Mrs. Harrington perched tentatively on a piebald vector.

"In my husband's absence, may I mix you a drink?" she asked.

"Vodka, straight. If you've got it."

"We've got it." She came back with it in a minute. "What kind of chore does Len have you doing?" she asked, perching again.

"He wants to find out once and for all whether your son was killed in that much-publicized roundhouse blast five weeks ago."

"He's still on *that* kick?"

"Why do you call it kick, ma'am? Do you know something your brother doesn't know?"

"A mother's heart tells her things," she said, but ironically.

"Have you heard from Gerald since that explosion?"

"Not a word."

"When did you hear from him last?"

"All of two months ago. He honored us with a weekend visit—to think things out, he said."

"What sort of things?"

"He didn't take us into his confidence. He just lolled around in various chairs and hammocks and appeared to sleep most of the time."

"Sounds like a natural weekend for a young man carrying a heavy load at college."

"Well, he's been quite an activist, if that's what you mean."

"That's not quite what I meant, Mrs. Harrington. But now that you mention it, was Gerald the bomb-throwing type?"

"I never thought so, but I'm prejudiced, and quite alone."

"I gather Mr. Harrington and Gerald weren't on the warmest terms."

"You gather right. I'm going to have another drink. Are you ready?"

"I'm set, thanks."

When she returned, her manner was somehow different, as if she had taken a quick look into herself and found a great anguish. "If you want to know the truth, Mr. Pilgrim—what is your first name anyway?—if you want to know the awful truth—"

"Jake," I said.

"Ames actually hates Gerald and hates him for every reason in the book. Long hair verboten, intelligence verboten, rock music verboten, pop art verboten, brown eyes verboten, rebellion verboten, frequent visits verboten. Gerald didn't come here often because he never felt at home."

"How long have you and Harrington been married?"

"Since Gerald's first year of college—four years now. One great big mistake."

"This was to be his graduation year, then?"

"Yes."

"How old was, I mean, is he?"

"Twenty-one."

"When was his birthday?"

"April twenty-eight."

"Did you happen to send him a gift?"

"Of course I did."

"I don't suppose it was a cigarette lighter."

"Of course not. Gerald doesn't smoke. I sent him a check."

"A check. Did he cash it?"

"Yes, I'm sure he did. It was with the others in my last bank statement."

"Can we take a look at it? I think it will answer a big question."

"Why not?" She left the room in an opposite direction from the drink-mixing department and returned in four or five minutes with a sheaf of checks. It took her another minute to find the one made payable to Gerald Davies in the amount of one hundred dollars. She handed it to me and I turned it over to the endorser's side.

"Is this Gerald's signature?" I asked.

"It's not a forgery."

The bank-clearance date stamped on the back was May 13, nearly two weeks after the roundhouse explosion, and we all know these days that the bankers clear checks within 24 hours of presentation.

"Well, Mrs. Harrington," I said, "you've got more than maternal intuition to prove Gerald didn't die that day in East Riverton. You've got this." I indicated the clearance date.

She gave it an owlish look and then it dawned on her. "Why, of course," she said. "I wonder why I never thought of that."

"You'll find the answer to that later, maybe, and you probably won't like it."

She flinched. "You're not a very nice man, Jake."

"I'm an inquisitive one, though. Did your son have a special girlfriend that you know of?"

"He may have. I'm not sure."

"The last time he was seen, there was a girl with him. They went swimming together in a hotel pool."

"He did get several phone calls here during that week-end visit. At least one of them was from a girl. I know because I answered it myself."

"Did she give a name?"

Mrs. Harrington sipped thoughtfully from the highball glass. "I think she did. What was it now? Something rather poetic, as I remember. Leona, Lenore—Leonora, yes, that was it."

"No last name?"

"No, just Leonora. 'May I speak to Gerry? This is Leonora calling.' A soft musical voice. I intended to kid Gerald about it, but then something else came up and I forgot." She finished her drink and the dreamy look was now going drunk.

It was nearly ten o'clock when I left Queensport with the case pretty much sewed up. Fortunato had employed me to find out whether Gerald Davies was one of the victims of the roundhouse disaster. I had discovered he was not. The canceled check was irrefutable proof of this. In the course of my brief investigation, however, I had uncovered in the form of a cigarette lighter a modicum of proof of something else—that Gerald Davies was intended to be a victim one way or another. Why? And by whom? On these questions I slept soundly that night.

Next morning after vodka, breakfast and vodka, I scanned the phone book for Resnicks and Purvises. There were quite a few of the latter, several of them in high-income residential areas, but only one Resnick (Michael E.) with an address that spelled money. I dialed his number.

A feminine voice with an Irish brogue answered. "The Resnick residence, if you please," said she.

"Are any of the Resnicks available, mavourneen?"

"Not himself nor the missus. They're after taking a cruise."

"Who's holding the fort besides you?"

" 'Tis me and none other because, Lord knows, Miss Natalie listens to nothing all day but those hairy screeches singing on records."

"I want to talk to Miss Natalie," I said.

"A brave mouth to you."

Several minutes of silence ensued and then a hesitant, reedy voice said, "Who is this, anyway?"

"My name's Pilgrim, Natalie. I'm a detective. I'd like to ask you a few questions concerning your brother Bob. Did you know many of his friends?"

"A detective? Gee, I never talked to a detective before."

"Can we meet somewhere for a little chat, Natalie?"

"Sure, I guess so. Where?"

"How about right there?"

"Here? Okay. When?"

"In about thirty minutes," I said.

Just as I was leaving the apartment, the phone rang. It was Fortunato. "Congratulations, Mr. Pilgrim," he said.

"On what?"

"On the expeditious manner in which you established the fact that Gerald is still alive. My sister just phoned me and told me about the canceled check."

"I see. Well, sir, the check doesn't prove he's *still* alive. It proves only that he was alive a few weeks after the explosion."

"Oh, I'm certain he'll turn up soon," Fortunato said blandly. "And so is my sister."

"I think I might turn him up for you," I said.

"Don't bother, Mr. Pilgrim. You've already performed admirably."

"But I'm still holding six more days' pay and expenses," I said. "I hate to give refunds."

"Consider it a bonus, Mr. Pilgrim."

"If you say so, Mr. Fortunato."

Driving to keep my date with Miss Natalie Resnick, probable age 15, I asked myself a question: why did Fortunato want me to leave the case with the main end still loose? A glimmer of the answer was working its way through the convolutions of my brain, but it had not yet arrived as I drove up the semi-circular drive leading to the imposing front door of the Resnick mansion.

Natalie herself opened the door. In the background lurked a gray-haired woman in a white smock. Mine hostess dismissed her with the imperious suggestion that she betake herself elsewhere.

"You don't look like a detective," she said to me.

"None of us do," I said.

Natalie, however, looked like I wanted her to—short, somewhat pudgy, with mouse-colored hair worn long. Behind the granny glasses she looked wise beyond her scant years. If anyone in this house knew practically everything about everyone else, it was Natalie. Upon her round face was the satisfied expression of the confirmed eavesdropper bulging with luscious chunks of other people's private moments. She was already a better detective than I'll ever be.

"We can talk without *her* hearing in Daddy's study," she said.

I followed her lead. The room might have been a leathery nook wrenched from any of the exclusive men's clubs associated with ivy-league alumni.

"Do you drink brandy?" Natalie asked hospitably.

"No, thanks."

"How about a real Cuban cigar from Canada?"

"Much obliged, but no. That was an awful thing that happened to your brother Bobby," I went on. "Getting blown up like that."

"Power to the people," Natalie said, practically disappearing into a deep armchair.

"What's that?"

"That's what Bobby was always saying—he and his friends too."

"Did you know many of his friends, Natalie?"

"All of 'em that ever came here, and that was plenty. What a freaky bunch!"

"You didn't approve, I gather."

"I thought Daddy was right. They all had too much too soon and couldn't digest it. Daddy stopped giving Bobby an allowance, but that didn't bother Bobby. He told Daddy he could get all the money he needed from somewhere else."

"And did he?"

"Did he what?"

"Did he get money?"

"Cripes, yes. He always had plenty. And so did Johnny Purvis."

"He was the other lad killed in the blast, wasn't he?"

"Yes. It's a wonder they both weren't blown up a long time ago. They were always buying dynamite and things like that and taking it to places all over the country. Once they bought a couple of machine guns and drove them in Bobby's car out to some college near Chicago."

"You kept them under pretty good surveillance, Natalie."

"I might be an undercover agent when I get older."

"Did you happen to know Gerald Davies?"

"Oh, sure. He used to come around with the grass and they'd smoke it in the toolhouse behind the garage. But Gerald never liked the idea of dynamite and guns and all that. He was against violence. He was afraid a lot of innocent people might get killed. He was always saying things like that, and Bobby and Johnny and most of the others razzed him a lot. They called him a cream puff. You can't shake the rafters with a feather duster. Johnny was always saying that."

"Did the boys have any girls?"

Behind the granny glasses gray eyes flickered. "Oh, sure. To hear them rapping, specially when they were high on grass, they were all big studs."

I blinked, and smiled.

"But the only girl I ever saw hanging around," Natalie continued, "was that Watrous creep—Martha Watrous. She popped pills. You could tell by the way she couldn't stop talking. And her eyes bugged out, too. Her parents were divorced and married to somebody else. They lived in Europe or someplace and sent her cards at Christmas. She lived on a trust fund from an aunt. Martha's dead now."

"She is?"

"Almost for sure. Nobody's seen her since the roundhouse blew up. She was there, I bet—the third body."

"Have you retailed this tidbit to the fuzz?"

"I wanted to, but Daddy told me to keep my nose out of it, so I did."

"What about Gerald Davies? Did he have a girlfriend?"

"Oh, sure. Leonora Sypher. He used to write poems to her. When he was alone in the toolhouse he sometimes read them out loud, for practice, like. I heard him a couple of times. Leonora's not too creepy."

"I suppose you know where she lives."

"Oh, sure. With her parents on Rumstick Terrace. It's only a few blocks east of here."

Leaving, I told Natalie she could have a job as my assistant when she got a bit older. She beamed. Some sweet day she'll knock on my door.

Back at the office, I phoned the Sypher residence. A female menial informed me that Miss Sypher was employed from nine to three at The College Booksmith's on University Avenue. I was going to phone, then thought better of it. If Leonora Sypher was the girl who had taken a swim with Gerald Davies on his last day of visibility, she presumably knew where he was now. She had known for all these weeks and had kept silent. Why? To protect him, of course. From what? From the death that was supposed to be meted out to him by a cigarette lighter. And if that were the case, a phone call from a stranger in search of Gerald was bound to frighten her off and out of sight. I'd make a personal appearance at The College Booksmith's and play it diplomatically from there.

Before leaving the office, I equipped myself with a pocket-size tape recorder and pinned a lapel microphone behind an artificial carnation.

The College Booksmith's was on the lower and dirtier part of University Avenue, bracketed between a hock shop and a store advertising brand-name cosmetics cut-rate. The characters lolling or strolling in the area were costumed as characters. Fluorescence was the word for their garb. Beads and medallions abounded. The female element revealed as much thigh as possible, while the male with few exceptions concealed physiognomy behind hirsute aberrations.

Luckily, I found a parking stall halfway down the block. I nickled the meter and walked back toward the bookstore. As I passed the hock shop my attention was caught by a display of cigarette lighters in the window. I stopped for a closer look. One of the lighters, gold-plated, was almost exactly the size and shape of one now resting safely in the graveyard outside Queensport. It was ticketed for $3.98. I went inside and bought it.

A minute later I was smiling—most affably, I hoped—at Leonora Sypher across a table stacked high with the works of such modern geniuses as Rod McKuen, Jerry Rubin, Jean Genet, and Eldridge Cleaver. She was an extremely attractive girl with glistening blonde hair worn straight and long. She was returning my smile with a show of fine white teeth, but her eyes, I thought, held a hint of apprehension.

"May I help you?" she asked.

"I think so," I said.

"Name it and we probably have it."

"My name is Pilgrim, Jake Pilgrim. Do you mind if I call you Leonora?"

The apprehension deepened. "How do you know my name?"

"It's come up in connection with the name of Gerald Davies."

Fear came to her eyes now. "Who *are* you?"

"A detective, private. Can you take a coffee break, Leonora? It's important that we talk about Gerald."

"I've nothing to say."

"What if I told you Gerald's life is in danger?"

"We know that—I mean, I'm not saying another word, sir."

"I'm on your side, Leonora. Believe that."

"Who hired you?"

"Gerald's uncle."

"Then you're not on our side, definitely."

"He fired me this morning. Does that help my defense, your honor?"

"Why did he fire you?"

"Because I found out Gerald is alive, and that's all he wanted to know. But I'm afraid the boy won't be alive long unless we get to him first."

She wrinkled her lovely brow in thought. Then, apparently arriving at a decision, she walked to the back of the store, disappearing behind the tall racks that formed aisles. A moment later she reappeared with a tall, thin, shaggily-bearded young man gangling behind her.

"Herbert's agreed to take over a while," she said. "There's a greasy-spoon sort of place on the corner."

We left together, going in the direction of my car and the greasy-spoon sort of place. I said, "We don't have much time to waste, Leonora. Where is Gerald holed up?"

"I don't know why I should tell you that, Mr. Pilgrim."

"Call me Jake. And tell me something, were you the girl who went swimming with Gerald at the Meridian Motor Lodge?"

"How did you know that?"

"I keep busy. He'd had a birthday a few days earlier."

"You do keep busy."

"Somebody sent him a gift—an expensive cigarette lighter."

"That was from Leonard."

"Uncle Leonard Fortunato?"

"That's right."

"How come Uncle Len didn't know his favorite nephew hadn't acquired the nicotine habit?"

"Len knew that. He probably gave him the lighter for grass."

"So Len knew about the grass, did he?"

"Len introduced Gerald to grass. He introduced a lot of kids to it. He had a source."

"Lucky for Gerald he didn't try the new lighter."

"He was going to send it back. A few weeks earlier he'd

sworn off the stuff. He was finished with the whole bag—
the picketing, the riots, the bombs, the underground press."
She paused, then said, "Lucky. What do you mean *lucky?*"

"Unless I'm badly mistaken, Uncle Len's gift is fueled
with enough glyceryl trinitrate to blow a man's head off.
That's why he was so positive Gerald was a victim of the
roundhouse blast."

"And that's why Gerald wanted him to keep thinking
that way," Leonora said, as if learning an important fact
for the first time.

"But Uncle knows better now," I said.

"Oh, yes."

"He'll be checking on a few obvious hiding places."

"Oh, Lord!"

"It's that obvious, then."

"My father's hunting lodge. A gang of us used it a few
times last winter for skiing. I'm certain Gerald told Leonard about it. Why, sure. He even borrowed a deerskin
parka from him."

"Where is this hunting lodge, Leonora?"

"In the Berskshires, a few miles beyond Pittsfield."

"Here's my car," I said. "We can drive there in less than
two hours."

She got in. Five minutes later we were on a northbound
interstate highway.

During the trip I asked a lot of questions and got a lot of
answers. The story which emerged was, for these times, a
painfully familiar one, but with sinister overtones that
made it distinctly different.

It was the story of a boy who had lost his father before
he was old enough to know him. It was the story of a boy
raised by a pretty young mother who was somewhat self-
indulgent. The relationship was often prickly with jealousy
from either side. The mother still had a lot of life to live,
the growing boy needed an ideal to worship, a maternal
goddess, but in the final analysis what he got was a frail
human being, a human being who loved him, of course, but
who also had needs of her own, needs that could be ful-
filled only by a man.

By the time Mrs. Davies became Mrs. Harrington. Gerald was disillusioned. Soon he became alienated. He
searched for purpose and found it in the ferment of the
college campus. He established a bi-weekly newspaper

called *Thrust* and apparently shook the spleen out of his system with editorials against all that represented the traditional establishment and in favor of all the wonderful but unhappily impossible dreams which youth has been pursuing since time immemorial.

Thrust, it seems, was not a paying proposition. Sometimes it skipped an issue. This fact came to the attention of Leonard Fortunato. He offered financial assistance. Gerald and his little band of editorial radicals accepted it, and they were soon accepting the business executive as well. Fortunato was over 30 but, unlike many others over 30, he could be trusted. He effortlessly bridged the so-called generation gap by flaunting sideburns, endorsing the radical point of view, blowing a stick of griffo with the fraternity, never batting an eye when the talk touched on TNT and arson and pig-sticking, being helpful even when certain wild ones suddenly needed transportation money from one jurisdiction to another. Yes, though a dozen years older than most of the boys, Leonard Fortunato was almost considered one of them—almost, which doesn't make it.

As time went on, Uncle Len's role began to nag at Gerald's consciousness. It somehow embarrassed his basic good sense. There was something wrong here. Quite by accident he discovered what it was.

Six weeks ago he had gone to New York to cover an anti-pollution demonstration for *Thrust.* After the speeches, he went alone to a cafeteria on East Forty-second Street near First Avenue. Sitting near the window over a cup of coffee and danish, he looked out to see his uncle pass by in the company of a short, bearded man who was wearing a black beret. Impulsively, he got up from the table and rushed from the restaurant.

Fortunato and his companion were weaving their way rapidly through the flow of other pedestrians. Gerald followed. It was his intention at first to overtake them, but then he noticed how deeply they were engrossed in conversation and he decided to wait politely for a break.

The men crossed First Avenue and walked to the entrance of the United Nations headquarters, where they came to a halt but continued to converse for another five minutes. Gerald watched them from a distance, his curiosity piqued. Who was this little man who so commanded his uncle's complete attention? Why, he was nearly obsequious in the presence of the man, quite out of urbane character.

Then, brusquely, the man in the beret terminated the conversation, pivoted on his heels and entered the great building. Fortunato stood for a moment rigid, as if on parade inspection, and then walked away.

Unobserved, Gerald hurried into the United Nations building in time to see the beret crossing toward the elevator bank. He touched a guard on the sleeve and asked, pointing, "Could you tell me who that gentleman is?"

The guard looked. "I do not know him by name," he said, "but he is a member of the Cuban delegation."

We were now passing through Pittsfield.

"Gerald began to see the light?" I asked.

"Oh, but definitely," Leonora said. "The very next day he went to Leonard's office for a confrontation."

"What happened?"

"Leonard simply laughed and asked what all the excitement was about. When Gerald asked point-blank if certain projects at the school—even the newspaper—were being financed by foreign money, Leonard readily admitted it. Money was money, he said, and ideas were ideas. He suggested that Gerald reread the back numbers of *Thrust* and then explain how his editorial position differed from some of the views expressed over the years by Castro or Mao or, for that matter, Lenin."

"Quite a gut puncher, our Len."

"Anyway, Gerald thought the matter over for a few days and then decided to print an exposé in the paper unless Leonard promised to sever all connections with the Cuban secretariat."

"Gerald sounds like he's still wet behind the ears."

"He's an idealist, if that's a sin," Leonora snapped.

"I simply mean that Leonard could no more cut and run than, say, the gent who wrote *Doctor Zhivago*. Pasternak."

"Gerald realizes that now."

"What made him catch on?"

"The dynamite."

"What dynamite?"

"The dynamite Leonard obtained through devious channels for Bobby Resnick and Johnny Purvis. He told Gerald about it to prove how deeply everyone was involved. If

Gerald blew the whistle on Leonard, he was also blowing
it on two of his closest friends and consequently on himself
as well."

"What did Gerald say to that?"

"He phoned Leonard from the Meridian Motor Lodge
the day I went swimming with him. He told him he was
going to take Johnny and Bobby into his confidence. He
was sure, once they learned they were being *used*, they
would change their views."

"He never got to them, though."

"An hour later they were dead."

"So goes the revolution."

We drove another few miles in silence. After a while I
asked, "Hungry?"

"A little," Leonora said. "There's always something to
eat at the lodge. We take the road to the right around the
next bend."

I took that road. It climbed and twisted for at least a
mile and then flattened out on a plateau lush with silver
maples and staghorn sumacs. I saw the sports car before I
noticed the roof of the lodge fairly hidden behind the
screen of green leaves. Turning off the ignition, I rolled to
a quiet stop.

"Fortunato's wagon?" I asked in a low voice.

Leonora nodded, her sweet face very pale.

"I'd like to listen before I knock," I said.

"Follow me," she whispered.

We approached the house from the side by an almost
indiscernible footpath hedged with fern and chokecherry
and something with brambles. It brought us under an open
casement window. Through the screen, voices were clearly
audible. I turned on the tape recorder.

". . . no choice," Fortunato's voice was saying. "If you
don't agree, somebody will be assigned to take care of you,
and there's not a damned thing I can do about it."

"Once and for all, I'm not going to Cuba," said an angry
young voice I'd never heard before—Gerald's. "I'd be
practically a political prisoner there. You admit that."

"You'd be alive."

"Maybe. I tell you I don't trust you Commies."

"I've been ordered to hand you an ultimatum, Gerald.
It's an extremely distasteful task, I assure you. But I must
pass your decision on no later than noon tomorrow."

"Well, you've got it."

"You're quite sure you won't reconsider?"

"As sure as I've ever been of anything in my life."

"In that case, I'm sorry, Gerald. Very sorry indeed."

"I know it's breaking your heart, Len."

"More than you'll ever know, Gerald."

There was something in the tone of Fortunato's voice that caused me to move fast. I went around the corner of the house, Leonora following me, over a rough-hewn banister that belonged to six rough-hewn steps and through a rough-hewn door that led directly into a large room built around a huge fireplace.

By the astonished expression on Fortunato's face, I could have been Nikita Khrushchev coming out of retirement. The gun in his right hand sagged down from the line it had been drawing on Gerald Davies' chest.

"What are *you* doing here?" Fortunato asked uncordially.

"Earning my pay," I said. "What's your excuse?"

"Gerry darling," Leonora cried, running into the young man's arms.

"Quite a reunion," Fortunato said, slipping the gun into his coat pocket and producing a long, guaranteed-to-be-Cuban cigar. He removed the wrapper carefully, clipped the cigar's end with his square white teeth, and smiled. "I wonder how much you know, Pilgrim."

"Plenty."

"I wonder how much you can prove."

"Plenty."

"I'm not so sure of that." He placed the cigar in the middle of his mouth and began rummaging around in his pockets for something with which to light it.

"Permit me," I said, making quite a production of getting up the hock-shop lighter.

Fortunato looked at it and asked quaveringly, "Where'd you g-get that?"

"From Gerald's luggage." My thumb was dramatically poised to strike for flame.

"Don't," Fortunato said in a voice suddenly gone husky.

"Why not?"

"You'll kill us all."

"How?"

"The lighter's loaded with nitro."

"How do you know?"

"I loaded it myself."

"And sent it to Gerald?"

"Yes."

"A birthday gift?"

"Yes."

"You're some nice uncle," I said. My thumb flicked up the flame for Fortunato's cigar, but I didn't light it because he fell forward in a faint. He damaged the cigar irreparably when he struck the rough-hewn floor, and he didn't do his face much good either.

THE DAY OF THE PICNIC

by John Lutz

"South into the hot barren country of southern California, east all the way into Arizona, that's the range of the California condor."

"Those birds fascinate you, don't they?" Judith asks. It was another of her stupid questions that were beginning to annoy me more and more.

"They are magnificient," I tell her, bracing myself for a bump as the jeep speeds over the rocky land. Of course they are magnificent; with a wingspread of over ten feet that carries them up, up in spiraling circles over a mile high, then enables them to ride the air currents in sweeping arcs for up to a hundred miles in search of carrion. "There are only an estimated fifty or sixty of them left, you know," I say.

Judith says nothing. She *is* beautiful—except, perhaps, for her rather prominent nose. Despite the heat that has been withering us for over an hour, she still looks fresh in her tan safari jacket and gray slacks. Her blonde hair is drawn back and tied with a black ribbon. Appropriate, I think.

The jeep bounces high into the air. There is a metallic sound and the horn rim drops into my lap, then onto the floor to rattle beneath the seat.

"For heaven's sake, Norton, watch where you're driving!"

She says nothing about the horn rim. Secretly she feels that I'm cheap; I know that. Perhaps that is one of the things about Rod Smathers that appeals to her, his undisciplined spending habits. She thought I should buy a newer jeep, from a registered dealer, but why should I when Harry Ace's Premium Motors had just the vehicle I needed. As I told her, I am an experienced naturalist, and I know just what type of transport is best for my purposes.

didn't know, of course, that I immediately had a new muffler put on the jeep, for it's against the law to drive in certain areas of the vast condor preserve, and today, especially, I didn't want to attract unwarranted attention.

It was I who suggested this little picnic outing. I waited a full three months after buying the jeep from Harry Ace, for I am by nature a cautious man. Also I am a possessive man, and I couldn't live with the fact that behind my back Judith was seeing the loud and freewheeling Rod Smathers. Let us call it the territorial imperative.

The steering wheel shimmies in my hands and I let up on the accelerator as the jeep lurches over some especially rocky terrain.

"It's terribly hot, Norton!" Judith complains. "Couldn't we have gone to the mountains for this picnic, where there are trees and some shade at least?"

"I suppose we could have," I say, watching her take a long drink from the canteen. "But I wanted you to see these birds. It's a sight I wouldn't want to share with just anyone." She offers me a drink but I refuse with a curt wave of my backhand. "Be watching the sky," I say, and dutifully she turns her face to the sun.

"I'm hungry, Norton," Judith says in her protesting whine.

"We'll eat soon," I tell her, thinking of the dry sandwiches she's packed that are bouncing on the rear seat. "If you eat now, it will just make you thirstier in this sun." At the mention of water she takes another drink. Judith has always been the pawn of suggestion. I suppose Rod Smathers knew that instinctively.

"There!" I say, downshifting and braking the jeep to a halt.

Judith's eyes, the exact shade of blue as the cloudless sky, wander aimlessly as they search the airy void ahead of us. Then she sees the tiny black form off to the west. It has to be a condor!

Getting out my secondhand binoculars, I focus them on the dark form. Only one bird flies like that, huge wings outspread and curving gently upward to end in five guiding feathers, spread like the reaching fingers of a hand. The giant bird wheels to the east, giving the impression that it is somehow suspended from above, then turns gently and glides lower. I start the jeep and drive slowly forward,

handing the binoculars to Judith. "You watch him," I s.
and she fits the lenses to her searching eyes.

The condor has landed.

I stop the jeep and motion for Judith to speak quietly.
"Bring the canteen," I say. "We'll walk from here."

She obeys, and we move forward over the sun-baked,
uneven ground. We stop behind a cluster of rock, and we
have a perfect view.

"I wanted you to see one up close," I say. "We're in luck
today."

"He's huge!"

I am strangely thrilled by her enthusiasm. It is a big condor, with a wingspread of perhaps eleven feet. It is feeding
on a half-eaten pronghorn antelope, recognizable only by
its horns, for the condor has turned the carcass inside out
to reveal the gleaming skeleton and sun-dried meat.

"They always do that," I say. "They tear at the navel or
rectum of their prey with their beak and pull the innards
out before feeding."

"How terrible!" Judith says, her eyes riveted on the huge
bird.

The condor knows we are here, I am sure, but as long as
we keep our distance he will ignore us and not flap away in
wily caution. As we watch, he lowers his bare orange head
and neck and digs at the half-eaten carcass with his curved
beak.

Then a dark shadow moves slowly over the terrain and
we actually hear the whir of wind through the wing tips of
the second huge condor that glides over us and lands near
the carcass. Dark as its own shadow, dragging its massive
wings, it walks in clumsy lurches toward the antelope and
begins feeding.

"Sometimes," I tell Judith, "they gorge themselves so
that they can't take off for hours. Though what's left of the
antelope isn't enough for that to happen."

"It's disgusting," she says, but she is hypnotized.

We've had a hot walk, and I offer her the canteen. She
takes a long drink, and I smile at her.

"What's funny?" she asks, blinking heavily at me.

"Perhaps the whole world," I say, watching her face
closely. "I wanted especially for you to see these birds close
up, to see the talons and the curved beak, and to know how
they feed, using the unique sharp tools nature has given

…m to disembowel a carcass." I screw the cap on the half-
…apty canteen and lick my lips. Perhaps the sun is affect-
…ng me slightly.

The strapless binoculars drop from Judith's hand and she
crouches there, making no attempt to pick them up, not
realizing that she's dropped them.

"You see," I tell her, "I know about you and Rod
Smathers, about what you've been doing behind my back.
So I pulled a little trick on you, Judith, and loaded the
water in the canteen with enough barbiturates to stop the
hearts of ten unfaithful women. But the little trick isn't
over."

From a hundred yards beyond us comes the muffled flap
of a huge wing against the ground. Judith stares at me with
sleepy eyes held wide by horror-arched brows. "Oh, no,
Norton!" She slumps from her crouching position to sit
with her back against a rock. Her jaw moves, and she tries
feebly to raise both hands, but cannot.

When her eyes close, I undress her and carefully fold her
clothes. Then I drag her body out from behind the rocks,
listening to the flapping of kite-like wings as the condors
take to the air behind me. I lay Judith on her back on the
bare ground and press my ear to the still warm flesh beneath her breasts, listening for a heartbeat. There is none;
she is quite dead. She is carrion. I have no feeling at all.

Leaving Judith there, where telescoping eyes can see her
from miles up, I gather her clothes and walk back to the
jeep. I get a drink from the other canteen and notice with
satisfaction that my hand is not shaking. Then I drive some
distance away and stop, training the binoculars on the two
condors still circling above the scene I've left. Presently
they are joined by a third condor, and at last the three of
them glide downward in ever narrowing circles.

I cannot stop laughing for a long time as I put the jeep
in gear and speed northward. Judith's bones might not be
found for months, and then who will know how the
bleached and nameless skeleton met its fate? The thing
now, I realize, is to get clear of the area as quickly as possible, and I urge the bucking jeep on to higher speeds.

What's that?

Something dark, bouncing out in front of me, *a wheel!*
Suddenly the left front of the jeep digs into the earth and I
am hurled forward and up. *Smash!* against the windshield

frame. *Smash!* onto the hard ground and I slide, my
bent grotesquely beneath me! There is the distant ren
of metal and tinkling glass, and then with blinding pain
neck and shoulder slam into a rock and I am lying still
my back. Time seems to have ceased.

Above me the sky seems to waver like rising heat fumes,
and hours and hours pass.

Finally, I roll onto my side and try to rise, but I cannot.
My left shoulder is scraped to ugly red and burning raw-
ness but there is no pain in my legs, only a creeping numbness. I try to crawl but lack the strength to do even that.
Waves of nausea assail me as I see again the bouncing,
free-rolling loose wheel. *Harry Ace has done this to me!*

Or is it Judith's fault—and Rod Smathers'?

I try to control myself, lying here in the searing heat. It
doesn't matter who is responsible. The front wheel of the
jeep came off and here I am, and it is up to me, Norton
Saltt, to get myself out of it. If only I could move!

There is blood running from a cut on my head into my
eye, and I remove my torn shirt and dab at the painful
wound, then wrap the shirt about my forehead. Again I try
to crawl, but I drag my crippled body forward only a matter of inches before the pain and numbness overcome me.
My heart begins to pound unreasonably fast, as if it pos-
sesses some secret knowledge.

I do not see it land, but I turn my head and it is there—
a very large condor, about a hundred feet from me, with
huge soot-black wings spread and resting partly against the
ground as it balances awkwardly. It fixes a saucer eye on
me that is not the eye of a warm-blooded animal like myself, but the eye of a bird. In weighty, clumsy lurches it
moves toward me, its gnarled talons clacking on the hard
ground, and I wave an arm weakly and scream as loudly as
I can through my parched throat.

It stops.

When I lie still, my body vibrating with my pounding
heart, the condor lurches forward again and rests not more
than fifty feet from me, watching. I watch too, the red-
orange and wrinkled skin of its neck and head, the whitish
curved beak, the unbelievably long and wicked talons. *I
have never known such fear!*

I glimpse above me the spread of mammoth black wings
with a flash of gray beneath, and a huge shadow moves

ss the land as another condor soars low, then glides
vard to arc in slow and lazy circles.

Then I see that the circles are narrowing, *and that I am
their focal point!*

Through my horror I try desperately to dredge up every
bit of information I've ever learned about the giant condors, but as I lie there watching those narrowing, swooping
circles, listening to that clacking, feathered walking, one bit
of information on which even the experts disagree burns in
my mind like an agonizing, glowing coal. No one really
knows if the great birds wait until their prey is completely
dead before they begin to feed.

No one really knows.

They took to the streets with more deadly
purpose than the criminals they hunted!

DEATH SQUAD

Another Sgt. Edmund Roersch thriller
by **HERBERT KASTLE**
author of *The Gang* and *Cross-Country*

The Death Squad were cops who were tired of
playing tug-of-war over the law with corrupt
officials, exasperated by the revolving door of
criminal courts, disgusted by the pimps, junkies,
rapists, and murderers who held the city hostage.
In the tradition of **Death Wish,** they became
vigilantes by night. Discover what happens when
the law stops working!

A Dell Book $1.95

IT BEGAN WITH JUST
AN ORDINARY LITTLE DOG.

by David Anne

John and Paula had thought they had
found the perfect way to end their
holiday in France. They had had fun
outwitting the authorities by
smuggling a dog into England. And Asp
was a beautiful, loving corgi with
soft fur and limpid eyes. But the
horrible virus she concealed paralyzed
first a town, then the nation with fear.
As the disease mutated and became
airbone, it lashed out to terrorize the
entire world!

A DELL BOOK $1.95

Dell Bestsellers

IN 1942 THE U.S. RATIONED GASOLINE

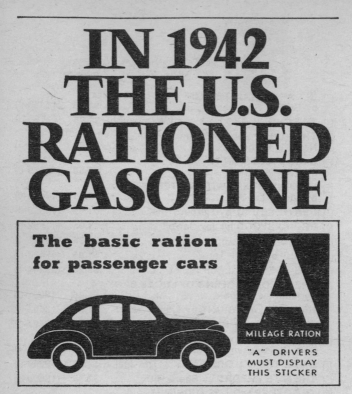

The basic ration for passenger cars

A

MILEAGE RATION

"A" DRIVERS
MUST DISPLAY
THIS STICKER

That was wartime and the spirit of sacrifice was in the air. No one liked it, but everyone went along. Today we need a wartime spirit to solve our energy problems. A spirit of thrift in our use of all fuels, especially gasoline. We Americans pump over 200 million gallons of gasoline into our automobiles each day. That is nearly one-third the nation's total daily oil consumption and more than half of the oil we import every day . . . at a cost of some $40 billion a year. So conserving gasoline is more than a way to save money at the pump and help solve the nation's balance of payments; it also can tackle a major portion of the nation's energy problem. And that is something we all have a stake in doing . . . with the wartime spirit, but without the devastation of war or the inconvenience of rationing.

ENERGY CONSERVATION -
IT'S YOUR CHANCE TO SAVE, AMERICA

Department of Energy, Washington, D.C.